DEATH DROPS THE PILOT

ALSO BY GEORGE BELLAIRS

DEATH DROPS THE PILOT

AN INSPECTOR LITTLEJOHN MYSTERY

GEORGE BELLAIRS

OPEN ROAD

INTEGRATED MEDIA

NEW YORK

ISBN: 978-1-5040-9266-1

This edition published in 2024 by Open Road Integrated Media, Inc.
180 Maiden Lane
New York, NY 10038
www.openroadmedia.com

To Dorothy Quick

DEATH DROPS THE PILOT

1

QUEER BEHAVIOUR OF THE FALBRIGHT JENNY

The impatient clanging of a ship's bell. Ten-thirty and the last ferryboat was ready to leave Elmer's Creek for Falbright just across the River Hore. If you knew the schedule of cross-river sailings, you could tell the time of day by the ferry bell, just as in the fields of France the peasants follow the passing hours by the tolling for the offices at the parish church.

A lovely autumn day had been followed by a pitch-black night. The last thin suggestion of departed daylight lingered on the horizon to the West beyond the Farne Deep and the intermittent flashes of the Farne Light.

The *Falbright Jenny* stood moored at the end of the long stone jetty, two deck-lights fore and aft and a glow shining from her innards where the engineer was putting coal on the boiler fire. Shuffling, unsteady footsteps along the quay, and the last two passengers crossed the gangway. Two half-drunken seamen who had been spending the evening in the taproom of the *Barlow Arms* at the top of the jetty. The engineer closed the furnace door, emerged from his lair and, single-handed, hauled in the gangway. As he did so, the engine room telegraph clanged for half astern.

Time to shut up shop at Elmer's Creek. The last boat cut the village off from the rest of the world altogether until six in the morning. Unless, of course, anyone wanted to walk along the riverbank to the bridge at Chyle, five miles away. A few natives and one or two modest holidaymakers remained; the rest returned to Falbright, a mile across the river estuary.

The *Falbright Jenny* backed her way out of Elmer's Creek. Her reversed engines towed her a little way upstream, then halted. After a momentary hush, the bell clanged for full-ahead and she took a straight course for the light on Falbright pier-head.

A small steamer, built like a river tugboat, which held about two hundred passengers at a pinch. She was old and the Falbright Borough Council talked of replacing her by a motor vessel, but every year convinced themselves that she was good for another twelve months. Old John Grebe, the captain, had been piloting her for thirty years. The handyman, Joe Webb, who ran the engines and fired the boilers, made up the crew of one.

This night there were about forty people on board. Unusual for the time of year, with the holiday crowds gone home, but the Elmer's Creek Methodists had been holding a Sale of Work and a contingent of Falbright Mothers' Union had been over, headed by the parson, to help them.

The Rev John Thomas Jingling, BA, was filled with a vague melancholy as he watched the lights of Elmer's Creek recede and those of the opposite bank approach. The beauty of the night moved him deeply. The glow in the sky which came from the large town of Falbright, the lamps on the promenade looking a bit forlorn now that, the season over, they had removed the festoons of coloured lights which joined them in summer. A cluster of lighted cottages round the jetty at Elmer's Creek. The illuminated portholes of the mail boat from Ireland, which had arrived earlier in the evening, tied up at Falbright pier. And the buoys which indicated the Hore channel, twinkling in and out almost as far out as the Farne lighthouse which flashed in the distance.

Sailing over the flood to the distant shore! Mr Jingling made a mental note for next Sunday's sermon and almost without knowing it started to hum a tune. A woman at his elbow took it up in song and soon the whole boatload, except the tipsy customers from the *Barlow Arms*, were chanting to the vibration of the ancient engines.

> O Beulah Land, sweet Beulah Land,
> As on thy highest mount I stand,
> I look away across the sea,
> Where mansions are prepared for me,
> And view the shining glory shore...

It was then that Mr Jingling noticed that the *Falbright Jenny* was behaving queerly. She wasn't heading for the shining glory shore at all, but out to sea in the direction of the Farne Light.

It was with difficulty that the parson refrained from crying out aloud. Instead, and still shouting his chorus, he peered ahead at the bridge, but seeing no sign of Old John there, made for the engine room and staggered clumsily down the short iron staircase.

"We're heading out to sea, Joe!"

Joe Webb was standing at the steam valve, his short pipe held a foot away from his mouth, which was wide open.

"Where mansions are prepared for me..." he was yelling. He had a vague idea that a good hymn might counteract the unlucky presence of a sky pilot aboard.

"Wot?"

"We're heading to sea."

Joe shook his head contemptuously. He'd been on the *Falbright Jenny* for twenty years and she'd never tried those sorts of tricks.

5

"You're mistaken, Reverend. The skipper's jest takin' a wide sweep on account of the tide."

"Come and see for yourself, then. Quickly...quickly..."

But it was too late. The *Jenny* had already run a course between two buoys in the twisting river channel and with a quick shudder plunged her nose into a bank of sand. And there she stuck, her engines going, her screw thrashing vainly, her passengers terrified. Joe Webb closed the steam valve and there was silence for a minute. Then pandemonium broke out.

The engineer ran on deck and met the rushing stream of panic-stricken members of the Mothers' Union.

"Stop where you are... Jest where you are... You don't want her to 'eel over, do you? It's all right but stop where y'are."

He wobbled across the deck as fast as his large bulk would permit and up the ladder to the bridge. There was nobody there.

"Where's he gone?" Webb asked the binnacle light.

But there was no answer and Webb hadn't time to wait, for those ashore at Falbright had seen everything and men with lights were crossing the sandbanks to the *Jenny*. It was quite safe at low tide. She was stuck on the Elmer's Creek side, with a narrow stretch of deep channel between her and the rescuers, who eventually brought a motor launch to take the passengers off.

"The skipper's disappeared..."

If Joe Webb said it once, he said it a score of times before dawn. He shouted it to the first of the men who arrived across the bank. He said it softly to the women as they were disembarked one by one from the *Jenny* to the launch and thence home. He whispered it in an awful monotone to the tipsy mariners from the *Barlow Arms*, who said they didn't believe him and kept shouting "Women and children first".

Then, he had to tell it to the police at one in the morning.

They gave Webb a large cup of tea, at which he looked

disgusted and said he was starved through. They then added a tot of rum. Webb smiled. "It was like this..."

Webb was a small, very fat man of a little over fifty. He had a large, round red face, too, with protruding eyes of washed-out blue. He moved and thought slowly and with difficulty.

"It was this way..."

Mr Jingling had already given a coherent account of the tragic trip to the glory shore and gone home. All the police wanted was to know at what point the skipper disappeared.

"I got his orders over the telegraph awright till he was half over... I can tell jest where we are in the river, you know, havin' crossed so offen."

The sergeant of the borough police raised his eyes as if praying for patience.

"Do you think Old John had a stroke and fell off the bridge, like?"

"Eh? Fell off?"

Webb had to stop to think. He eyed his empty cup and the bottle on the desk, but nobody took the hint.

"How old was he?"

"Seventy... Talked of retirin' any time."

"Did he have a drink at the *Barlow* before he came aboard for the last trip?"

"Perhaps he did... And then, perhaps he didn't... When we put in at Elmer's Creek before the last trip back, the skipper took a walk up the jetty to stretch 'is legs. He always did."

"Did you go, too?"

"No. I stayed and tended the fire. It was warmer there, too. I've got a bit of a chill, you see, and the breeze was cold."

Webb eyed the bottle again, but there was no response.

"You're sure he came back on board?"

Webb looked utterly disgusted.

"Oo do you think gave orders from the bridge if he wasn't back on board? The devil himself? The skipper rang down jest like he always did. Astern out of Elmer's Creek till we turned in the river; then full-ahead..."

"And half speed ahead as you neared the pier on this side?"

"That's right."

"And before he could do it, he vanished, and the *Jenny* took the bit between her teeth and headed for open sea."

"That's 'ow it seems. I can't understand it. It beats me."

He pondered deeply, puffing out his cheeks like balloons.

"Where is Old John, then?"

"Your guess is as good as ours, Joe. Likely he had a stroke and fell overboard. The river squad are out now looking around for him."

Outside, the town was quiet. The Irish boat was almost in darkness, ready for the morning trip. A few fishing vessels, which that night were off to Iceland, were casting-off. A stiff little breeze whistled round the police station from the windows of which the whole of the river and waterfront were visible. The string of flickering lights on the buoys of the channel, the swinging lamps of the docks and harbour, the deserted promenade following the course of the river until it joined the sea at Farne Point, and across the channel, the navigation lights on the jetty at Elmer's Creek and a solitary illuminated upper room at the *Barlow Arms*. Overhead a plane droned its way to Ireland.

Joe Webb seemed disinclined to move. The room was cosy and there was a chance that they might remember to give him another tot of rum. He coughed hoarsely to remind them he wasn't very well.

"I'll 'ave to rub me chest when I get in. It's a cold night for the time of year."

"Try another little drop of this."

The sergeant poured a couple of tablespoonfuls of the liquor in a cup. Webb took it with eager fingers, frowned at the amount, swung it round in the cup, sniffed it, and threw it into his mouth. The sergeant was glad of a bit of company. With the exception of the search for John Grebe's body, there wasn't much doing.

"Did you know the skipper well, Joe?"

Webb rubbed his bristly chin and put down his cup.

"Yes...an' no. We'd worked together for nearly a score o' years. But I never knew much about 'im. A close sort o' chap."

"Did he come from these parts?"

"No. Blest if I know where 'e came from. A bit of a mystery. I've 'eard it said he'd a master's ticket. What 'e was doin' on a one-eyed little tub like the *Falbright Jenny* God on'y knows. Time was when shippin' was bad, when many a good captain took to a poor job. But never a one like that, with a crew of one, just pilotin' an old 'ulk across an estuary over an' over agen. Bitter, 'e was, too, but as far as I could see, 'e never tried to change 'is job."

"Bitter? What about?"

"Life, I suppose. I've seen holidaymakers crossin' the ferry try to get Old John to talk. Sort of tell 'em old sailors' tales. But 'e soon shut 'em up. Proper 'aughty-like when 'e tuck that way. Might have bin the capting of the *Queen Elizabeth*."

"A man with a past, eh?"

"Shouldn't be surprised at that."

"He lived over at Elmer's Creek, didn't he?"

"Yes. In the old 'arbourmaster's house. There used ter be an 'arbourmaster there, you know. Quite a sizeable port, it was, till it all got sanded up and Falbright grew instead. You know Old John's cottage. On the river jest past the jetty."

"I know it. Did he keep house for himself?"

"He'd a sort of housekeeper, who kept the place clean, but who didn't live in. Mrs Sattenstall...a widder who lives next door to 'im. Old John wouldn't 'ave anybody livin' in with him."

"And after the last ferry across, I suppose somebody rowed him back across the river."

"In winter season. In summer when there's two ferries, the

Falbright Belle leaves Falbright ten minutes after the *Jenny's* last trip and we both get 'ome on her. Which reminds me. 'Ow am I gettin' back to Elmer's Creek? I'll 'ave a job gettin' a row over now."

"If you'll wait a bit longer, the police launch'll take you. They should be in any time. They can't go on searching all night. The tide'll be in soon...4.27 high today."

"The *Jenny*'ll float off the sandbank before then. I could 'ave cried to see 'er there when we left 'er tonight. She's not much to look at...not much of a ship, but to see 'er there, like an old duck tryin' to swim in two inches of water... It cut me up, straight it did. I've been on 'er a long time."

"The harbour men are there now, looking after her."

"I ought to be with 'em, you know. Nobody knows them engines like me. Last time I went on me 'olidays and Mack Oliver took over as engineer for a week, the skipper went daft. They couldn't run the crossin' in the usual quarter-hour on account of not havin' enough steam."

"Is that so? Don't you worry. The old *Jenny*'ll be waiting for you in the morning."

"But wot about the skipper? That's wot bothers me."

"Jefferson'll have to pilot her across."

Webb looked for a place to spit.

"Jefferson! Skipper in the children's yachtin' pool, that's where 'e oughter be."

"He's all right. Spent a long time on the Iceland run."

"Do you remember the time he ran the *Belle* right into the pier? Frisky little ship, the *Belle*. The *Jenny* was always stiddy..."

The telephone rang.

A rapid conversation from the other end, punctuated by "Yes" and "No" from Sergeant Archer, a large, beefy man with a red face, slant eyes and heavy eyebrows like moustaches themselves.

"Phew!"

10

Archer laid the instrument down very gently.

"Poor Old John!"

Webb lumbered to his feet.

"What for? Why poor?"

"They've found him under the pier where the ebb must have carried him, and the new tide must have floated him out..."

"Is 'e dead?"

Poor Webb's protruding glaucous eyes stood out farther than ever.

"Dead as a door nail."

"Wot of? Was 'e drowned?"

"They didn't say. They're just bringing the body in to the mortuary, so you'd better come down with me and identify him."

"Won't somebody else do?"

Webb was a rough man but a soft-hearted one and he didn't like death, or anything connected with it.

"They asked if you were here and said you'd better..."

"All right. Are they 'ere now?"

"They will be. Better be gettin' along if you want to see Elmer's Creek before dawn."

They rose, went through a little inner door at the back of the office, and down two flights of spiral stone stairs. The place smelled of damp and old stone, like descending into a tomb. Webb shivered and put up the collar of his reefer coat.

They reached at length a small room with four receptacles like ovens let in the walls. The refrigerators of the unhappy dead who had left life suddenly or violently and waited there for the law to pass them for burial and peace. A door to the left led to the laboratory where the police surgeon worked.

Webb gazed round with startled eyes, dubiously watching the four closed doors as though fearful that, at any moment, they might fly open and reveal their grisly contents.

"You needn't look so scared, Joe. There's nothing in those

things just at present... Sometimes, in the holiday season, what with road accidents and such like, we get a houseful now and then."

"Don't... I can't stand it."

"We've all got to come to it."

"Not now, please, sergeant. I'm not feelin' very well."

Outside they heard the ambulance draw up softly with a gentle screech of brakes. Doors opened and then a procession, headed by the cheerful custodian of the morgue, who also helped the surgeon in his macabre research. A small man, like a robin, with a bald head, prominent false teeth, a shabby grey suit, and a sloppy shirt and soft collar.

"This way, gentlemen."

The guardian of the dead smiled, displaying all his dentures like a ventriloquist's dummy.

The sheeted remains of Captain John Grebe were wheeled in on a trolley. The custodian opened one of the ovens and with delicate fingertips drew out a rubber-tired shelf to which the body was transferred.

A police Inspector joined the party, carrying a sheaf of notes in one hand and his flat cap in the other.

"You Joseph Webb?"

Webb nodded. He couldn't speak. His throat was dry and constricted with a great fear.

The Inspector gently drew back the sheet and revealed a face, peaceful in death, in spite of all that had been done to its owner.

A long face, rugged and tanned, covered with close-clipped whiskers ending in a small torpedo beard. A mighty Roman nose, a firm jaw, and hair receding from the broad, highbrow and leaving a bald patch between the large well-shaped ears. They had closed the blue eyes in their deep sockets, lined with tiny wrinkles.

"Recognise him?"

Webb nodded and tried to speak but only made a noise which sounded like a great sob.

"John Grebe?"

Webb nodded again and then remembering he'd been brought up a Catholic, even if with the years he'd drifted away, he crossed himself awkwardly, more out of a desire to show some kind of respect for the dead than anything else.

"Was 'e drowned?"

"No. Stabbed in the back and probably pushed overboard."

Webb stiffened and then sagged like a sack of flour.

"Come on."

The kindly sergeant could see he'd had enough.

From the direction of the sea they heard the triumphant siren of the *Jenny*, now back in the river.

Webb held on to the white-tiled wall for a minute and then pointed upwards as though about to ask if his old captain would now be safely in heaven.

"Could I 'ave jest another tot o' that rum? This 'as turned me up good an' proper."

"We'll see what we can find."

"Who'd 'ave wanted to do poor old Captain John in?" Webb was asking it as they corkscrewed their way slowly up the stone stairs again, back to the humdrum and routine of life in the police station.

And the local police were still asking the same question three days later, in spite of all their inquiries, when the Chief Constable decided to call in Scotland Yard.

2

SEVEN LOST YEARS

The violent application of brakes almost rolled Chief Inspector Littlejohn out of his berth in the sleeping car and he awoke to find the train slowly gliding into a station. He rose and slid down the shutter over the window.

Tidmarsh. It was still dark, and the lamps illuminated the long, deserted platforms. Littlejohn looked at his watch. Five-thirty. He'd been on the way since midnight and there was still an hour to go.

A truck rumbled, somebody shouted incoherently, doors were slammed, and a whistle blown. The London-Falbright-Belfast train slowly drew away.

In the next compartment, Sergeant Cromwell slept and snored undisturbed by all the racket.

Littlejohn took up the file he'd been reading when he fell asleep somewhere about Watford on the night before.

GREBE, John (69) Born Rosslare, 1886, English parentage.
Went to sea at 14. Master's Certificate, 1913.
1914-18. Transport service in Middle East.

1925. Arrived at Falbright and took Pilot's Certificate for River Hore.

1927. Master of ferry for Falbright Corporation...

He laid down the file on the blanket, took off his spectacles, and looked through the window with unseeing eyes. Transport service in the Middle East during the first World War and then... A gap of seven lost years and suddenly Captain John Grebe arrives at Falbright, a God-forsaken little port on the west coast and lives out the rest of his existence ferrying people across an obscure river. And his record closes with a stab in the back and a sordid end in the waters he'd so often navigated.

Outside it was growing light. By easing himself up in his berth Littlejohn could see the flat pasture lands through the window, acres and acres of them dotted with farms, some of them with the smoke of early morning rising from their chimneys, others still sleeping. The railway line, too, seemed built on ground with no gradients whatever; the train slid along at high speed with hardly any vibration.

Then, suddenly, they ran into thin mist and from the very taste of the atmosphere on his lips, Littlejohn knew they were nearing the sea. The attendant arrived with tea.

"Falbright in half an hour, sir."

He passed on to the next compartment and suddenly the snoring there ceased.

Littlejohn sipped his tea as he shaved; then he tapped on the communicating door to the next compartment and thrust in his head. Cromwell was on the floor, his body raised on his hands and tiptoes, performing with difficulty in the narrow space, his morning exercises. He screwed round his head, smiled, and struggled to his feet.

"I've had an awful night, sir."

"Didn't sound like it, judging from the snores."

"I slept all right, but the rolling about gave me a shocking nightmare."

He ignored the teapot on the tray and started to make himself a drink of Strengtho from a tin he carried in his luggage, measuring two teaspoonfuls carefully, mixing it into a paste, thinning it with water from the jug. Then he drank it with apparent relish and satisfaction.

They were now crossing a series of complicated points on the railway lines and through the window they could see the estuary of the River Hore. The tide was ebbing, leaving a thin channel straggling its way seawards between stretches of mud and wet sand. The line ran for several miles along the riverside, on which chemical works and factories making fertilisers from fish offal rose and spoiled the skyline.

The railway threaded between trucks and wagons marshalled in extensive yards and past rows of shabby houses and small workshops. Finally, the station with its three platforms, offices, third-rate hotels, familiar posters, and knots of porters and officials waiting for the train.

FALBRIGHT (MARITIME).

Littlejohn and Cromwell gathered together their odds and ends of shaving tackle, reading matter and pyjamas and thrust them in their luggage. Cromwell rammed his belongings in the large portmanteau he always took away with him and which contained, *inter alia*, books on police law and procedure, toxicology and forensic medicine, handcuffs, chest expanders, revolvers, and reserve supplies of Strengtho.

They emerged from the train. Through a large archway at the top of the platform they could see the masts of ships and the funnel of the Irish Mail, emitting black smoke ready for the trip. A thin trickle of passengers made their way to the quayside. The smell of the sea and the faint odour of tar mingled with the aroma of coffee and the acrid fumes of burnt toast emerging from the refreshment rooms. A porter intent on cleaning the platform swept with a large brush clouds of dust in the path of the passengers.

Three men in uniform stood at the ticket barrier: a customs officer and two police officials. One of them, wearing the uniform and insignia of a Superintendent, detached himself and approached Littlejohn. Superintendent Lecky, a man in his forties, alert, fresh-complexioned, dark eyed and wearing a small dark moustache and thick eyebrows. The other, an Inspector, followed; a tall, heavy, fair man, with a large chest and huge hands and feet. A pleasant round-faced countryman.

Lecky singled out Littlejohn at once and advanced quickly.

"Delighted to meet you, sir."

Passers-by, struggling with their luggage, turned to see what was going on. The newspapers had been full of the Elmer's Creek affair and the editions of the evening before had hinted that Scotland Yard had been called in. The travelling crowds seemed torn between the group of policemen and the Irish Mail, which to help them make up their minds emitted three roaring blasts from her siren.

"We felt we needed some expert help. We're at the end of our own resources. A boatload of women, a parson, and two drunks. You understand? We haven't even a suspect yet."

Lecky seemed anxious to excuse himself from the start.

Littlejohn smiled and handed over his bag to a waiting policeman who had been gesturing that he was there to act as porter. Satisfied, he reeled under Cromwell's heavy load and put the luggage in a waiting police car.

"I'm not here to interfere, Superintendent. You quite understand that. My colleague and I will help all we can, but the case, of course, is yours."

Lecky looked relieved. He'd expected someone a bit officious and overbearing from London, somebody who would make all their local men look like amateurs. He smiled and his eye followed the direction of Cromwell's, who was trying to read the menu stuck in a brass frame at the door of the refreshment room. It contained the noon ordinary of the day before.

"You've not had breakfast?"

"No."

"We'd better make that the first job, then."

Outside the station, the road divided. One branch led into the town; the other to the landing stage, a huge structure of heavy old timber with several storeys, each of which came into use according to the state of the tide. At present, the Irish boat was lying low in the river. Passengers were descending to the lowest stage of the pier and filing across a rickety gangway to the ship. Another blast on the siren reminded them that the boat left in five minutes.

Across the river they could see the jetty at Elmer's Creek, with a cluster of houses on the riverside, the *Barlow Arms* towering above them and then, on the road beyond, a row of red brick boarding houses. The early morning was dull and the waterfront chilly. Over the water a thin mist. From Elmer's Creek the coast swept into the wide, flat, desolate expanse of Balbeck Bay.

Fishing boats in the river, a noisy dredger busy keeping the channel clear, and across the wide expanse of sandbanks which composed the estuary of the River Hore between Farne Point at Falbright and Elmer's Creek, men were gathering shrimps and digging for cockles.

The police car pulled up at the Terminus Hotel, a large rambling Victorian edifice, with an expensive sun lounge tacked on it, from which the whole of the waterfront was visible. Before the advent of sleeping cars, this had been the refuge of cross-channel passengers from Ireland who didn't care for the overnight train journey to London, or for those who, crossing from Falbright, used to arrive on the previous day to catch the morning mail. Now, its main purpose finished, the hotel was empty, forlorn and shabby and gave one the impression of having innumerable closed rooms and vast empty corridors full of old rotting furniture and smelling of damp and decay.

They served the Scotland Yard men with a tolerable meal of bacon and eggs following heavy porridge. As they sat eating, they could see the Irish boat slowly manoeuvring her way down the channel and then, as soon as she was clear, the ferry from across the estuary put out.

"That's the *Falbright Belle*, sister ship to the *Jenny* on which the murder happened. We've laid up the *Jenny* for the time being, sir. We thought you might like to look over her."

Lecky was sitting smoking a pipe in one of the creaking basket chairs of the sun lounge where his friends were dining. The Inspector, appropriately named Silence, had also squeezed his huge bulk in a basket chair and looked highly uncomfortable, expecting it at any minute to disintegrate.

"Inspector Silence has been on the case and will take you round when you're ready, gentlemen. It's court day for me and I've to see to one or two cases before I'm free."

Silence turned to nod and smile, but the chair creaked and groaned and wiped the smile from his face and gave him a look of intense and ridiculous anxiety.

"Would you like to stay here whilst you're in Falbright, Chief Inspector?"

Littlejohn looked around at the vast empty dining room, the decrepit waiter, the ancient badly polished sideboard.

"Or would you prefer across the river at Elmer's Creek? That's where Captain Grebe, the murdered man lived, and it's easily accessible by ferry. Or the police launch could take you to and fro. The *Barlow Arms* there is quite a comfortable little pub, mainly frequented by yachtsmen and sea fishermen who come at weekends. You'd get the local colour there."

"Yes; good and proper."

Silence felt he ought to say something and his sudden ejaculation made them all turn their heads in his direction, whereat he blushed and coughed and made his chair expand and squeal again.

The Scotland Yard officers finished their meal. Littlejohn felt happy when it was over. They kept having silences, as though the two local men were overcome and embarrassed by the reputation and urbane presence of the Chief Inspector.

"You'll have to take us as you find us, sir. This is a small provincial town and you two gentlemen being used to the ways of London and the up-to-date atmosphere, as you might say, will perhaps find us a bit..."

"I was born and brought up in a small town, Superintendent. So was my colleague here. We'll be all right and you needn't worry about our being comfortable. We'd like to stay at the *Barlow Arms*. As you say, we'll get local colour."

"You'd like to get over there, then?"

"As soon as convenient."

Silence drove the car to the landing stage, and they boarded the *Falbright Belle*, which was there waiting, and the crew of one had just rung the bell to warn passengers that they were ready to draw in the gangway and make the trip.

By the side of the landing stage was a small slipway, and there the *Jenny* had been hauled high and dry on the last high tide, her rusty keel showing, her sides barnacled, her propeller raised in the thin air.

"That's the *Jenny*," said Silence as he shepherded his charges on board the *Belle*. He looked very self-important and gave the skipper, standing on the bridge, a sideways glance to see if he had noticed the two VIPs now gracing the ferry.

"Hullo, Alf."

The captain shouted down at Inspector Silence in a voice like a megaphone. "Still huntin'?"

Silence gave the ferry master a sickly grin and indicating his companions with a large thumb, said out of the corner of his mouth in what he thought was *sotto voce*, "Scotland Yard."

The name of that famous place floated across the water almost to the opposite bank of the river. Two small boys, four members of a girls' school off on a natural history lesson in charge of a mistress, two workmen crossing to build a bungalow on the marsh, passers-by in boats, all raised their heads and gazed in awe at the massive, pleasant figure of Chief Inspector Littlejohn and the man by his side, Cromwell, now struggling to keep on his bowler hat in the teeth of the stiff river wind. One of the schoolboys, after a consultation with his companions, crossed to Littlejohn and secured three copies of his autograph.

The engine room telegraph clanged loudly and, although the skipper might just as well have shouted his orders over the rail to the fireman engineer below, he manipulated the brass handles in various directions on the dial as if he were handling a huge liner.

Half astern.

They backed out into the river.

Looking upriver, Littlejohn could follow the thin channel to where it turned and seemed to vanish among green fields. A vast tract of flat country stretched as far as the eye could see, broken only in the foreground by the factories along the river-bank which he and his colleague had passed in the train. Down river, the estuary, with the stream winding among jutting sand-banks and then spreading itself across the Farne Deep, with the Farne Light, a squat erection on steel feet, straddling the water two miles out at sea. The channel was full of small craft, private launches, sailing boats, fishing smacks, and two or three trawlers returning from the fishing grounds. In the far distance, larger vessels passed on the skyline, the trade route between the larger northern and southern ports.

It took about a quarter of an hour and Littlejohn wandered about the deck smoking his pipe, until, finally, the skipper invited him to the bridge. There was hardly room for two, but the skipper didn't take up much of it. A thin, lanky man with half-closed blue eyes, a large straggling moustache, and a broken nose. He swung the wheel casually, describing a wide arc to keep in deep water and then running parallel to the opposite shore for a stretch until he drew level with the jetty at Elmer's Creek; then he turned sharply and drew alongside.

"Bit of a bobby-dazzler about Old John," he said, as the crew cast out the gangway and made the boat fast. "I've known 'im ever since he came here. I was a nipper in those days. Always a bit of a mystery, but I never thought..."

He shook his head and spat over the side.

"I hear he did good work in the Middle East in the First World War."

The skipper took out a short pipe and filled it with tobacco which he carried loose in his jacket pocket.

"So I heard. He'd never talk much himself, but I did hear once that he lost two ships troopin' in the Mediterranean in those days. Gallipoli, or somewhere."

Littlejohn paused and tapped his own pipe out against his heel.

"Can you remember who told you, captain?"

"Can't say I can. We meet such a lot of people on these boats, 'specially in the holiday season. If I do remember, I'll let you know. You'll be here for some time, I expect?"

"Yes. We're staying at the *Barlow Arms*. Call in for a drink with us some time. Do you live this side?"

"No. I'm a Falbright man meself. But I'll call one night after the last ferry and have a yarn."

"How long do you stay here between trips?"

"All depends. Winter schedule, which came on at the beginning of this month, we have quarter of an hour's stop. Summer, it's less."

"All the time?"

"Yes."

"I see from the report that Old John went off his ship the night he died, took a walk along the jetty, and then came back just before the ferry sailed."

"That's right, I believe."

"He'd have time to get home and back?"

"Just about. His cottage is at the top there. The one with the white gate. Whitewashed walls. See it?"

"Yes. He was buried yesterday?"

"Yes. In the cemetery here. A big turn-up. He wasn't what you'd call popular, but 'ighly respected."

"Well. We'll be seeing you then, skipper."

Inspector Silence gave the bags to a lounger on the jetty, who shouldered Cromwell's with a sigh and a heave and shuffled off to the hotel. The trio followed slowly. A man passed carrying a large conger eel.

"They catch 'em at the point here," said Silence. "Devils they are, too, if you don't watch out. Bite like a dog."

A passing tramp offered Cromwell a bunch of bulrushes.

"Threepence the rush."

At the *Barlow Arms* the landlord met them at the door. He nodded to Silence and raised one eyebrow. A huge man, fattened by beer and lack of exercise, with a large moustache and sly little brown eyes. He was in his shirt sleeves.

"Have you two rooms free?"

"How long for?"

"A few days."

The landlord who, according to the licence notice over the door, was called Frederick Braid, eyed the three of them up and down.

"I'll see."

Littlejohn didn't like the man and was just about to suggest to Silence that they tried one of the cottages or boarding houses instead, when the landlady arrived. She looked like Braid's mother and was obviously the boss. A pleasant, elderly woman, clean, efficient, countrified, and with a smile.

"We've two nice rooms facing the sea."

The inn smelled of spirits and cooking. There were a lot of flies buzzing about. A modernised place, constructed from an older foundation. A bar, a homely dining room, and a kind of parlour where the locals gathered. In the latter four men were playing darts and drinking beer.

Fred Braid was back with a shabby hotel register.

"Better sign in."

He eyed Silence up and down to show he was keeping to regulations. The two newcomers filled in particulars. Fred Braid turned round the register and read it. He eyed them both slyly, but his impudence had vanished.

"You the famous Scotland Yard chap? My name's Braid, but call me Fred."

The men in the parlour had stopped playing darts. Two of them looked uneasy; loafers, probably up to no good.

"You here on the Old John case?"

Silence intervened.

"Don't be so inquisitive, Braid. It's your job to make the two gentlemen comfortable, not to be quizzing as soon as they get here."

Braid shrugged his shoulders and went to the foot of the staircase, a broad affair with a graceful handrail, probably part of the original structure.

"Lucy! Carry the gentlemen's cases to their rooms."

He made no attempt to do it himself.

"We'll do it..."

"That's what she's here for. Let her carry 'em."

A tall, well-built maid appeared, bent her head as she saw the detectives, seized the bags, and hurried aloft. Braid's little eyes followed her until she vanished round the turn in the stairs.

The dart players were shuffling out after drinking up from

their glasses. Two young fellows, a man like an old salt with a reefer jacket and shabby old trousers, and finally a middle-aged man with a bald head and reddish hair surrounding it like a halo. He was sloppily dressed and flabby, gone to seed through drink and idling. His glassy grey eyes watered as he looked at the new arrivals. A little snout of a nose and ruddy cheeks hanging from his jawbones.

"You the two Scotland Yard men?"

His voice was educated, but husky from drink.

"Yes."

"The police said you were coming. I didn't catch your names."

Silence introduced them in a mixture of respect and disdain.

"Mr Brett, the parish clerk."

"Have a drink with me?"

"No, thanks, sir. We're just going to see our rooms."

"You'll be comfortable here. Old Mrs Braid's a good cook. Perhaps you'll have a drink another time. So long then. Official duties call me."

He left the place with uncertain steps, lingered on the doorstep smelling the air, and then disappeared in the direction of the village.

The two detectives, led by Braid and followed by Silence, mounted the stairs to their rooms. As they turned the corner of the corridor, Littlejohn came face to face with Lucy, the maid. She started and hurried past.

Littlejohn was sure he'd seen her somewhere before!

3

THREE POSTCARDS

Before returning to his duties across the water, Inspector Silence took his two colleagues on a sightseeing tour of Elmer's Creek.

From the jetty, the road followed the coast past the *Barlow Arms* for about half a mile and then forked. A signpost indicated *Pullar's Sands* along the coast road and *Peshall* to the right of it where the main highway turned inland.

The tide was out leaving a vast tract of shining sands right across Balbeck Bay, which swept to the North for miles and ended in a dim range of hills rolling inland. Already fishermen were digging for bait and women were picking samphire. There was a diminutive promenade, a rough affair of asphalt, stretching as far as the signpost at which the village ended. One or two seats on which idlers were enjoying the fine day. Two navigation marks between the benches, large wooden diamonds seen far out at sea.

The village itself consisted of a number of cottages built along the riverbank, their front garden gates almost reached by the tideline. Half a dozen modest boarding houses along the road to Pullar's Sands. A village stores, which also held the post office, a couple of second-rate cafes with seedy chairs set out in front, and two Methodist churches. Difficult to imagine whence, in their heyday, the chapels drew their congregations. Now one of them, with a foundation-stone marked *Bethel United Methodists*, had been turned into a factory. *Drink and Enjoy Grebe's Dandelion and Burdock. Health in Every Glass.*

Littlejohn paused.

"Grebe? Is that anything to do with the murdered man?"

Inspector Silence nodded.

"His brother. They weren't on speaking terms when John Grebe died."

"Why?"

"Tom Grebe, that's the owner of this place, is a big Methodist and he didn't approve of his brother's carryings on. I believe when he spoke to Captain Grebe about it, the captain kicked him out of his cottage."

"Drink? Or language? Or what?"

Silence shook his head and smiled.

"Women."

"Oh. A lady-killer?"

"Not exactly. From time to time he'd go on leave. Nobody knew where he went. But this spring, he came back with a woman. The girl you saw at the *Barlow Arms*. Lucy. He persuaded Mrs Braid to find her a job. She was a waitress and a good one, and as such girls are hard to come by these days, Mrs Braid didn't hesitate."

"What was wrong about that?"

"Well... In a village like this... People soon got talking. She used to call to see the old man at his cottage. Tom Grebe objected and got kicked out for his pains. I don't say there was anything wrong between Old John and Lucy, but you know how folks are. There'll be more talk when they hear about Old John's will. He's left all he has, cottage and money, to Lucy. Tom doesn't get a cent."

"Who has the will?"

"Flewker, the lawyer in Falbright. Old John wasn't buried till yesterday and the Superintendent asked Flewker to keep the will quiet for a bit."

"Was Old John a wealthy man?"

"I wouldn't think so. Perhaps a thousand or two, but you never know."

A man had appeared at the door of the soft drink factory and nodded to Silence and eyed his companions suspiciously.

"Morning, Inspector."

A tallish, flabby man with an unctuous manner. Bald head, long red face, heavy red nose of an alcoholic rather than a teetotaller, and small blue eyes, which remained hard although the face wore a continual smile.

Silence introduced Littlejohn and Cromwell.

"They're here to investigate the case of your brother's death."

The little eyes grew shifty, almost afraid.

"Very sad. A great grief."

The voice reminded you of lather, rich and oily.

Tom Grebe didn't seem to want to talk. He kept looking up and down the road.

"Expecting a load of stuff from the railway."

He indicated a small edifice which Littlejohn made out to be a station. A single line ran from the sheds away into the country.

"We've a light railway here, sir. Used to carry passengers, but the buses have put it out of fashion. Now it's just for goods. Runs to Freckleby Junction where it joins the main line."

Silence was having to make conversation. It was obvious Tom Grebe was uneasy about something and was anxious to get rid of his visitors. He opened the large main doors of the building, revealing the dismantled chapel, with brewing and mixing vats, casks, bottles, carboys and boxes. The interior had been whitewashed, but the gothic windows had been retained and dimly through the whitewash above the three at the far end could be read, like a truth which human effort could not eliminate. *Praise God from Whom All Blessings Flow.*

They bade the soft-drink merchant good morning and left him.

"He seems a bit put out, sir. Perhaps he thinks you'll suspect him for quarrelling with his brother."

They had reached three detached houses at the end of the village. One a bungalow, occupied, Silence informed them, by a retired bank manager. The other two needed no explanations. A brass plate on the gate.

A Horrocks, MB, Physician and Surgeon.

The plate was tarnished and the lettering almost obliterated by weather and metal polish.

"Dr Horrocks is getting a bit past it now. Not that he ever had much of a practice. He's money of his own and spends a lot of time fishing in his boat, or at the *Barlow Arms*."

Next door, a neat red building with a signboard in the garden.

Swine Fever.
Join the Civil Defence.
Pause before you Cross the Road.

A tidy garden full of autumn vegetables and potatoes and among them the large rear of a man rooting up a row of carrots. He straightened himself as he heard footsteps approaching.

"Morning, Dixon."

PC Dixon was speechless for a moment. He wasn't used to morning calls from his superiors and he hadn't been forewarned officially of the arrival of Scotland Yard, although there had been rumours.

"Mornin', sir. Mornin', gentlemen."

He sniggered and regarded his dirty hands as though wondering if they were really his and how they'd got in such a state. Behind him, at the window of the police house, appeared the faces of his three children, enjoying a holiday locally known as "teachers' rest", with their mother in the background, buxom and pretty.

Dixon himself was huge and ruddy and was wearing an old regulation suit, minus the official buttons, from which he looked about to burst at any minute.

"Just enjoyin' an hour off, sir. Got to keep the garden tidy..."

Silence introduced the two Scotland Yard men. Dixon looked at his soiled hands again, but Littlejohn stretched out his own and was seized in a huge iron grip.

"Pleased to meet you, sir."

Cromwell was eyeing the soil. He was a bit of a gardener himself when not engaged in his other hobbies: birdwatching, Lads' clubs, rifle-shooting, yoga, and singing in the choir of the Metropolitan Police.

"Good for carrots? Nice and sandy, eh?"

Dixon smiled.

"You should see my asparagus."

Silence coughed. He hadn't all day.

"These two gentlemen'll be staying at the *Barlow Arms* for a bit, Dixon."

"Yes. I heard so."

"They've only just decided..."

"News travels fast in Elmer's Creek, sir. Mr Brett passed on his way home, sir, and told me."

"Hm. Well, it's up to you to see they have all they want and any help they require, Dixon, although I'll be coming over quite a lot."

"Very good, sir. I'll jest get into me uniform, then."

"No need to bother for the present, Dixon. We'll go back as the Inspector goes. It'll soon be lunchtime. Get on with your digging."

Dixon smiled broadly at Littlejohn.

"Very good, sir. I'll be along soon, then. I'll 'ave a word with Braid, like. If I 'ear any complaints about you not bein' comfortable, God 'elp him."

He turned and saw the fixed, round eyes of his offspring watching through the window, and waved to them officiously. They all disappeared like a conjuring trick.

"It's rude to stare like that," he told them all later.

"You've been through Grebe's cottage, Silence?" asked Littlejohn on the way back.

"Yes, sir. Just superficially, like. There were no letters of any importance. Nothing in the way of *clues*."

Silence uttered the last word with emphasis.

"But perhaps you'd like to see over it, sir. You might find something that we've missed, though I doubt it."

"I'm sure you've not missed anything but, all the same, it'll be interesting to see where the old man lived. Give us a bit of background about his life and habits."

The cottages were approached by a path on the riverbank. The traffic of the estuary passed the front door and as they made their way fishing boats, the ferry in midstream, and the dredger were visible.

Three small, whitewashed houses with their gables tarred to keep out the weather. Grebe's was the middle one and was larger and better kept than the other two. There was a net spread out to dry in front of the end one.

A small garden in front, untidy, with a fuchsia hedge and the dead plants of summer lying across the beds. A black door with a large keyhole, a brass knocker and letter slit, and an old-fash-

GEORGE BELLAIRS

ioned latch. A bow window overlooking the river from the ground floor and two small sash windows upstairs.

Silence took a large key from his pocket and unlocked the house.

"Perhaps you'd like to keep this, sir?"

He handed the key to Littlejohn.

A small passage with two doors leading into the downstairs rooms. The stairs rose straight and narrow from the end of the lobby. A hat stand in the hall and an old-fashioned sea picture hung on a nail. A barometer and an old wooden sextant on the wall.

The place smelled damp and airless and Silence left the front door open.

A living room in front and a kitchen behind. They turned in at the first door. A snug place with old-fashioned armchairs, a table covered with a green plush cloth, chintz curtains at the windows, and a few geraniums blooming on the windowsill. An array of dishes on a welsh dresser, a tallboy, a grandfather's clock still ticking, a shelf of books, with *Pilgrim's Progress* and a Bible prominent among them. A worn carpet on the floor and a rug made of pieces of rag in front of the hearth. The fireplace was an old broad iron one with a dead fire in it. On the mantelpiece a ship in a bottle and some photographs, faded from sun and sea air.

"The chest there has linen in it and the dresser drawers have the cutlery and such like. There were some bills in one of them, too. Perhaps you'd like to look through yourself some time, sir."

"Yes."

Littlejohn was imagining Old John Grebe about the place, especially at night after the last ferry had gone. There was an oil lamp on the sideboard, a brass affair with a large white porcelain shade. The place was wired for electricity and there was a bulb with a coloured bead shade hanging from the roof in the middle of the room. But Grebe seemed to prefer his old lamp.

32

Pipes on the mantelpiece, too. Short, stumpy ones with well-bitten stems and battered bowls. Over the mantel shelf a framed picture of an old woman, perhaps Grebe's mother. On the wall opposite, a framed sampler of an embroidered house and all the letters of the alphabet in stitching.

Ann Bowley, her work, 1868.
Rock of Ages, Cleft for Me.

Littlejohn looked round the room again. Two old newspapers under the cushion of the spindle backed armchair by the fire, a pair of leather slippers, twisted spills of paper in an old jam jar in the hearth.

He could see the old man sitting there before bed, wearing the steel-framed spectacles still on the chest, his slippers on, his old pipe going, reading the news by the light of the lamp. And the passing boats could see his windows from the river.

The kitchen was tidy and strictly utilitarian. A small electric cooker, pans, a kettle. A worn porcelain sink, a rough wooden table, a larder with a few eatables still there. Just enough for one man and his wants.

The narrow stairs with a strip of carpet down the middle led to a small landing from which two rooms were entered. Only one was furnished. A large iron bed with brass knobs, perhaps a family inheritance, chairs, a chest, a wardrobe. Oilcloth and a couple of mats on the floor and a seaman's chest in one corner.

Silence pointed to the chest.

"Nothing special in it. His papers...mariner's certificates and the like, passport, bank books, some old letters from pals he must have had at one time, but they weren't important. They're still there. He might have expected something to happen to him, because if he had any letters or papers that would lead us anywhere, he's got rid of them. We searched his pockets. The stuff's still at the police station. Nothing much."

They stood in the spartan bedroom wondering what they were doing there. Littlejohn felt a vague feeling of depression. The damp house, the forlorn property of the dead man looking as though it was going to remain there forever, the feeling that Old John Grebe might return at any time and ask them what the hell they were doing among his private things. And, on top of it all, the same question, over and over again: Why would anybody want to murder Old John?

The other room was a lumber dump. Odds and ends of furniture, an empty trunk, a suitcase, empty boxes, old magazines and books, and in the middle a large tin bath where, presumably, Old John took his daily or his weekly tub. Three pairs of sea boots, all clean, and a very old leather hatbox. Littlejohn opened it and revealed an antique silk hat.

"Hullo... Hullo... Anybody there?"

A quavering voice from the hall below. Littlejohn looked over the landing rail and could see the foreshortened form of a little old woman looking up at him.

"What are you doin' up there?"

Silence joined Littlejohn and looked down, too.

"It's just us, Mrs Sattenstall. I'm showing the Chief Inspector over the house."

"Oh. I thought it was some more of them newspaper men or nosey parkers. They've never bin away since the murder."

She didn't seem afraid of murder. On the contrary, she rolled the word round her tongue with relish.

The policemen descended and joined her.

A small old woman who lived in the cottage next door and had kept house for John Grebe in his lifetime. A widow of a retired customs officer, she looked about seventy, but was surprisingly nimble and intelligent. She wore black clothes and her white hair in a bun on the top of her head. Her bright dark eyes missed nothing. She held her head on one side and hunched her shoulder against it...probably a deformity.

DEATH DROPS THE PILOT

"I've had reporters round, offering me money to get in the house, but Mr Flewker, the lawyer, said nobody except the police was to come in unless he said so... Is it true that hussy Lucy Binks from the *Barlow Arms* has come into Mr Grebe's money and this house? Because, if it is, I've finished."

"I really couldn't say, Mrs Sattenstall. Mr Flewker'll be over after the will's published."

"I wouldn't put it past her to have wheedled it out of him. After all, since he quarrelled with Mr Tom, Mr Grebe hasn't had anybody in the world as far as I know. Just what that hussy wanted."

"Chief Inspector Littlejohn will be coming to look round. I've given him the key."

"That's all right."

"Nothing else, Mrs Sattenstall? Reporters and sightseers. No post or anything?"

The old lady fumbled in her pocket, which was somewhere in an underskirt beneath her voluminous outer clothes. She finally produced three postcards, which she held firmly, in spite of the efforts of Silence to snatch them.

"These didn't come by post. I mean, not since Mr Grebe died. He must have got them before."

"But we searched the place."

Silence was getting nettled.

"They were in the teapot there."

On the shelf of the dresser stood an old-fashioned pewter teapot, glistening from Mrs Sattenstall's elbow grease.

"He used to keep some loose change in it, and I went to it when I had to pay the milkman and the grocer and the like."

She clung to the cards, intent on telling a full tale before surrendering them.

"This mornin', the bread man came to say we owed for last week, two and fourpence, so I went to the teapot for it. There I found these three cards. Mr Grebe must 'ave put them there for some reason or other. Why, I don't know. Here you are."

They took them to the window to examine them.

All three were cheap coloured picture postcards, sold for a penny or two-pence because the views were out of date.

A picture of London Bridge with horse traffic crossing but bearing the postmark of a week ago. The message and address were printed in bold illiterate pencil.

MR J GREBE ESQUIRE,
ELMER'S CREEK.

So you've hiden youself away there have you.
I'm on my way you old swine, Leo.

Littlejohn examined it carefully. It was grubby and like the other two, bore a two-pence half-penny stamp. Probably it had been handled too much for fingerprints to be of any use.

The second card was of Warwick Castle and dated two days later than the first by Warwick Post Office.

Getting a bit nearer you dirty dog
Be seeing you soon and then. Leo.

The last effort bore a Tidmarsh postmark on the day before John Grebe's death. A cheap view of a main street.

Right on your dorstep now eh. You'll soon get vats coming to
you dear old pal (I don't think—) Leo.

Littlejohn put the three cards in his pocket.

"We'll be crossing for the conference with the Superintendent and the rest of you after lunch, Silence. I'd like to keep these cards till then."

They thanked Mrs Sattenstall, locked the house, and then Littlejohn and Cromwell saw Silence off on his trip back on the *Falbright Belle.*

"What do you make of it, Cromwell?"

They were walking along the jetty back to the *Barlow Arms.*

"Who's Leo, sir? He seems to have been out for Old Grebe's blood. It looks as if the case won't be so difficult after all. Once we can lay our hands on Leo, whoever he might be."

"That may not be so hard, either. Did you get a look at Lucy, the waitress at the *Barlow Arms?*"

"I can't say I did. I didn't see her face."

"She didn't want either of us to see her. I just happened to get a quick glance by accident. I was sure I'd seen her somewhere before but couldn't bring to mind where. The name Leo has brought it all back."

"Lucy Binks, Silence called her."

"Yes, but it's not Binks, at all. She's Lily Fowler."

Cromwell halted in his stride.

"Lily Fowler! Well I'll be damned! But as I said, I didn't get a look at her face. The Balham Bank robbery."

"That's it. Her brother was involved, and she appeared in court to give him an alibi, which was rejected, and she almost went down for perjury. Her brother got four years and, from my calculations, should just be out of gaol...Leo Fowler."

Cromwell thumped the palm of one hand with the fist of the other.

"An open and shut case. Old Grebe has been carrying on with Lily, or Lucy, while her brother's been in gaol, and now that Leo's out, he's after the old man's blood."

"Yes, but why? John Grebe seems to have treated Lily very well. He's even left her all he's got."

"Leo knew it and put Old John out of the way so that he and Lily could get it."

"A bit risky."

"The next thing is to find Leo."

"The first thing is to have a word with Lily, or Lucy. Here we are."

A smell of cooking in the *Barlow Arms* and a few guests, mainly locals, already starting to eat in the dining room. Fred Braid himself was acting as waiter and didn't look pleased about it. He shambled from the kitchen to the tables and back again, a scowl on his heavy, unpleasant face.

"Lunch is served," he said over his shoulder as Littlejohn and Cromwell hung up their hats. Then he halted.

"New job for me. Lucy's done a bunk. Waits till lunch is nearly ready and then clears out, bag and baggage, and after all we've done for 'er... What's bitten 'im?"

Littlejohn was in the telephone box dialling the Falbright police.

Silence had just got back. No, Lucy Binks wasn't on the ferry. There was, however, a bus which left just before for Freckleby. She might have got that and hoped to catch a train at the main line there.

"Lay it all on, then, Silence. She might even have thumbed a lift. She mustn't get away. If necessary, put down roadblocks."

"Whatever's the matter, sir? She's only a waitress and, besides, she was on duty when the ferry left the night Old John was killed. We checked that when we questioned the Braids."

"She happens to be Leo's sister."

"Leo? Who...? Good Lord!"

Littlejohn joined Cromwell in the hall.

"Nothing more we can do for the present, except be patient, not only with Lily, but also with Braid's table manners. Come on. Let's eat."

Through the window of the dining room, which gave a full view of the promenade and the whole of Balbeck Bay, they could see first Mrs Dixon emerge from the house and address her husband still among the carrots. Presumably the telephone.

Dixon slowly followed his wife and in next to no time emerged clad in uniform and running. With all speed, he vanished in the direction of the main road.

With trembling hands, Braid served steak-and-kidney pie, swearing under his breath.

4

THE LONG QUEST OF JOHN GREBE

A very unilluminating conference with the Falbright police. The Chief Constable, Superintendent Lecky, Inspector Silence, and the two Scotland Yard detectives sat round a table and talked for two hours, examining reports and photographs, all to little purpose. Specialists came in and out when required. The fingerprint experts had been all over the cottage and the bridge of the *Falbright Jenny* but produced nothing helpful. The medical report was formal but made by a very intelligent and careful man. A stab in the back had passed through the aorta and killed Grebe instantly. It also revealed cirrhosis of the liver which would soon have put paid to the old captain in any case. One sentence of the autopsy report interested Littlejohn:

> *The wound was a strange one. A savage gash, fairly deep, and then a long tapering wound right to the heart. It is difficult to even guess the type of weapon. Like a stiletto wound with part of the handle thrust in as well.*

"Grebe was a heavy drinker then?"

Littlejohn was leaning with his elbows on the table and his

cold pipe between his teeth. He was bored and wanted to get the session over, return to Elmer's Creek, and live again for a while against the background of Old John Grebe.

"I never saw him drunk, but he could shift rum with anybody. When Grebe and his buddies settled down for a proper session...well."

Silence nodded to emphasise his point.

"Who were his buddies?"

Littlejohn thumbed over the duplicate file they'd given him. It contained to the last detail all the points which the pompous fussy Chief Constable insisted on airing over and over again. But no names of Grebe's friends.

"Mainly Captain Bacon, from Peshall Hall, and Dr Horrocks. Sometimes Brett, the parish clerk, joined them. Grebe spent a lot of time with Bacon."

"Who's Bacon?"

"A retired director of a shipping line. A small set-up with about four coasters which plied between here and Liverpool and generally took short cargoes to and from places like continental ports just across the Channel, Scandinavia and Ireland. Bacon had some shares and was a sort of commodore of the fleet. Then, when he got past tossing about in the little tubs, he joined the board of the line. Six months after that, they got themselves taken over by one of the larger companies and Bacon, among others, made quite a packet. He bought Peshall Hall, which was empty at the time, and did it up. It's not a large place, but too big for him, and what with his drinkin' and such, he's let it go to ruin again a bit. It's said he bought it because it once belonged to his family and he'd always sworn if he ever came into money..."

It looked as if Silence was going to talk indefinitely and the Chief Constable was clearing his throat ready to stop him when the door opened, and a bobby put in his head.

"Excuse me, sir, but we've got them."

"Who?"

"Leo and Lily Fowler. The Freckleby police found them at the Junction waiting for the London train, sir. Lily had got a lift with the guard on the goods line from Elmer's Creek, and Leo was waiting for her."

"Where are they?"

"Over at Elmer's Creek, sir."

The Chief Constable turned mauve.

"What the hell are they doin' there?"

"There must have been a misunderstanding about the instructions. Freckleby thought Chief Inspector Littlejohn's headquarters were at the police station at Elmer's Creek."

Littlejohn daren't catch Cromwell's eye, otherwise they'd both have laughed.

"Well...Tell 'em to bring the pair of them over here right away. Were you saying somethin', Chief Inspector?"

"Perhaps I could see them over there first? After all, they aren't under arrest. Unless you think it better, sir."

"The case is in your hands, Littlejohn. Do as you like. But I'd have thought... Are you goin' over now?"

"Yes, sir. There's nothing to detain us here at present?"

"No. Keep me fully informed."

Over the river again and along the road to the Elmer's Creek police station. It was a simple place, a little police office in the front room and a house behind. PC Dixon was waiting for them at the garden gate, saluted them, opened it, and led them inside. They could hear the children noisily playing and a dog barking in the back. Dixon left them for a minute to restore quiet.

"What are you all doin' kicking up a row indoors? Go and play on the shore for a bit."

Dixon insisted on Littlejohn occupying the only chair in the office. Cromwell leaned against the wall. There was a large map of the district on one wall, police notices on the others, and a coloured picture of Winston Churchill over the small fireplace which held a gas fire.

PC Dixon must have been holding Lily and Leo Fowler in the cells, for he quickly disappeared and returned hustling them in front of him like a dog with two sheep. Leo was tall and thin. A bit elegant in a flashy kind of way. A long narrow face, with bright little dark eyes, a thin hooked nose, a sharp chin. His eyelids were heavy and hooded his eyes, and he looked exhausted. His thin hair receded from his narrow forehead and he wore it long in the neck. He had on a blue serge sailor's suit with a shabby reefer jacket, and yellow shoes with narrow toes. He entered the room reluctantly, obviously opposed to anything the police wanted him to do.

This time they got a good look at Lily, too. She wore a costume with a green jumper underneath it. Out of her black waitress's dress she looked better, even in her ill-fitting ready-made clothes. She was dark and plump with fine eyes and a firm neck and voluptuous bosom. But now she wasn't at her best. She seemed defeated. Her make-up was thoroughly dilapidated and the lipstick which remained here and there on her mouth was smeared about anyhow.

"Find them a couple of chairs, Dixon, will you, please?" Leo looked hard at Littlejohn and smiled with slow insolence.

"So it's you, is it? And what are you doing in a one-eyed hole like this, Inspector?"

Cromwell took his hands out of his pockets and looked ready to smack Leo.

"That'll do, Leo. Speak when you're spoken to."

"I wasn't speaking to you. And by what right are we brought 'ere? You 'aven't anythin' on us. And you've kept us waitin' long enough, too. Sittin' in a stinkin' little cell."

"I gave you some tea, didn't I?"

Dixon struggling with a couple of huge dining chairs from his house behind, was quick to defend himself.

"Tea! What I want to know is…"

"Did I tell you to shut up, Leo?"

Cromwell advanced half a step.

"We're here of our own free will, then, and don't you forget it."

Compared with Lily, Leo was a poor type. They were said to be brother and sister but with the exception of the way in which Lily had tried to protect him in the past, you wouldn't have thought it. Leo was a corner-boy, a smart Alec after easy money; Lily looked respectable, even in her shabby black suit.

Littlejohn lit his pipe and gave Leo and Lily a cigarette apiece.

"You first, Leo. Let me see, how old are you?"

Leo got to his feet and Cromwell pushed him down again.

"Behave yourself, Leo. It'll be over all the sooner."

"How old?"

"Twenty-five."

"And Lily?"

"Twenty-eight."

The answer came from the girl herself in a quiet resigned voice.

"Brother and sister, aren't you? Is that a straight blood relationship?"

Lily replied.

"I'm his half-sister. As you know already from the other case, I was illegitimate, and I was nearly two when Leo's father married my mother and took me on as his own kid. Leo was born a year after they got married."

"And you took his name?"

"For convenience. It avoided awkward questions, like."

"You're fond of Leo, aren't you, Lily?"

"Mother died when we were seven and ten. I'd to look after dad and Leo."

Leo shuffled in his seat and ground out his cigarette under his heel on the floor.

"What *is* all this? No need to go into all the fam'ly 'istory, is there?"

Littlejohn looked him in the face.

"I just couldn't understand her being so fond of a chap like you, Leo. However... What were you doing here till you left a few nights ago?"

"A chap can call to see his sister, can't he?"

"Was that all you came for?"

"What else?"

"Did you send for him, Lily?"

"He only came out three weeks since. I went to the prison to meet him. Nobody here knew, but *you* know about it all. He wouldn't come with me right away. Wanted to see some friends, he said. I told him I could get him a job here. A week ago, he arrived."

"Broke, I suppose, and after some money from you?"

Her eyes flared.

"After a stretch in jail, what do you expect? He wasn't rolling in it. Matter of fact, he hitchhiked all the way here from London."

"Sending postcards on the way?"

Leo suddenly looked interested.

"What do you mean?"

He was used to the police by now and there was malice in his voice.

Littlejohn took the three postcards from his pocket and flung them across the desk. Leo picked them up and examined them and Lily rose and looked over his shoulder.

"I never sent these."

"I thought not. You wouldn't be such a fool, would you, Leo?"

"Look 'ere. Wot the 'ell? Are you tryin' to pin the old buffer's death on me? Because, if you are..."

"You've never seen those cards before?"

"I said so."

"That's not your writing?"

"Look. I'm not an educated bloke, but I can do better than that. W-A-T...wot. D-O-R-S-T-E-P...doorstep. I'm not as bad a speller as all that. Besides, I never set eyes on the captain before I got 'ere."

"Are you sure?"

"What he says is right, Inspector."

Lily was obviously speaking the truth.

"How did you come to know Grebe, Lily?"

"I met him in a transport cafe in Southwark, down by the docks. He called one day. I hadn't been well and I nearly fainted at the time he was in. He was very kind and called to see me a day or two after. I said I was all right; just a bit run down. Then, what does he do, but offer to get me a job here? I wasn't struck on the idea because I'm a London girl and I get bored when I'm out of town, but I wasn't well and I wanted a change. So I came for the season. He looked after me all the time I was 'ere and said I needn't feel short of a home. I could always call to see him at his place. Which I did, a time or two. Nothing wrong."

Leo turned with a scornful gesture.

"I should 'ope not, and him nearly seventy. You'd be hard-up."

"Don't talk like that about him, Leo. He never..." Littlejohn lit his pipe again.

"But he was very friendly with you. Why was that?"

"I suppose he took a fancy to me. It wasn't my fault."

There was a coquettish look in her eye, and she patted her dark hair almost instinctively.

"Did he ever suggest you went to live with him?"

"Yes. He asked me to come and keep house for him. He'd a spare room. I said I couldn't. That sort of job didn't appeal to me. Cooped up with an old man. I'm young enough yet to want younger company. Mind you, I won't have a wrong word said about the captain. One of the best."

"When did you intend going back to London?"

"When the winter came on, I guess. I couldn't stand this place much longer. Too quiet altogether."

"Did you tell that to Captain Grebe?"

"Can't think I did. Matter of fact, I put off telling him deliberately. I knew he'd take on."

"You perhaps planned to leave without telling him?"

"Perhaps."

Outside the sun was shining and making the sands sparkle. High clouds floated across Balbeck Bay, and far out a few sailing boats were making for home.

A tall, angular man, carrying a string of small plaice arrived at the gate next door and entered. A man of about seventy, rather bad on his feet, and dressed in tweeds with a fishing hat.

"Is that Dr Horrocks?"

"Yes, sir."

"A friend of Captain Grebe's?"

"Yes. He's just come from his boat, by the look of him. Been fishin' at the Farne Deep. He used to take the captain often enough."

Littlejohn turned to Lily.

"Did you know Captain Grebe had left you all he had? House, money...the lot?"

Lily's eyes opened wide and a smirk slowly appeared on Leo's ugly face. You could almost see him calculating the gains and getting ready to borrow all he could.

"It's not true."

"It is. You'll be hearing soon from the lawyer. Now why should Captain Grebe do that?"

"I don't know. I suppose he'd nobody else."

"He'd his brother."

"He hated him."

"He told you so?"

"Yes. His brother tried to suggest that...that between the captain and me..."

"So I believe. Any idea why the brother settled so near the captain?"

"Captain Grebe said he was a good-for-nothing who'd always sponged on him. He followed the captain here years ago and later borrowed from him to start the business down the road there. They never got on, but the captain always said blood was thicker than water and he couldn't let his brother starve."

Littlejohn turned to Leo again.

"What are you doing in that get-up, Leo? Sailor clothes, I mean?"

"I can wear what I want, can't I?"

Lily looked distressed again.

"Why can't you be civil, Leo? It only leads to trouble. He came to see me in a light-grey suit. With that on, nobody here would find him a job. It made him look as if he didn't *want* work. So I bought him one more in keepin' across at Falbright."

"And a bright cut I look in it, too! Talk about 'I didn't rear my boy to be a sailor.' I don't know what the boys in London would think of me now."

There was a pause. They could hear the waves breaking on the shingle outside. The front door was open and a fresh bracing breeze blew in and made the official notices flap on the walls.

"What made you suddenly decide to clear out, Leo?"

"I'm free to do as I like, ain't I? I don't like it here. It's not my line of business workin' on the waterfront in a cockeyed little port."

"I'm sure it isn't. But your sister was doing her best to keep you straight. What were you doing on the ferry that ran adrift after the captain had been killed on it?"

"Look here..."

"It was you who crossed half-drunk, then."

No answer.

Littlejohn turned to Lily.

"He was on the last ferry…the one on which Captain Grebe met his death, wasn't he? Don't deny it. That was why the pair of you were so anxious to get away. The reason why you, Lily, took to your heels when you saw me arrive, wasn't it?"

"Leo didn't do it."

"Nobody says he did. But you thought perhaps he *might* have done it, didn't you?"

She looked resigned and a bit faded again. A kind of despair had taken hold of her. A weariness at always having to get Leo out of trouble and his getting into it again as fast as ever.

"He told me he'd not done it, although he was on board when the boat ran on the sandbank. I've never known Leo tell me a lie."

"Why the hurry? Why the hasty retreat on the last ferry? Where was he going at that hour?"

"He'd arranged for a lift on one of the fish lorries as far as Manchester and he said he'd thumb another lift to London from there. The lorry was going about midnight. We had a bit of a row about the way he was drinking at the *Barlow Arms* and he packed up and left for the ferry."

"Is that right, Leo?"

"Are you hintin' Lily might be a liar, becos…?"

"That'll do. You sponged on your sister till you couldn't do it anymore and then you made off for London. Why were you at Freckleby, then, instead of off on the fish lorry?"

"It 'ad gone when I got there. It took them so long to get us off the sandbank and take our names."

"You gave the wrong name and address, I suppose."

"What do you expect? I'd just done a stretch. They'd have blamed it on me."

49

"So you decided to go by train, and you hid out for a bit and then telephoned Lily?"

Silence.

"You wanted more money to get away, so you got in touch with Lily who arranged to meet you?"

It was Lily who answered.

"He telephoned the next morning and I told him to stay at Freckleby till I met him and telephone me every day. I couldn't leave till I'd drawn my pay. I needed it. Then, when you came, I thought I'd better pick up Leo and the both of us get away."

"Panic, Lily?"

"Call it that if you like. But neither Leo nor me had anything to do with Captain Grebe's dying. Why should we?"

"Those postcards, now. Did anybody know you had a brother called Leo?"

"A lot of the regulars at the *Barlow Arms*. You see, when Leo came out of…came out…I wanted a few days off to meet him and I just said to Mr Braid I'd want them because I was going to see my brother, who was home from abroad. He said he never knew I had a brother and what was his name. I'd no more sense than to say Leo. Mr Braid thought it a funny name for a brother of mine. He used to tease me about it before the customers. 'How's Leo?' he'd say and tell them I'd a brother with a posh name. They all got to know."

"You see, don't you, Lily, that these three postcards give one the idea that Leo was on his way here to settle accounts with Captain Grebe? And those accounts might have concerned *you*. In other words, they give the idea that Grebe had led you astray or wronged you…"

Littlejohn turned to Leo again.

"You're sure you never knew Captain Grebe before you came here? It's useless to tell me you never saw him in your life. He used to come and drink at the *Barlow Arms* and he was on the ferry every day. You saw him and I'm surprised you didn't try to touch him for a loan on account of his good-feelings for Lily."

"Well, I didn't."

"No, sir, he didn't. I wouldn't let him even speak to the captain and I didn't tell the captain Leo was my brother. I told Leo I'd never speak to him again if he tried to borrow money from Captain Grebe."

"Well, I've only one other thing to ask you, Lily. I don't understand Captain Grebe's excessive fondness for you. He picked you up in Southwark, got you a job, looked after you, and left you all he had. Why? He never made any improper suggestions to you, did he?"

"Never! He wouldn't have done such a thing."

"And he wanted you to live with him and keep house."

"He was a lonely old man, but I just couldn't. It wasn't my line."

"Why? A better job and more security than serving at the *Barlow Arms*."

Lily was growing afraid. Her face was pale and strained and she tore at the small handkerchief she had been using.

"How long had Captain Grebe been looking for you when he found you in Southwark, Lily?"

Leo's mouth opened and his puzzled eyes turned to his sister's face.

"I don't know what you mean."

"Every year as soon as he got his leave, Captain Grebe went off, nobody knew where, seeking something, wandering about alone. Then, he found what he wanted, brought her here, died, and left her all he'd got. Did he never tell you he was your father, Lily?"

Dead silence again. Even Leo seemed to hold his breath waiting for the answer. The waves dragged at the shingle on the beach, and in the river a tugboat hooted excitedly.

"He never said so and I never guessed, except that he often

asked about my mother and how she died and how she went on before she married. When you told me he left me his money in his will, it suddenly struck me. If it's true, he must have sought me all over the place. I was born in Gravesend. My own father went to sea without marrying my mother because he didn't know she was going to have a baby. Then Leo's father, my foster father, came and my mother took him, and he was good to me."

"What happened to him? Is *he* dead, too?"

"I don't know. He was a tugboat captain on the Thames. One day, when I was twelve, he went off to work and never came back."

"That was before the war?"

"Yes. We all thought he'd somehow fallen overboard in the river but when we inquired about him, it turned out he'd given up being a pilot over twelve months before. It was all a mystery. He was presumed dead in the end."

"I wonder why Grebe never told you if you were his daughter. He took enough trouble to find you."

"Perhaps he was ashamed to tell me, considering the way he treated my mother."

Littlejohn stood up and knocked out his pipe in the fireplace.

"Well, you can both go now and don't try to get away again, because we certainly haven't finished with either of you. You'd better go back to your job, Lily, and if Leo doesn't want to stay at the *Barlow Arms*, he'd better get a room at one of the fishermen's cottages. Have you enough money, Leo?"

Lily was quick to his assistance.

"I'll look after him. He slept over the garage at the *Barlow Arms*. There's a cheap room there that some of the chauffeurs use in the season."

"Well, get along, the pair of you. And if you try to get away, we'll bring you back and lock you up."

They left with scarcely another word and as he watched them through the window, Littlejohn could see Leo rating Lily and angrily gesticulating at her, presumably because she'd not told him everything she knew.

Dixon accompanied the two detectives to the door of the police station, from which they could see the broad stretch of sea and sands between the Hore estuary and the far end of Balbeck Bay, with the sun beginning to set across them. It was chilly and lonely and the figures still gathering bait and netting for shrimps on the tideline looked insignificant. Overhead flew a flock of wild geese, honking their way home from their feeding grounds, and along the road, dead drunk, shuffled the tramp who, earlier in the day, had tried to sell some bulrushes to Cromwell.

"Penny the rush..." he managed to say to the party at the door of the police station, and then wobbled away to sleep off his drinks in his favourite haystack somewhere on the marsh.

5

EVENING PATROL

A fter the drunken tramp had left them and vanished round the bend in the road, the trio of officers stood silently at the door of the police station, looking across the stretch of clean sand with the tide slowly coming in across it. The sun declining in the West cast a shimmering crest of gold across the waves. It was one of those moments of beauty and silence which are surrendered reluctantly.

"I'd better be movin' on, sir. You won't mind if I leave you. I've the evenin' patrol to do. I'd better be gettin' out my bike."

Dixon had his job to do, looking after the joint parishes of Elmer's Creek and Peshall. He seemed quite capable of the task. A hairy giant, with a heavy moustache and eyebrows. Tall, benevolent, with a copper-coloured complexion from wind, sun and sea air. His sandy hair had been bleached fair by the sunshine of his garden.

"How far does your beat take you, Dixon?"

"Along the road to the far edge of Peshall and then back to the *Barlow Arms*. Nothin' much ever happens...but then, you never know, sir, do you?"

"I'll come with you, if I may. It'll be a nice walk before dinner."

Dixon's eyes opened wide. This meant a five-mile walk, instead of a steady cycle ride. All the same, he didn't mind, provided it didn't happen too often.

"It'll be a pleasure, sir."

"And on the way, you can tell me all about Captain Grebe, his habits and his friends."

"No difficulty there, sir."

Littlejohn was anxious to get an idea of a day in the ferry master's life. In fact, of many days' methodical routine of a bachelor, who hadn't very much to do in his spare time.

"And while I'm away, Cromwell, you might call on Tom Grebe, the captain's brother, and get to know, if you can, what brought him here in the first place, his relations with the dead man, and what they thought of one another. I'll see you at the *Arms* in time for dinner. Don't drink too much dandelion and burdock."

Cromwell jumped at the suggestion. Sitting on a barrel, talking to Tom Grebe, with perhaps a drink of his infernal brew now and then to lubricate the interview, appealed to his sense of curiosity much more than pounding the beat with PC Dixon.

"Right, sir."

Dixon removed the cycle clips from the bottoms of his regulation trousers and shouted indoors to his wife that he was off on his rounds.

The road forked at the signpost about two hundred yards from the police station. Littlejohn and Dixon took to the right, navigated two hairpin bends, and found themselves in Peshall village, where the road broadened half reluctantly to accommodate two shops, a couple of cafes, and a small church with a spire. One of the shops embraced the post office and the postman was just emerging with his delivery bag.

"Afternoon, Percy."

Dixon greeted his uniformed rival with unusual zest. He was proud of his distinguished companion and anxious to introduce him.

"This is Percy Fothergill, our postman, sir. Chief Inspector Littlejohn, of Scotland Yard, here on the Captain Grebe case."

The postman nodded his head agreeably several times, not knowing whether or not it was quite the thing to offer a handshake, until Littlejohn showed the way. Even then, there was an atmosphere of reserve about the meeting. The postman was jealous of the policeman on many counts. They were rivals at all the local flower and vegetable shows and the only two men who wore official uniforms on government business in the little community.

Furthermore, Fothergill often spoke of Dixon as a timeserver. He accused the bobby of always being "after his stripes", as though in some way the villages were suffering through Dixon's struggles to become a sergeant. Dixon, in turn, ponderously deprecated Fothergill's incessant efforts to get himself a little red van for deliveries, instead of his old red bike. Whichever came first, red van or stripes, would be a tremendous official feather in the cap of the lucky one of the rival pair.

"Good afternoon, constable. Good afternoon, sir, to you. We're very pleased to welcome you 'ere to solve the case which our local men are quite out of their depths in."

Fothergill was tall and lean, dark and hairy, with a moustache larger than his rival's, malicious little dark eyes, and a thin long nose. It was suggested in the village that he steamed open all the interesting letters. He certainly knew as much as the constable about what went on, good or bad. He had his good points, though. He was always ready to open and read the letters he delivered to the blind, the illiterate, and the busy people. He even wrote letters for those who couldn't write.

"Did Captain Grebe get very much mail, Fothergill?"

The postman raised his bushy eyebrows, looked profound, and coughed.

"My duties are, of course, confidential, sir, but..."

He gave Dixon a searching look as though the poor sweating bobby were tempting him to break his trust.

"But as it's official police, I don't mind sayin' that a few days before his death, the captain received three queer postcards."

"The Chief Inspector's got those, Percy."

One up to Dixon. The postman couldn't have recoiled more from a blow across the mouth.

"Oh, indeed."

The postman then gathered himself together to fire a retaliatory shot.

"But do you know, sir, that before his death, the captain was regularly sendin' money to a London detective agency once a month?"

Fothergill stepped back a pace and a satisfied smirk came on his face as he threw a look at Dixon.

"How long for?"

"He'd been at it for two or three years on and off."

"How did you know it was the captain and he was sendin' money?"

Dixon's eyes grew small and malicious as he shot his question. He knew how Percy knew, of course. With the help of the steaming kettle. But he wasn't going to miss a chance like this.

"A suspicious chap, aren't you, Albert? Well, one of the letters was unsealed...by accident, I prezhume...when posted, so I stuck it up. But not before seein' five pounds in notes in it. Ought to 'ave been registered, by rights. The address was there plain as a pikestaff...Hamster's Detective Agency in the Strand, London. I knew the captain's writin', of course."

Hamster's, eh? Littlejohn smiled. Hamster had once been a constable at Scotland Yard and had 'retired'. Now he was running a little private agency of his own. He made a note to have a word with Hamster, if necessary.

"What was the captain doing with the detective agency, Fothergill? Do you know?"

The postman thought hard. He wanted to show his superior knowledge, but it needed a bit of careful handling.

"I think he was tryin' to trace somebody."

"Who?"

"Well, if what I say might be regarded as under the umbrella of, shall we call it, official secrets, I'll tell you. It was Lucy at the *Barlow Arms* he was seekin'. But the name's not Lucy. It's Lily, Lily Fowler."

Dixon was on him like a shot.

"How did you come by that information, Percy?"

"Perfec'ly legitimately. Always a suspicious one, Albert, aren't you? Everybody guilty till they're proved innercent. It's not British, Albert; it's not British."

Dixon turned a dusky red as Fothergill told his tale to Littlejohn.

"The detective agency sent a receipt on one occasion. It was in an open envelope, as such things usually are, and the flap wasn't tucked in. As I tucked it back, I 'appened to see words to this effect on the bill. 'To inquiries re Lily Fowler (Lucy Biggs).' And then the amount of five pounds. I've a good memory, you see. My job depends on it."

Dixon's mouth was slowly opening to question the procedure, but Littlejohn glared at him to keep quiet. The postman certainly hadn't come by this flaunted information in the way he said he had. In the first place, Hamster's would never write about anything in an unsealed envelope; no private detective worth his salt would do such a thing. The kettle had been at work again, but it was as well not to suggest it. Much might depend on Fothergill's good will. So they bade him good afternoon and he left them grumbling that he had to deliver a solitary ruddy circular for a free sample of detergent at Peshall Hall two miles away.

"They ought to get me a van for me rounds, and if you're ever questioned on the point either 'ere or at Whitehall, Chief Inspector, I'll take it as a favour if you'll put in a good an' appropriate word for me."

The beat took them through the village and as the houses began to peter out, Dixon indicated Peshall Hall in the distance, standing in a small forest.

"Used to belong to the aristocracy, sir."

He sighed loudly, lamenting the passing of the class who, at Christmas, used to give the local constable a turkey and five pounds for ensuring their safety over the past year.

"Captain Grebe was regular in his habits, Dixon?"

"Yes, sir. A real sailor. Like clockwork."

"What did he do with his time, then?"

Dixon gave Littlejohn a startled look as though the Chief Inspector might be putting one of the burdens of Hercules on his back.

"Well, sir..."

"About his work on the ferryboat... Was he at it all day?"

"Not exac'ly. There are three captains, sir. Two on duty and one off. That's in summer. In winter, when the schedules are changed and there aren't as many boats, one captain is sort of laid off on furlough and only one boat's used. The other two do eight hours at a time."

"How is it worked, this timetable? I don't want a full schedule. I can get one from the ferry office. What I'm after is the leisure of Captain Grebe and how he spent it."

"The first ferry from here is at six, summer and winter. That's for the market men and early workers. The last in winter is at ten-thirty and in summer, till mid-September, it runs till eleven. So, in winter, one captain works six till two; the other then takes over till half-past ten. They swop shifts every week.

In summer, it's a bit different. Three captains run two boats between 'em for seventeen hours all told."

"And when Grebe wasn't on duty, how did he spend his time?"

"When he was on duty in the mornin', he'd take a walk every afternoon, more or less over this very round we're doin' now. Do his shoppin' in Peshall, walk along this road to see Captain Bacon at Peshall 'All, and stay there a bit. Then you'd see 'im walkin' back home to tea. At night, he'd have his tea and then turn out at about seven. If it was dark, he'd go to the *Arms* for a drink; if it wasn't dark, he'd have a gossip on the jetty with the fishermen there."

"And when he was free in the mornings?"

"Then, he'd still have his walk. Kept him from gettin' set in his body, he'd say. A chap tends to stiffen up, like, always on the bridge of a little boat."

"He saw his cronies every day."

"Yes. Dr Horrocks and Captain Bacon. They'd go off fishin' two or three days a week in good weather, the three of them. Brett, the parish clerk, would go sometimes. The four of them would meet for a drink at the *Barlow Arms* every night, too. Brett wasn't quite *in* with them, if you see what I mean, sir. The two captains and the doctor were really pals; Brett just an 'anger-on. Captain Grebe never got on real friendly terms with anybody else. Not even his brother."

"He didn't like his brother?"

"No. Mr Tom's a religious man. A Methodist...and the Captain was a bit too much for 'im. Language, and the like."

"How did Tom Grebe turn up here? Did the captain bring him?"

"Yes. Don't know why he did. He wasn't fond of him, so why have 'im on the doorstep, so to speak? Perhaps he wanted to keep an eye on Mr Tom, so's he'd not get in mischief. Mr Tom's a poor businessman. I did hear from somebody 'ere on 'oliday, who knew him and once lived in the same town, that he'd been bankrupt once and it was known there that his brother, the captain, paid his debts and took him away with him, quick like. Perhaps the disgrace was too much for a straight man like Captain Grebe and he took Mr Tom under his wing to stop him goin' bankrupt again."

And from the bobby's simple suggestion Littlejohn got an idea.

"Dixon, did it ever strike you that Captain Grebe was hiding here out of the way of someone?"

Dixon stopped in his stride to think it out.

"What makes you think that, sir? It never struck *me*."

"Perhaps you haven't seen the file on the case. Captain Grebe, a master mariner, for some reason and when quite a young man, decided to tuck himself away in this obscure spot, became first a river pilot and then a ferry master. Rather a waste of talent for a man who, during the first war, was a troopship captain."

"Yes, sir. But perhaps he liked the place after all, and if his needs were few, he might have preferred a bit of peace here to a lot of money and responsibility elsewhere."

"Yes, that's quite reasonable. But then there are the post-cards. Whoever wrote them — Leo, or somebody else — suggested that Grebe had been hiding and that now the writer had found him out."

"Yes. There's that."

"And then there's an idea you've just put in my head. Grebe brings a brother he doesn't like, to live on his doorstep, perhaps because the brother's been bankrupt and likely to repeat his failure. So Grebe puts him where he can keep an eye on him."

"Well... What of that, sir?"

"When a man goes bust, his bankruptcy's advertised in the newspapers, he's publicly examined and reported on, and his disgrace is made as public as possible, so that he can't take in the public again. Suppose whoever's looking for Captain Grebe, finds the news of a Grebe who's bankrupt. By contacting Tom Grebe, he can soon find John. In other words, John took Tom off the bankruptcy market to keep him from leading somebody to his brother."

"But who could Captain Grebe have been runnin' away from all this time?"

"I don't know. If we find that out, we'll probably solve the case."

"Evenin', Dixon. Deuced hot, isn't it?"

In his concentration on the conversation, Dixon was ignoring passers-by. The one now greeting him was an elderly, clean shaven, tall man, dressed in tweeds and a soft hat. He carried a large ash stick and had a spaniel trotting at his heels.

"Evening, Captain, evening. It's 'ot, I agree."

Dixon replied in an eager, shrill shout which made a passing milk horse prick up its ears in surprise.

The man walked on without stopping but gave Littlejohn a keen searching glance as he passed.

"That's Captain Bacon from Peshall 'All, sir."

"Looks more Army than Navy, Dixon."

Which was right. Bacon was slim and had the tottering gait and bandy legs of a cavalryman.

"When he came home from the sea to retire here, sir, he was a fine, stout, well set-up man. He's aged of late years. The death of Captain Grebe's been a bad shock to him, you can see. They were good pals."

The road was thinly lined with new bungalows and behind them, allotments and market gardens. Two fields away to the West, Littlejohn could see the land slope down and eventually merge with the tideline.

Now and then, the workmen and occupants in the gardens and smallholdings raised themselves to shout greetings to Dixon, who was on good neighbourly terms with them all. After all, what's the local bobby for, but to be a friend in need? That's what Dixon used to tell himself in his hours of meditation. Sort of shepherd of the flock, to keep 'em all in order and protect them from other people. The last house before Peshall Hall. This too was built in a small grove of trees and was approached by a long drive closed from the road by large wrought-iron gates. On the stone gatepost the name: *Solitude*.

"That's Mrs Iremonger's 'ouse, sir. Now *there's* a character for you, if you like."

Dixon paused. Opposite *Solitude* there was another large house behind brick walls, which had been turned into a girls' school. The girls were in the habit of baiting Dixon as they walked in a crocodile for nature study or church service, hailing him one after another. "Good afternoon, Constable Dixon." Twenty or more of them, and blushing, he had to keep returning their greetings. Now, rather than run this gauntlet of energetic young femininity, Dixon had developed the habit of dodging round corners and hedges. He looked to right and left, saw nobody, and sighed with relief.

"Why is she a character?"

"Drunk as a lord most of the day. Drink with anybody *and* drink most of 'em under the table. Facts is often stranger than fiction, sir."

They were still walking briskly and Littlejohn made no reply. He knew that Dixon wouldn't be able to refrain from his tale. It soon came.

"She's a friend of Captain Bacon, and of Captain Grebe, sir, when he was alive. Her husband was one of the party and he owned a big yacht, the *Euryanthe*, on which they'd sometimes go for a trip when Captain Grebe had time off. Mr Iremonger was a millionaire, I believe. Made 'is money abroad. Well… They say that one day in London a girl offered to sell him a posy. Whether she was in a shop, or a street seller, I never quite got to know. But he bought the buttonhole, took a fancy to 'er, and married her."

"Quite a romance."

"You're tellin' me, if you'll pardon me puttin' it that way. They hadn't been married long before they started drinkin' like a pair of fish. They'd give parties on the yacht and once, when they were moored in the river 'ere and gave a swell dinner, the pair of 'em got so drunk they walked off the ship and into the River Hore. He died about fifteen or more years since. The gossips say, she started him drinkin' so he'd booze himself to death and leave her his fortune. Which he did. And now, she can't stop drinkin' herself, so there's a sort of 'eavenly justice in the case. She's known as Little Chickabiddy. That's what 'er husband always called her and if I was to introduce you to 'er now and you was to say, 'Pleased to meet you, Mrs Iremonger,' she'd jest say, 'Call me Chickabiddy. They all do.'"

"And she was a friend of Grebe and Bacon and Dr Horrocks?"

"Yes. They're in a sort of syndicate for buildin' houses on the road we passed along. Bacon owns some of the land and Mrs Iremonger a part of it, and they made a pool to try and make more money than they've already got."

They paused at the gates to look down the drive. Gardeners were busy on the borders, and in the distance, the house, built on colonial lines with a low roof and a spreading white facade, looked deserted.

"She's in there...probably tight and with the shutters all drawn."

They could just make out one of the chimneys faintly smoking.

"I saw Dr Horrocks comin' out this way this mornin'. Perhaps she's got the DT's. She has 'em now and then. When she's sober, she's as nice as pie, but when she's proper drunk, she's a devil. They say there's gipsy blood in 'er. She can only

keep staff by payin' 'em twice as much as anybody else. Well...
She can afford it."

"Did Grebe call here much?"

"Now and then, but mostly with the other two. They'd all be
together here sometimes. I'd see Dr Horrocks's car and often
meet the other two comin' away a bit the worse for drink.
Directors' meetin's of the building trust, likely as not."

"Was Grebe in the trust?"

"It's said he was. Perhaps all bein' friends, they let him in and
have his cut."

"How long had they been friends?"

"Dr Horrocks has been here for donkey's years, sir. He was a
pal of Captain Bacon, who belongs to these parts. He was born
here, was the captain. Then, Captain Grebe arrived. All before
my time, of course, but I hear things from the old people, you
know. Grebe seemed to know Horrocks and Bacon, because I've
been told they were on visitin' terms right away, as soon as he
came. Then, just before the war, the Iremongers arrived and the
other three were soon pals with them, all drinkin' together."

They had reached the gloomy gates of Peshall Hall, great
wrought-iron spikes, with spear-tops of tarnished gilt, and
rampant lions on the gateposts. A dark avenue of elms swept
from the gatehouse to the hall, which was only dimly visible
from where the two men stood.

The gatekeeper was smoking at the door of his lodge. He
eyed Dixon and Littlejohn craftily.

The policeman and the gatekeeper stared at each other, each
trying to discover what the other was wanting and thinking. For
a second, the looks exchanged were ones of hatred. Then they
both relaxed.

"Afternoon, Charlie."

"Afternoon. On the snoop again, eh?"

Dixon recoiled. He knew Charlie was being offensive simply
to show him, in front of a spectator, that he didn't care a damn.

A rough countryman in leggings and with a face like a goat. He spat in the drive in a gesture of defiance.

"Not come to see the captain, 'ave yer? Becos you've had a wasted journey. He's out."

"We met him going to the village."

"Well, is it me you want?"

"No. I'm on my beat and well you know it, and this is Chief Inspector Littlejohn, of Scotland Yard, and I'll thank you to be polite when you speak to us."

"Ha! Landidah! If you and the Inspector are round 'ere tryin' to find out about Captain Grebe, you're wastin' your time."

"Who said we were?"

"That's what it is, isn't it?"

In the house behind, a slovenly woman was peeling potatoes. Now and then, she turned her head and watched them through the window. A good wash and her hair properly combed and she'd have been very good looking, with her dark eyes and her fine nose. She looked years younger than Charlie Withers, locally known as Charlie the Cheat, because he'd once been half killed by a drunken sailor for cheating at cards.

The wrangling between Dixon and Charlie might have gone on longer, but in the lodge a bell rang, presumably on the private line from the hall.

"You're wanted up at the house, dad."

The woman with the potato bucket shouted without even answering the phone and Withers, muttering obscenities under his breath, went indoors.

Littlejohn and Dixon turned about. This was the end of the beat for the patrolling bobby. The next stretch was along the shore.

They made their way down the road they had come until they passed *Solitude*, and then a track through two fields led to the shore and the by-road between Elmer's Creek and Pullar's Sands. As Dixon was showing Littlejohn the stile, a car travelling towards *Solitude* pulled up. There was a chauffeur in front and a woman behind. She lowered the window.

"Dixon!"

"Mrs Iremonger," said the bobby to Littlejohn out of the corner of his mouth as he turned.

"Yes, Mrs Iremonger."

"Dixon, tell the post office, or whoever it is keeps damn well sending them, that I don't want any more forms asking me if I've paid my wireless licence. My set broke down in the summer and I threw the damn thing out of the window. I won't be pestered. Don't forget."

Littlejohn stood smoking by the stile, watching Chickabiddy bullying the bobby.

A good-looking woman still, in spite of incessant drink and the ravages of time. She looked between forty and fifty. She was black-haired, and nature was assisted in this matter by art; for there wasn't a sign of greyness. No wonder some said she had gipsy blood. Her features were strong and regular. A bit coarse, but aquiline still and handsome. She wore a tweed costume with a white blouse fastened at the neck by what appeared to be a single stone diamond brooch. A stone which, if genuine, was worth a fortune. She was smoking a cigarette.

Dixon was answering some muttered questions from Mrs Iremonger. He returned to Littlejohn.

"She's heard you're here and asked to meet you." And lowering his voice: "She's stone sober."

Dixon deferentially introduced the pair of them.

She was cordial but didn't suggest the familiarity of Chickabiddy.

"I'm glad they've put the case in responsible hands. We simply can't let a decent fellow like Grebe die and not find out who did it, now, can we?"

She looked Littlejohn straight in the face and the Chief Inspector remembered the encounter between Dixon and Withers, ten minutes before. Here it had passed to a higher level, but the looks exchanged between him and Chickabiddy might have contained similar hatred for a brief second. Then they both smiled politely.

"Call at my place for a drink, Chief Inspector. Any time. Just call. I was a friend of Captain Grebe and so was my late husband. I may be able to help you. I've read about some of your cases. Don't forget. Call soon."

She nodded to the chauffeur who slipped the engine in gear and drove her off without another word.

"So that's Chickabiddy, is it, Dixon? A silly name for such a woman. More like Lady Macbeth."

"Beg pardon, sir."

"Is that the stile? Let's get going, then."

From the coast road, they could see the unbroken stretch of Balbeck Bay until its line vanished into the haze far away. In the foreground, a clump of buildings which must be Pullar's Sands.

"That's Pullar's Sands, sir. There's a few houses and a pub and shop there. When the tide's out, you can cross the sands and get away north, but when the sea's in, you've another three miles round to the bridge at Parth to go. That's what you might call the excuse for the pub bein' there. The *Saracen's Head.*"

Littlejohn wondered what Saracens had to do with such a forsaken spot. There was nothing much on either side of the coast road between Pullar's Sands and Elmer's Creek. To the West, the sea with a tideline marked by old cans, corks, seaweed, driftwood, and other junk. It was Dixon's duty to patrol there twice a day to make sure nobody was drowned and needing removal from among the rubbish, and to see that nobody misbehaved on the foreshore. The tide was coming in and the shrimpers, cocklers and bait-diggers were retreating before it.

On the other side of the road, flat fields protected from the high tides by a long causeway along which the highway also ran. The dykes which drained the fields formed an intricate network, emptying themselves into a main ditch which flowed to the sea. The backs of *Solitude* and the other buildings along the inland road were plainly visible. From where he stood Littlejohn caught the glint of the sun reflected on glass and turning in the direction of *Solitude* made out Mrs Iremonger following their course with binoculars. As soon as he turned, she withdrew from the upper window and closed the shutters.

He felt that, somehow, Mrs Iremonger and he had already embarked on a battle of wits about how Grebe died.

"Here's Jumping Joe again."

Dixon, his eyes shaded against the western sun, was watching a figure tottering towards them along the embankment.

"Who?"

"The tramp fellow who tried to sell the rushes to the sergeant a little while ago. Nobody knows what his proper name is. It's Joe, but as for the rest... He rarely keeps to the road, crossin' the fields and jumpin' the ditches like a goat. That's how he got his nickname."

Jumping Joe was already upon them. He was more sober than when last they saw him and judging from the soaked state of his long shaggy hair, he'd been cooling his head somewhere.

"Hullo, Joe. You ought to've had a good sleep, you know. You'd had one above the eight when we met you a little while back."

"My own business entirely. Drink if I want to. Can pay for all I need. Out of my way, policeman."

A cultivated voice, coarsened and harsh from too much drink and neglect. The sentences were clipped, and the words well spoken. The man himself wore a tattered grey suit which fitted anyhow, a knotted silk scarf, a dirty cloth cap, and heavy boots without socks. His face was clean enough, but unshaven. A grey stiff beard, rough grey hair, a massive roman nose, and loose lips. The eyes were blue, round and small, with a film

69

across them which prevented you from seeing what Joe was thinking. Nobody knew whence he came. Five years ago, he'd suddenly turned up off the ferry and settled down, sleeping in barns, cadging, selling mushrooms, cobnuts or blackberries, carried in his hat, or bulrushes cut from the ponds.

"I've plenty of money. And more where that came from. Can pay my way."

"Don't overdo it, then, Joe. Don't end up in the cells like you did last winter."

"Don't care where I end up. As for overdoing it... After what I've seen I need somethin' to help me forget. Ghosts on the marsh, I tell you. Ghosts. Never believed in ghosts, but this time, I've seen 'em... Gospel truth. Ghosts..."

He shambled off to the nearest pub, walking like one eager to shake off an unpleasant companion. As he went, talking and shouting, the gulls rose from the marsh and haunted him further with their sad cries.

6

SOFT DRINKS

I f the shop's shut, you'll find him in the 'ouse at the back."
A passer-by, taking the air with an aged bulldog, shouted
to Cromwell who was trying the door of Tom Grebe's soft-
drink brewery.

Cromwell thanked the man and looked around. The village
had grown suddenly animated, for the ferry which brought the
workpeople home for the night from Falbright had just come in.
Workmen, shop girls and a few women who had been over the
river to do some shopping hurried home to tea. Some who had
stored cycles at the ferry-head mounted them and pedalled furi-
ously off into the country. Then, the boatload having dispersed,
quietness fell over the place again. You could almost imagine the
inhabitants seated at tables, chewing their food and taking
intermittent swigs of tea.

In its heyday, the superannuated chapel had supported a
chapel-keeper who lived in a house behind, and Tom Grebe had
made this into a home for himself and his wife. Cromwell
ploughed an unsteady course through a small loading yard
littered with old boxes, crates, bottles, barrels and carboys to the
door of Grebe's house, an old, ivy-covered cottage, badly in

need of a coat of paint, two up and two down, bath and internal sanitation included.

Mrs Grebe admitted Cromwell. A large, dark woman with the traces of a handsome youth still remaining.

"Is Mr Grebe in?"

"Yes. What do you want? I'm his wife."

A surprise for Cromwell. He'd thought, somehow, that Tom was a bachelor, like his brother. But Tom had passed through a single purple patch of existence in his younger days when he'd been good looking. He'd run away with an Italian ice cream merchant's wife. Agostini's Pure Ices. His wife had not been as innocent as his ice cream and had done most of the running after Tom. Then Mr Agostini had obliged by dying soon after her fall from grace. Tom Grebe, who was cooling off, found himself obliged to make an honest woman of her. In recompense for his ever-growing marital disappointment, Tom had then turned religious.

"Police. Could I have a word with your husband, please?"

Mrs Grebe still barred the way with her huge body. Her fine eyes opened wide.

"It isn't the motor lorry again?"

Tom Grebe ran two decrepit vehicles which delivered his drinks and were always in trouble.

"No. Just a few questions about his late brother."

"Oh, him. I'd forgot."

Mrs Grebe thought nothing of John, who, in his lifetime, had made no bones about denouncing his brother's folly.

"Come in, then."

A small, cosy room furnished with odds and ends and Tom Grebe doing his books at a ramshackle old desk stuffed with papers almost to collapsing. He rose, pushed his glasses up on his forehead, and eyed Cromwell up and down. He had a limpid, short-sighted look and a perpetual mirthless smile bared his dentures. This fixed porcelain grin never left his face, even when Tom Grebe wept. There was a faint smell of kippers and mothballs about the place.

"Police."

"What about...John?"

"Yes, sir."

Mrs Grebe entered and removed a pack of cards from a small table by the window, which was screened by three lush geraniums. They were a rum, ill-assorted couple, the Grebes. He and his religion and she preferring to trust in fate as disclosed by a pack of cards instead of her husband's gawd, as he called Him. And had not a tall, dark man just arrived to bear out the recent prediction? She made no effort to leave the men alone. Instead, she sat in a rocking chair, slowly heaving herself to and fro, her arms crossed on her ample bosom, her inquisitive dark eyes moving first to one and then to the other.

Cromwell eyed Tom Grebe up and down, in turn. He had seen the photographs and the description of John Grebe on the files of the case and he was surprised how alike the brothers were. The same good height, sturdy build, shape of head and face. Only whereas John had been dark, Tom was fair — or as much as was left after time had turned his blond hair white. John had been tough, too, and Tom was soft and flabby.

It was obvious that the business was in low water. Bills and invoices scattered about the desk as though thrust aside in despair. Making and bottling soft drinks and then distributing them in two old lorries in the district was a declining trade. Too much competition; too many large-scale opponents. Tom Grebe was on his way to the bankruptcy courts again and this time John wasn't there to save his bacon. He was unkempt, shabby, and his shoes were down at heel. There was a bitter sneer mixed with the dental grin now and then.

"I came to ask if you'd any helpful ideas about your brother's murder, sir. Have you any views about who might be his enemies?"

Grebe sniffed and two large tears gathered and rolled down his cheeks. Tom was a good weeper. He could do it at a moment's notice. He was full of self-pity and was able to recite his misfortunes and the shabby tricks of fate in the same, solemn orderly way in which his wife recited her rosary.

"I've no idea. We didn't see much of one another. He left 'ome early in life to go to sea. He had all the luck and left me behind with the responsibilities of the family and a widowed mother. All the same, 'e was my brother, and the wheel is broken at the cistern, as the good book says."

"How did you both come to live in the same place, then, after being so long apart?"

"After all I'd done for 'im, Mr Cromwell, in the way of supporting our widdered mother, he owed me quite a lot. I'd a bit of bad luck in a furniture business I was running near Oxford and he found me and paid what he owed me by rights and set me up in this place, which 'e bought cheap. If I'd had my choice, you'd never 'ave found me in this forsaken hole, but beggars can't be choosers and John was set on it."

"He owned the property?"

"Yes. He ought to 'ave made it over to me by rights. After all, it's my business, isn't it? I'll be in the cart good and proper if he 'asn't left it me in his will."

Another tear. Grebe wiped it away with the back of his hand before it reached his chin. He was feeling badly treated.

Cromwell smiled gently at the thought of Lucy inheriting a chapel. Would she turn Grebe out when he couldn't pay his rent? Or...and Cromwell's imagination ran riot...or would she start a religious sect of her own with her legacy?

"You knew a fair amount about your brother's comings and goings, didn't you, sir?"

"Of course he did!"

Mrs Grebe couldn't resist interfering. She was ready for a

right good gossip, a right good washing of John Grebe's dirty linen, and she was determined to have it.

"Your John and that chit of a woman from the *Arms* he brought here with him! A barmaid, and him old enough to be her father, *and* her grandfather, as well."

She had long forgotten her own affair with Tom Grebe in Agostini's days.

"When did he bring Lucy...or Lily, here?"

"About six months ago. Treated her better than his own brother, spending his money on her and her playing up to him for what she could get out of 'im. The hussy...I've seen her sort before."

Tom Grebe raised a large hand to stem the flow.

"He knew my views in 'is lifetime and quarrelled with me about my principles. Let 'im rest in peace now...if 'e can."

"Did you see much of him after he left home to go to sea, sir?"

"He wrote now an' then. But he didn't get 'ome much. He was on tramp ships all over the world."

"Yet, when you were in financial difficulties, he found you and helped you."

"Yes. I wrote to 'im about it and he was livin' here at the time. He was down in Oxford next day in a rare tantrum for some reason. He paid all my debts and set me up 'ere, as I just said. What he owed me for looking after our widdered mother and other fambly responsibilities must 'ave laid 'eavy on his conscience."

Outside, one of the lorries was entering the yard lamely, driven by a young man with a dirty face and a shock of unruly black hair. It struck Cromwell how few fair people there were among the natives. They were like a swarthy colony of foreigners. The vehicle looked to be just managing to hang together. The driver got down and started to unload boxes of empty glass bottles and shove them in an old wooden shed.

Mrs Grebe watched the young man's every movement, apparently torn between going out to help and staying to listen to the conversation. She had obviously been waiting for his return and her eyes melted and her breath came faster at the sight of him. At length, she rose and went to the door.

"I'd better go help Len to unload. It's a lot for one and as you're..."

The door closed behind her and Cromwell saw her hurry away to where the vehicle was parked and start smiling at the young driver as he heaved the boxes about. In the same shed stood a contraption which Cromwell finally made out to be a battery of captive hens, which started to cackle and flap about as the activities of the pair outside disturbed their peace.

"How long have you lived here, Mr Grebe?"

Grebe's malicious little eyes turned from the window to Cromwell.

"Nearly ten years. Times are bad now and I'll 'ave to be thinkin' of retiring if my brother's will is as I think it should be. The grass'opper's becomin' a burden, as the good book sez, and I'm not so young as I used to be."

Cromwell wondered what would happen when the news leaked out.

"Do you know your brother's friends here?"

"Yes. Thick as thieves, he was, with that Dr Horrocks and Captain Bacon. A proper lot of 'eavy drinkers, they were. I was surprised at our John. 'E was brought up a good Methodist. But I suppose the sea gets men they don't care. He knew what I thought about his friends. Besides, they weren't 'is class. More money and more expensive tastes than our John could afford."

"Did Captain Grebe ever tell you he was afraid of anyone? In danger in any way?"

Tom Grebe's eyes opened wide.

"Why, no! *Was* 'e in danger?"

"It's evident someone owed him a grudge or had a score to settle. As far as it's known, it wasn't theft."

"No; his watch and wallet and money were there. But his uniform cap and overcoat had gone when they found the body."

"Is that so?"

Details of this hadn't been on the file, or if they had, Cromwell had passed them over as unimportant. Cromwell made a brief note in his large black book and snapped the elastic band and put it away again.

"Perhaps he lost his 'at when he fell overboard, Mr Cromwell."

"But his coat couldn't have fallen off, could it?"

"It was suggested that somebody found the body, took away the hat and coat, and left it."

"Maybe. There was no evidence of a scuffle, as far as I can remember from the report."

"No. But there must have been, mustn't there? If somebody tried to get on the bridge when the ship was in midstream, our John would have done his best to stop them. He took 'is responsibilities seriously, like a captain on a liner, Mr Cromwell, and wouldn't 'ave any intruders with him when 'e was navigatin'."

"You seem to know a lot about your brother's habits, sir, considering the pair of you didn't get on very well."

Grebe looked at him gravely and then said with unction: "I was the older of the two of us and I kept an eye on 'im for 'is own good. I knew more than he thought."

"He seemed to keep an eye on you, too, sir. Didn't he bring you here to keep you from going bankrupt?"

Grebe rose in indignation and raised his large paw again as if to fend off any further outrageous comment.

"He did not, Mr Cromwell. He did not. I'm quite capable of looking after my own business, thank you. But this brings me to the point you jest mentioned. Was our John afraid of anybody?"

Grebe thrust his face close to Cromwell's own. His breath smelled of flag root, which he chewed for indigestion. "Maybe he *was* afraid, come to think of it. The wicked flee when no man pursueth, as the good book sez. Not that 'e was all that wicked; jest self-ohpinionated. I wouldn't think he'd be afraid of anybody doin' him in. He was afraid of the fambly name being advertised in the bankruptcy courts, that's what it was. A very commendable sentiment an' I give 'im full marks for it. I remember it now. It all comes back. 'What will it look like,' he sez to me as he offers to put matters in order for me. 'What will it look like, our fambly name in all the papers and gazettes, in disgrace?' He owed it to me as a juty, as you might say, to keep me out of court. After all I kept our widdered mother."

So that was it! John Grebe didn't want the family name in the papers. Not for the disgrace, however. That wouldn't bother a tough nut like Old John. He didn't want someone to see it and trace him through it. That was what it looked like, at any rate.

"Do you think your brother was well-off financially, sir? In a position to retire comfortably, shall we say?"

Tom Grebe licked his lips and the wooden grin returned.

"Yes, Mr Cromwell, I think he was. We'll soon know when the lawyers 'ave finished their dilly-dallyin'. I've been over to see them twice. We ought to 'ave known long since. It's not fair or legal, all this delay. These lawyers are a weariness of the flesh, as the good..."

Cromwell veered off the subject.

"Where did his money come from?"

"Don't ask me. He must 'ave picked it up from somewhere. He's been 'ere as ferry master 'eaven knows how long and *that* didn't pay his expenses, the way 'e drank and carried on. You might say, Mr Cromwell, that he relied on it purely for pocket money. He was as good as retired. Out of the way in this quiet little spot."

Out of the way in a quiet little spot. Yes, that was probably it, and Cromwell remembered it later.

"Did he make his money at sea, then?"

"As a tramp captain? I ask you. No; I think he must have done some speculatin' somewhere. P'raps a bit shady, too. He wasn't above it, although I won't speak ill of the dead. Or I'd not be surprised if Horrocks or Bacon or that Jezebel, Mrs Iremonger, he was so friendly with, might 'ave put him up to somethin'. They were all as thick as thieves, as I told you. People of that class are always findin' opportunities for increasin' their money."

Tom Grebe gazed sadly in the fire.

"Wot does the good book say...? To them that 'ave shall be given, and from them that 'ave not shall be taken away even wot they 'ave."

A tear flowed as Tom Grebe thought with pity of his own unpaid bills and empty bank account, as well as the uncertainty of his late brother's intentions.

"Where were you the night your brother died, sir?"

Mr Grebe couldn't believe his ears.

"Eh? Yo're not thinkin'...?"

"Of course not. Just a formality. Where were you, sir?"

Here was a man, financially on the rocks, who had quarrelled with the brother who had regularly subsidised him and whose will he thought might not yet have been altered, in spite of recent high words. He'd fully expect to benefit and, in desperation, might have...

"I was 'ere, Mr Cromwell, when the last ferry left. I 'eard the bell go. The wind was in this direction at the time and it was very plain. I recollect lookin' at the clock."

Mr Grebe thereupon looked at the clock again, as though to get it to speak in confirmation. A cheap case clock with brass weights and a large brass pendulum, which had punctuated the conversation with a steady tick-tock and struck the quarters with a rusty sound as though the gong had bronchitis.

"Was your wife in?"

"No. She was with friends in Peshall. She offen goes there."

Mrs Grebe was welcomed by a certain section of the village on account of her soothsaying, a solitary talent which her husband wished she'd bury and never dig up again.

"So you'd no alibi, sir?"

"None, but a clear conscience, Mr Cromwell."

Tom Grebe drew a deep breath and thrust out his chest as though his conscience resided there and was confirming his statement.

"Wot does the good book say? A good name is better than precious ointment. I'll ask you to bear that in mind."

"Your brother never married?"

Grebe looked a bit put out. His own wilful past was forgotten, but the mention of "Luv", as he called it, still embarrassed him.

"Far be it from me to speak ill of the dead. As the good..."

Cromwell was wanting to get away. They'd taken long enough, and the airless, musty smell of the house was depressing him.

"Never mind quotations now, sir. Had your brother any love affairs?"

"He never went steady with any girl to my knowledge. But his behaviour with that Mrs Iremonger and Lucy at the *Barlow Arms* was too free altogether. Perhaps 'e had a girl in every port!"

Mr Grebe so far forgot himself as to grow excited at the very thought, and a note of jocularity filled his voice. Then he coughed and suppressed it with a guilty sidelong look at Cromwell.

"No. Not with my knowledge."

"I think that's all, thank you, sir."

"I must be gettin' along, too. I've the lime juice and the 'op ale to see to for tomorrow. This warm spell's cleaned us out. It'll want mixin' and bottlin' for the mornin' delivery."

Looking across to the tumbledown old chapel where Mrs Grebe was still rolling her eyes at young Len, Cromwell wondered how Grebe managed to make anything there and how long it would all last!

Mr Grebe seemed to read his thoughts.

"I do 'ope our John didn't forget me in 'is will. If he did, I don't know. I couldn't bear it. I couldn't..."

He paused.

"Go on, sir."

"Nothin', Mr Cromwell."

They were standing at the door of the house and Cromwell was firmly fixing his bowler hat in place against the sea breeze. He looked Grebe full in the eyes and the guilty look again returned.

"What does the good book say, Mr Grebe? A living dog is better than a dead lion."

And with that he left him.

7

THE LAST FERRY

I can't make it out, at all."
In the little group gathered round the fire in the dining room at the *Barlow Arms*, Dr Horrocks was holding the floor. Angular, dark-skinned and tall, he held himself erect like an army man, now and then fingering his small silver moustache.

"Why should anybody want to kill old John Grebe?"

The same old question.

Littlejohn and Cromwell had dined and then Lucy had cleared up and, by pushing back the dining tables, converted the small room into a private lounge. This was the place where Horrocks, Captain Bacon, and John Grebe, when he was off duty, had met with a few friends to talk and play cards.

Bacon had arrived first, at about half-past eight. A tall man, too, with a tanned face and florid cheeks. His thin dark hair was plastered flat across his head. A type of country squire who wore check tweeds and beautifully polished shoes. He walked more like a bandy-legged cavalryman than a sailor. His spaniel, always at his heels, followed him into the room and at once drank the milk put down for the cat.

Littlejohn was sitting alone smoking in front of the fire

82

when Bacon entered. Cromwell had gone off into the nether regions of the hotel into rooms labelled SNUG and SMOKE ROOM. In the latter, the lowlier elements of the village were gathered for darts. Charlie Withers, Charlie the Cheat, from Peshall Hall, was playing with Fothergill, the postman. Fothergill had his jacket off and his sleeves rolled up. He was a good player and the captain of the local darts team when they met other clubs. He didn't like Charlie the Cheat but had taken him on for a bit of practice and as the only one present worthy of his steel. A small cigarette smouldered in the corner of Fothergill's mouth and looked in imminent danger of setting fire to his large moustache.

"Evenin', Mr Cromwell. Play darts?"

Fothergill knew Cromwell already and had summed him up from the card he'd seen him post earlier in the afternoon. It was the usual picture-postcard which Cromwell always sent to his wife and family to announce his safe arrival on a case. Fothergill had cleared the box, read the card, ascertained from the handwriting and the address that Cromwell was a modest, middle-class public servant, like Fothergill himself and worth making a friend of.

"Play darts, Mr Cromwell?"

"Now and then, Mr Fothergill."

The postman puffed out his chest a bit. It was nice to be recognised and addressed by name in front of all the rest, especially by a man from Scotland Yard. Cromwell, too, knew all about Fothergill. "Self-opinionated postman you've got here..." he had said to the constable's wife whom he'd met on the road on his way back from Tom Grebe's. Fothergill had passed them, walking with the swanking gait of one who knows he's a somebody in a small community, and greeted them pompously. Mrs PC Dixon could tell a tale once you started her.

Fothergill took a deep swig at his pint of beer and wiped his large moustache on the back of his hand. Then he drew in a deep breath which sucked the moustache into his mouth where he again squeeged it dry. He passed a handful of darts to Cromwell.

"Let's see wot you can do, Mr Cromwell." He said it like a master testing the mettle of an apprentice.

In the dining room Horrocks had joined the other two. And then Brett, the parish clerk, had almost sneaked in. He liked to think himself a member of the most select company in the hotel, insinuated himself in the private room whenever he could, and sat there listening, rarely speaking except when he was spoken to. Small, pot-bellied and red-haired, he lived alone in a cottage down the road, ate gluttonously, and could be seen sometimes in summer peeping round the curtains of his front room and lecherously eyeing the half-clad girls who passed on holidays.

Lucy brought in drinks from time to time. She had returned and settled down to her old job without a word or an explanation, after her interview with Littlejohn. Leo was nowhere about. "He's gone over the river," she'd told Cromwell when he asked about her brother. Cromwell had smiled, thinking of the evangelical hymns he used to sing as a small boy. Leo, who was sleeping over the stables until the police said he could go, sought his pleasures across the ferry. "This dump gives me the willies," he kept saying.

Braid, the landlord, heavy and pear-shaped, entered finally.

"I'll see to the rest. You can knock off now," he said to Lucy, who retired meekly, followed out of sight by the hungry little eyes of Brett.

The curtains of the private room were drawn and the chairs pulled up to the fire. As a rule, the local party played cards for an hour. Now, with Littlejohn there, they felt more like talking about the murder and how the investigation was going on.

"Why should anybody want to kill old John Grebe?"

He'd no enemies. They all agreed about that. A bit surly and bad-tempered now and then, but otherwise, a harmless sort of a man who seemed to want nothing but a quiet life in which to do his job and enjoy his leisure.

"Did he call here for a drink just before the last ferry left on the night he died?"

They all looked at one another after Littlejohn's question, each wondering who must give the answer.

"Bacon and I left at ten. We usually do. And you went at the same time, didn't you, Brett?"

Dr Horrocks seemed to separate Brett from himself and his friend deliberately, just to keep him at arm's length.

"Yes. That's right, that's right, that's right."

Brett replied eagerly as though he greatly appreciated being spoken to at all.

Horrocks took a sip of his whisky and gently and deliberately put down the glass. His hands were noticeably long and delicate and he wore a large intaglio signet ring on his little finger.

"You see, the last ferry leaves Falbright at ten now on winter schedule, takes a quarter of an hour or twenty minutes to get over here, and then returns at ten-thirty. Grebe was never one for a quick drink; he liked to take his time. He'd only ten minutes over here and then he'd to take the ferry back. He used to walk to the top of the pier, just to stretch his legs, he said, and then go back on board. A man of habit."

"That's right. Very set in his ways," said Bacon, who was also set in his ways and slightly resented the intrusion of Littlejohn in the party which had spoiled the usual game of cards.

Littlejohn nodded.

"So you and Captain Bacon left at ten and went straight home, doctor?"

Bacon raised his eyebrows.

"You don't want an alibi from *us*, do you, Inspector?"

"It's as well to gather as many alibis as we can in a case like this, Captain Bacon. You and the doctor walked home?"

Horrocks answered. He seemed anxious to keep his peppery companion from stirring up trouble.

"We walked home, yes. Bacon left me at my door. It must have been about ten minutes past ten. He hadn't his car with him. He'd come in on foot. It was a nice night and he walked home, didn't you, Bacon?"

"Yes. Why not?"

"We were busy talking as we went, Inspector, and I left my stick behind. You can see it in the corner there. The one with the silver knob. I missed it at the gate and strolled back to get it after I'd told my housekeeper to go to bed. I got here just after they'd closed, and Braid will tell you I knocked him up. He was a bit surprised at seeing me, but I'm a bit fussy about the stick. Given to me by colleagues at a hospital I served in years ago."

Braid nodded to confirm this.

Littlejohn made a note on the back of an old envelope.

"And you, Captain Bacon, you went straight home?"

"Of course, I did. This is no place to be wanderin' about in at that time of night. My servants can no doubt confirm I got in before eleven. In any case, I don't see the point in all this. Why should any of us want to follow old John Grebe back to the *Jenny*, creep on the bridge, kill him, and chuck him in the river? Ridiculous to me, the whole business of alibis."

"Don't get upset, Bacon. The Inspector's got the job to do and he knows best. You see, all of us have alibis here, haven't we, Inspector? We were all seen that night. Braid and I saw one another, the servants saw Bacon, and what about you, Brett? Did you go straight to bed after you left us at your cottage?"

"Eh?"

Brett started as though he wasn't involved in the matter at all.

"Did you go straight to bed after you left us?"

"Yes, oh yes...yes, yes."

Brett answered eagerly without thinking for a moment.

"You didn't, you know, Mr Brett."

All eyes turned on Braid, standing about waiting for orders. He cut into the conversation malevolently, with relish, because he didn't like Brett.

"What are you talkin' about? Are you callin' me a liar, Braid?"

The fixed grin left Brett's face and he stood up, uncertainly facing the landlord.

Braid was like a cat playing with a mouse. He put his hands on his pear-shaped paunch and looked pleased with himself.

"You want an alibi, now, don't you, Mr Brett? It 'ud be dangerous to give the police untrue information, wouldn't it?"

Horrocks was on his feet, too.

"What are you gettin' at, Braid? Out with it and then bring us another round instead of hangin' about."

Braid flushed.

"Better ask Brett, then, while I bring the drinks."

"What is all this, Mr Brett?"

Littlejohn removed his pipe and turned a bland look on the little fat parish clerk.

"I'd forgotten, Mr Littlejohn. I took a stroll down to the end of the jetty to watch the last ferry in. I felt I wouldn't sleep if I didn't get a breather after sittin' in here with these two gentlemen all night."

"Did anybody see you there?"

Brett looked uneasy.

"I daresay. There were quite a few said good night..."

"Includin' Miss Clara Lewcock, Mr Brett."

Braid entered with a tray of glasses just in time to add his comments.

"I'll trouble you to leave her out of it, Mr Braid."

"I saw you with her, Mr Brett, walking along the jetty as I stood at the front door. She's a servant at *Solitude* — Mrs Iremonger's place — and Mr Brett 'as taken a fancy to her."

"Look here, Braid...I warned you. For two pins I'd smash your damned face in."

The rabbity Mr Brett was growing pugnacious under Braid's taunts and was obviously making threats in his rage which he couldn't hope to carry out.

"Why you...you..."

"That'll do, Braid. Put down the glasses and then get out. You've been offensive enough. Go on...get out."

"Very well, Captain, but you just ask 'im."

Braid left the room with as much injured innocence and dignity as he could muster.

"This Clara Lewcock can give you an alibi, Mr Brett?"

"I suppose so. I jest walked up the jetty with her. I'd rather she wasn't asked, though. Don't want any unpleasantness."

Bacon unexpectedly guffawed.

"Tryin' to persuade her to join you in your cottage, Brett, eh?"

"Really, Captain Bacon. As if I'd do such a thing."

Outside in the bar, shouts were raised as Cromwell humbled Fothergill at darts. The sergeant, too, was captain of a team which met at a pub in Shepherd Market. It was a red-letter day for the regulars at the *Barlow Arms* to see the haughty postman well and truly beaten.

Jumping Joe, the tramp from the marsh, was making most of the noise, too. He didn't know properly what the excitement was about, but it was infectious and got in his blood. He offered to stand drinks all round.

"Where's all your money come from, Joe?" asked Sid the pot man, as the jumper produced a pound note.

"Never you mind. Plenny more where that come from."

And he pulled out six or seven more.

After that they refused to serve Jumping Joe with drink and persuaded him to leave the place. He was getting too noisy and if Dixon happened to find them supplying him in his present condition, there'd be hell to pay.

"Righ'... I'm off... Don' want to stop where me company's nod wanted."

With his usual sublime drunken good humour, Jumping Joe rose, hiccupped, and then wobbled out into the dark.

"You oughtn't to leave him flounderin' about in the dark outside, Sid. He'll break his neck."

"I've seen him worse than that many a time. He's safer when he's drunk than when he's sober."

Sid wasn't going to miss a minute of the postman's discomfiture.

"I'm not very well tonight," Fothergill was saying. "Some pork I 'ad for my lunch was a bit off. I can't see proper."

"Go on with you, Percy. You're beat. Admit it."

The clock in the hall struck a quarter to ten. Littlejohn rose from his armchair in the dining room.

"Well... Thank you, gentlemen, for your help and your company. I'll leave you now. Just take a breath of fresh air along the pier and back before bed."

"Have another before you go, Chief Inspector?"

"No, thanks. I'll bid you good night and be on my way. Good night."

"See you again, Inspector. What about tomorrow night? We'll be here."

"Thanks, Doctor. I'll most likely be about. Hope to see you."

Littlejohn paused in the hall and could hear Cromwell's quiet modest voice encouraging and making excuses for his opponent, and Fothergill saving himself from being put completely out of countenance by agreeing eagerly.

"It's that pork you ate, I'm sure."

"That's it, Mr Cromwell. It's the pork. It must 'ave been a week old if a day and not kept in the frig at that."

Littlejohn let himself out by the back door, which led into a small stable yard. The *Barlow Arms* was built on a spit of land reaching into the estuary and twenty yards beyond the gate from the yard lay the river, just turning into the sea. The Inspector made his way to the road.

Four or five lamps illuminated the length of the jetty and there was a large bulb hanging from a post at the end where stood the ticket office and the mooring bollards for the ferry-boat. There was nobody about. Across the river the lights of Falbright illuminated the sky. Houses on the waterfront with drawn curtains, the railway station, and the quayside with the Irish Mail boat tied up and lights streaming through her port-holes. Littlejohn could see *Falbright Belle* across the river at the landing stage, with a booking office and the pier-head lamps nearby. As he looked, someone rang the bell warning latecomers that the ferry would leave in a minute.

The Chief Inspector strolled down to the end of the jetty. The tide was low and by the glow from the shore he could make out the mudbanks on the riverside. In midstream, a long string of buoys flashed and twinkled. Across the water, the *Belle*, with a hoot of her siren, detached herself from a cluster of lights and slowly began her last trip over to Elmer's Creek for that day. Littlejohn followed her course, first in the direction of the sea, then with a sharp turn back to shore. He caught the swish of her bows in the water, she chugged nearer, and then slowly glided to the jetty.

The man from the ticket office caught the mooring-rope which Joe Webb flung to him and slipped it over a bollard; then the pair of them hauled out the gangway. A few passengers landed. Two or three men returning from a spree in town, including Leo, drunk and shambling back to his bed over the stables. A family home after a visit. Some noisy lads and girls back from the pictures in Falbright. They climbed the sloping stone causeway to the road and slowly vanished in the darkness of the village.

All went quiet again. The only sounds were those of the water lapping the pier and the ferryboat; the voices of the skipper, Joe Webb and the ticket-man at the water's edge; the ceaseless fret of the distant sea. The rhythmic flashes of the Farne Light swung round and round, picking out buildings and landmarks on their way.

Then odd people began to appear, leisurely making their way to the last ferry. Two or three men who'd come over from Falbright for a change of beer at the *Barlow Arms*, a man with his wife and two children returning from seeing his parents, and an odd courting couple or two who haunted Elmer's Creek because it was dark and secluded.

Joe Webb rang the warning bell.

Littlejohn took a ticket, boarded the ferry, and walked round the deck until he found the engine room, which combined the duties of stokehold as well and where Webb was putting coal on the fire with a large shovel. Black smoke emerged from the funnel and was blown by the stiff little breeze back into Elmer's Creek.

"Hullo, sir."

"Hullo, Joe."

"Not going across, are you? How'll you get back?"

"You come back, don't you? I'll come with you."

"It's jest a rowin' boat, sir. I row meself over 'ere, then back in the mornin'. Sometimes think it 'ud be better to move over to Falbright, but the missus won't, and then, if I moved, they might change the arrangements and decide to 'ave the last boat finish up at Elmer's Creek. Then where would I be?"

"Excuzhe me, sir."

Joe Webb, pursuing his many duties as a crew of one, rushed on deck, moving with remarkable speed for one so small and fat, hauled in the gangway, ran back to his engines, and waited obediently for the engine room telegraph to clang.

Half astern... Stop... Half ahead... Full.

Littlejohn watched the manoeuvre and then went on deck.

The lights up and down river fascinated him, and he leaned over the rail watching them and quietly smoking his pipe. The knots of passengers were talking in hushed voices, except the lovers, who either sentimentally watched the water and the lights or else clung closely together in the darkest parts of the ship, kissing and caressing each other with pathetic eager ardour as though the end of the brief voyage would part them forever.

The Irish Mail towered above the little ferryboat as she nosed her way to the Falbright pier. On this side, the ferry had its own small landing stage above which hung the quays and the berth for the Irish steamers. Under the girders of the latter they had found John Grebe's body in the dark water.

Half, Slow, Stop. Finished with Engines.

Joe Webb had no sooner altered speed than another order arrived on the dial, heralded by a harsh clang on the gong.

The boat slid alongside and that was all for the day. Except, of course, Joe Webb's private trip back home, in which Littlejohn now joined him. There was a small rowing boat tied under a disused part of the pier, left there by a pal of Joe's for this very purpose. Webb untied it, after they'd both jumped in it, fixed the oars, and with easy skilled strokes, manoeuvred into the main stream.

"Could you row a course exactly like the one you took when Captain Grebe was killed, Joe? I'll take my turn with the oars."

"I could row all night, sir, and feel none the worse. Do you want the exac' way the old *Jenny* went when she kicked up 'er 'eels and run aground?"

"That's it."

Webb rowed silently and earnestly for a minute or two.

"Tide's comin' in, but I'll be able to manage."

They could feel the drag of the river on the boat and Webb strained to follow the course of the *Jenny* on the fatal night.

They described a wide arc sweeping in the direction of the sea and Webb had to keep rowing to maintain his progress as he talked.

"If you look upstream, sir, there...in the direction of the second flashin' light. That's where the *Jenny* sort o' took the bit between 'er teeth. Then, she off and ran to where we are now, sir. If I was to row dead straight now, we'd run on the bank on the Falbright side... See 'ow the buoys swings to the right from 'ere... That's the channel."

Webb struggled again to keep on his course.

"...Now, on the Elmer's Creek side, sir, to my right, if you was to drop a lead there, you'd find that two feet from where we are now, there's jest a foot of water. That's where the Elmer's Creek bank starts and it's a marvel to me, the course she took, that the old *Jenny* didn't pile 'erself up on both banks crossways and block the whole channel. She must jest 'ave turned in time and struck the Elmer's Creek bank o' the river."

"So, after Captain Grebe was killed and thrown overboard, the *Jenny* turned downstream, dodged the Falbright sandbank, and slewed round and got entangled in the Elmer's Creek one?"

"Yes, sir. You've got it."

"Would such a move by a boat without a man at the helm be natural?"

A pause whilst Webb changed course and started to make for the jetty at Elmer's Creek.

"Yes, sir, I reckon it might be. With the tide jest on the change and ready to come in. The current *might* have done it... All the same, I can't quite foller it. It must 'ave been jest before Cap'n Grebe turned in midstream to make for the jetty. We back out at Elmer's Creek and take a sort of half-circle ahead then. If the helm was left before the cap'n changed course...sort of left just as we'd reached the top of the half-circle...then we'd make out to sea."

Webb was obviously still a bit flummoxed about what had

actually happened and even more troubled about expressing it in words. All the same, Littlejohn got a rough idea of what it was all about.

"Thanks."

They drew alongside and climbed the stone steps high up the slope of the jetty and Littlejohn, after giving Webb a ten-shilling note for his trouble, walked with him as far as the *Barlow Arms* and there they parted.

All the lights were on in the pub and the place seemed to be overflowing with people, mostly fishermen and natives of the village. The helmet of Dixon was bobbing about in the middle of a group of men and Cromwell, looking harassed, detached himself from the party and greeted Littlejohn as though they'd been parted for years.

"I'm glad to see you back, sir. I wondered wherever you'd got to. I'm sorry, I was a bit engrossed in a game of darts when you went out."

Cromwell looked as if he'd thought the worst had happened to Littlejohn in the dark, and the Chief Inspector felt a guilty pang about not having warned his colleague that he was off for a stroll. The rest of the trip, the ferry, the journey down river and back with Joe Webb had all been done on the impulse of a moment.

"...I was looking for you, sir, to tell you that there's been another murder. The chap called Jumping Joe, the one who sells rushes about the place and is always tight."

"I know him. He was here tonight."

"Yes. He was there, standing drinks all round as we were playing. He seemed to have come into a windfall, too. Flashing his money about. The body's in the kitchen. The doctor's there and we got Dixon along. It's a nasty business."

"How did it happen?"

"He hadn't been robbed. The money's still in his pocket. A party of lads from Peshall, who came over on the last ferry from the pictures at Falbright, found the body in the road just this side of the village, in a dark spot where there are no houses. They thought he'd been knocked down by a car and stopped a passing motorist and brought him here. He was dead."

"So, it might have been an accident?"

"No. The doctor's had a look at him, Dr Horrocks... He says he's been strangled."

8

THE END OF JUMPING JOE

Police routine filled Elmer's Creek for almost a whole day after the death of Jumping Joe.

The police surgeon, who worked far into the night, said that Joe had definitely been strangled; throttled manually. He also said that if he hadn't met a violent death he'd probably have disintegrated physically before long. His heart, liver and stomach were almost rotted away by perpetual drunkenness, and he was undernourished through preferring liquid to solid refreshment.

Jumping Joe had died between ten and eleven in the night; probably nearer eleven.

"That leaves them nearly all without an alibi. They were all on their ways home about the time Joe was killed," said Superintendent Lecky, who arrived on the scene with the Chief Constable and wore on his face a pained expression, as though Littlejohn might have prevented the tragedy if he'd tried.

"What was he doing rowing about on the river at that hour? You'd think he'd something better to do than that, with this Grebe case on his hands and not a bit nearer being solved,"

Lecky complained bitterly to his subordinates, who, in turn, said behind his back that he was jealous.

Littlejohn took it all unperturbed, moving massively, smoking his pipe, and smiling now and then as one and another greeted him. The fingerprint men had been and gone; they'd turned up as a matter of form in case there were any prints to be had, and returned with the photographer, who'd taken a lot of pictures of the spot where Jumping Joe was found. Joe had been photographed, too, back and front, clothed and stark; an unpleasant sight indeed in his birthday suit!

"Who'd given Joe all that money?"

Everybody asked the question when they heard that the man who normally cadged drinks or sold rushes and mushrooms to get a pint, had been sporting pound notes in the bar and standing drinks all round. He'd even paid off Braid the four and fivepence he'd run up on the slate and told him to keep the change from a pound and open a running account with it for when he fell on hard times again.

Littlejohn strolled among the regulars and hangers-on round the *Barlow Arms*, asking questions, listening to the excited small talk, taking it all in and gaining a lot more background.

"He kept talking about meeting a ghost on the marsh, but he wouldn't say whose it was."

"Whatever he met he got a pocketful of the ready from somebody. Perhaps it was to keep quiet about what he'd seen."

"It wouldn't need much in the way of blackmail money to keep Joe's tongue quiet. He never talked sense when he was drunk. Just enough money to keep him tight and the secret was safe. That's what I think. Somebody gave him the money to keep him drunk."

"But what sort of a secret could Joe have found out?"

"Well, there 'as bin a murder 'ere, you know. How about if he saw who did for Captain Grebe?"

"Go on. Joe was nowhere near the *Falbright Jenny* when the

captain was done in. Joe was bein' chucked out of the *Arms*, blind-drunk and paralytic at the time..."

If you listened long enough, you got more information over a pint of ale than you'd gather all day by usual police investigation.

Superintendent Lecky, who had been directing routine operations with gestures and orders like a fire chief putting out a fire, put the direct question to Littlejohn at length.

"Who do you think might have killed Joe, sir?"

Littlejohn had just been having a long talk with Lucy, the waitress, and turned his head and smiled blandly at Lecky.

"I haven't a clue, Superintendent. But I think if we get Grebe's murderer, we'll get Jumping Joe's."

"You think they're connected?"

"Of course. Why two murders, one on top of the other, in a place like this, if they're not in some way connected?"

Lecky rubbed his chin. He felt he could have done better himself. The great Chief Inspector Littlejohn might be all right in London, but here, in this queer little backwater of coast, he seemed a bit out of his depth.

"I've got to get back and attend to some routine things in town. You'll keep in touch, won't you, Chief Inspector?"

"Of course, Superintendent."

Lecky and the Chief Constable went off in a police launch which seemed more in keeping with their dignity than the *Falbright Belle*, but if they could have seen themselves scrambling aboard their private craft and heard the comments of the fishermen on their bearing as they bobbed across the river, they'd probably have chosen the lowly, grubby ferryboat after all.

Nobody knew her real name was Lily; she was just Lucy at the *Barlow Arms*. Littlejohn found her laying the tables in the dining room for lunch, quietly and efficiently, in spite of all the commotion going on around. The *Arms* had become the headquarters of the two cases and Braid and his mother hoped they'd never be solved. The amount of liquor, of one kind and another, consumed was fabulous.

"So you've settled down again, Lucy?"

"Yes. What else can I do? If I try to go, you'll arrest me and Leo. Besides, I've my living to earn."

"You say you were born in Gravesend, Lucy. What part?"

"Down by the riverfront. Tenterden Street."

"What number?"

"Thirteen. Not very lucky. Why?"

Lucy searched Littlejohn's face with a half-scared look. It was as though she vaguely sensed some frightening idea. Perhaps Leo's past: perhaps something which would involve the pair of them further in the Grebe murder affair.

"You said you remembered your stepfather. He vanished when you were twelve...about sixteen years ago."

"Yes... Why?"

"What was his name?"

"I told you. Fowler, like me and Leo."

"What was his Christian name?"

"What do you want to know for?"

"We want to trace what happened to him exactly. You thought he was drowned or met with an accident?"

"Yes. He was a good father, and I was fond of him, although I wasn't his real daughter. He was very kind to my mother. You'd have thought..."

Lucy was talking thirteen to the dozen, saying anything to play for time.

"I'd better be going. Mrs Braid will be after me. I've a lot of work to do yet. There's the bedrooms still to tidy..."

"Not so fast. What was your father's Christian name, Lucy?"

"He'd nothing to do with these murders, I swear it. Why can't you leave me alone?"

Outside in the hall, Braid was getting annoyed at the knots of men, hanging round gossiping, hoping to get hold of the latest bit of news from the police. Even now, they were nudging one another: "The chap from Scotland Yard's questioning Lucy."

"Get out, the lot of you, now. It's a fine day. Are none of you goin' out fishin' today? You can't stay here."

Braid flailed the air. He hadn't shaved or washed himself; he'd started to be busy as soon as he got up at nine o'clock and had almost revelled in his unkemptness since.

"What was your father's name? We can soon find out, but you'd better save us the trouble, Lucy."

She threw back her head in a defiant gesture and her cheeks flushed, giving her almost a handsome look.

"It was Leo, like my brother's. Now are you satisfied?"

"So your father isn't dead?"

"What do you mean?"

"You know as well as I do, Lucy. *He* sent the postcards to John Grebe, didn't he? You and Leo knew all the time and you kept it dark."

"We weren't sure."

"You never saw him?"

"No. I swear it. He never came here."

"But he threatened Grebe on the postcards and was gradually getting nearer Elmer's Creek, judging from the cards. Why should he want to see Grebe and why was he so abusive?"

"I tell you I don't know."

"Was he ever in gaol?"

"What, father? No. He's not like Leo. He's a man, dad is."

"Can't you think why he should come here after Grebe?"

"He might have heard that Captain Grebe was friendly with me."

"How could he know?"

"I can't say. You're trying to trip me up, and I don't know anything. Why can't you leave me alone?"

"All right, Lucy. That will do for the present."

Flushed and panting, Lucy hurried from the room and ran

up the stairs like someone pursued. This was not lost on the men now being shepherded out by Braid: "It looks as if the Inspector's on to somethin'. He's found somethin' out from Lucy..." It went all round the village in no time.

Littlejohn strolled to the door. It was a pleasant, sunny autumn morning with a faint tang of approaching colder days in the air and a stiff little breeze which bellied the sails of the boats tacking down the river for offshore fishing round Farne Light.

The ferry was in midstream, lurching a bit in the wind and tide, smoke pouring from her funnel as Joe Webb fired-up. The Irish Mail had gone, leaving a large blank in the affairs of the waterfront. Four fishing boats were on their way to Iceland and the men aboard stood in little groups on deck, waving to their families on the pier. The river-police launch bustled about on an aimless looking patrol.

Cromwell was talking to Leo, who also looked as if he hadn't had a wash for weeks. His clothes were creased as though they'd been slept in, and he hadn't had a shave for two days.

"You crossed on the last ferry the night Captain Grebe was killed?"

"I've said so, haven't I?"

"Tell me again, Leo."

Leo had arrived back drunk the night before and had flung himself on his bed fully clothed and slept all through the excitement of Jumping Joe's murder. He, like the rest, hadn't a proper alibi. He'd been seen coming from the last ferry again, but for the rest, there was only his word for it, and he'd slept so soundly that he didn't know a thing.

"Yes. I crossed the last ferry. Now are you satisfied?"

He licked his dry lips. His tongue felt like leather. He hadn't had any breakfast because he didn't feel like it and in spite of that, he'd been sick. He looked a bigger villain than ever with his dirty face, his sallow cheeks and baggy eyes, and his nose slightly askew.

GEORGE BELLAIRS

"There was another sailor with you when you crossed?"

"Yes. A decent chap. He was goin' to Iceland with the fleet on the morning tide. We had a drink or two together and went off for the ferry. I lost him when the blasted thing went aground."

"What sort of a fellow was he?"

"Nice sort o' bloke who'd just come across for a spree before he sailed. He wasn't married and lived in Falbright with his maw."

He leered and showed his yellow teeth.

"Ask me, he was a bit sweet on my sister, Lily. But she never give 'im a second look. She's out for bigger fish, is Lily. She wants a chap as can give 'er a 'ome and money to spend. Not a ruddy mariner with a girl in every port."

"I thought you said he was a decent sort of chap."

"He was. What's all this about? Sailors, Lily, last ferries... Where's it all gettin' us?"

"I'll be the judge, Leo. What was the sailor's name?"

"Fred."

"Fred who?"

"How should I know? 'E was just Fred to me. Why should I want to know 'is name and address?"

"I thought you might want to send back the pound or two you touched him for."

"Well, I didn't touch him, see? And now I'll ask you to leave me alone an' let me get me wash an' brush up."

"You need one. I'd be the last to stop you."

Leo gave Cromwell a dirty glare and looked ready to say something else. Instead, he turned on his heel and shambled away.

Littlejohn thought how well Cromwell was looking. The sea breezes were suiting him. He had red cheeks and a red nose.

"Hello, Chief."

"Hello, Cromwell. I'm sorry to put an end to your little river-side gossiping. I want you to go over to the police station in

102

Falbright, contact the Yard, and ask them to make some inquiries in Gravesend."

"Something to do with Leo and Lily?"

"Yes. Their father's still alive, I think, and his name's Leo. Does that convey anything?"

"The postcards!"

"Yes. We want a full history of Leo, Senior, and what he's been doing since he vanished sixteen years ago. He seems to have hated John Grebe and he might have caught up with him here."

"But Jumping Joe... If Leo, Senior killed Grebe, he might have killed Joe as well. He must be around here somewhere."

"We don't even know what he looks like. Lily hasn't seen him since she was a kid and he's been out of circulation for quite a time. Go and get to know all about him and a description of him, if you can. He may have done a stretch in gaol. That might have put him away for a while. Inquire about that, too."

"Right, sir."

Leo Fowler, ex-tugboat captain on the Thames; 13 Tenterden Street, Gravesend.

Cromwell took it all down and then looked with relish at the river and the sea, the ferry tying-up, the old salts and young fishermen too busy with their gossip to get on with the day's work.

"The sooner you get off and do the job, the sooner you'll be back, old man."

"I'll go by the next ferry, sir."

"It won't take you long."

There was a bit of a stir on the jetty. The group of men who daily watched and talked about everything which came and went in the river and at sea, were watching a boat just rounding the Farne Light with her course set for Falbright port.

"It's the *North Star*. What's she back for? She ought to have been in the Iceland grounds by now."

A man who had just come from the ferry was eager to satisfy them.

"They've wirelessed the harbour office that they've had an accident. The galley boy was struck by a hawser and he's broke 'is leg in two places. They want a doctor and when they've landed the boy, they'll be off again to join the rest at the fishing grounds."

The motor vessel was hurrying upstream at a spanking speed, her engines full out, her bows ploughing into the choppy water and throwing up a huge feather of spray. They all watched her tie up at the pier and the boy was carried to a waiting ambulance. They could see his mother agitatedly fluttering on the edge of the little crowd and finally they put her in the vehicle with the boy.

Some of the crew went ashore. It looked as if the skipper was either effecting repairs or taking on more stores ready for the next tide.

One of the ship's company could be seen talking to a man who ran a little motor launch, a minor kind of ferry, which plied to and fro between the villages and factories on the riverbanks. They seemed to be striking a bargain. Then the sailor climbed in the launch which set out and crossed to Elmer's Creek.

"It's Fred Heath."

One of the old salts on the jetty shaded his eyes with a calloused hand and announced his discovery.

"What's he want? He seems in a 'urry to get over here?"

"Luve's young dream," cackled his companion, and all the rest of the party laughed. "He's keen on Lucy at the *Arms*, for some reason. Won't leave 'er alone. She won't 'ave nothin' to do with 'im, but he's made up his mind."

Fred Heath was landing from the motorboat and clambered along the jetty with the skilled movements of a real sailor.

"Stick at 'er, Fred. You'll bring 'er down yet," shouted the man who seemed to know so much about Fred and his amours.

The sailor paused, blushed, made a gesture of punching the air as though it were a man's nose, and then hurried along to the *Barlow Arms*. With long strides he vanished through the door.

Littlejohn followed him in.

Fred Heath met Lucy face to face as she hurried downstairs.

"Hello, Lucy."

"Hello, Fred. I can't stop. I'm busy. What are you doin' here? I thought you were in Iceland."

Fred looked pathetic. The sight of Lucy seemed to have taken all the strength out of his huge, powerful frame. He didn't know where to put his hands, moved from one foot to the other, stammered, and turned his cloth cap round and round in his great fingers.

"We've had a bit of an accident. Young Crowe, the pantry boy, broke his leg and we had to bring him back to 'ospital. We're goin' back on the afternoon tide and I've an hour to spare. I thought I'd... Maybe you'll just 'ave a drink with me, Lucy. I'd take it as a favour if you would."

Lucy was a bit cruel about it all. The sight of the huge sailor turned shy and awkward because he fancied her, made her long to shake him and tell him she preferred men who knew what they wanted and got it, without stammering and blushing. She wasn't used to men of Fred's sort.

"Why do you 'ave to come just as I'm on with the lunches, Fred? It's too bad of you. I can't stand about drinkin' with you now. Mrs Braid 'ud give me the sack as true as I'm here."

"I'm sorry, Lucy. I thought..."

"Well, I'm busy now. I'll see about it when you get back from the fishing. That is, if I'm still here."

"You aren't goin' away?"

His distress was pitiful to see.

"I don't know. I just couldn't stand this place in winter. It 'ud drive me daft."

"I'd make it up to you, if you'd stay on. I'd…"

"I've got to get on with my jobs, don't I tell you. I'll see you when you're in port again."

She left him standing there in his misery and the swing doors of the dining room flapped behind her.

"I'd like a word with you, Fred."

"What the 'ell do *you* want? Who are you anyway?"

Fred, now that Lucy had gone, had become a man again. He was ready, in his anger, to fling the massive man standing in his way right into the street. He'd take anybody on!

"My name's Littlejohn. I'm a police officer. You've heard of Captain Grebe's death?"

"Yes."

Fred Heath didn't care about John Grebe. Even a man who'd been killed and pitched into the Hore couldn't be more wretched than he felt. He told Littlejohn he didn't care a damn about old Grebe, and it was the ferry master's own fault if he'd come to mischief.

"…Botherin' around with Lucy, an old man like him. If it hadn't been for his age, I'd have chucked 'im in the river myself many a time. What did an old boy like him want with a nice girl like Lucy? A nuisance to her, that's what he was."

"All right, all right, Fred."

"It's not all right."

"You were on the ferry at the time old John was killed."

"What of it? I didn't do him in. I was being done myself at the time and I'd no time to see what was goin' on on the bridge."

"What do you mean?"

"Can't you leave me alone? I didn't do the murder."

"Nobody says you did, although you could be a good suspect, you know. You wanted old Grebe out of the way because he was paying attention to Lucy and pushing your nose out."

"I don't care who knows about what I think of Lucy. She's a fine girl. And I did want to break every bone in the old swine's body and that's how I'd have done for him, not sticking him in the back. And I'll thank you to leave me alone and I don't ruddy well care if you are police. I'm going back to my ship and nobody's goin' to stop me."

"You're wrong there, Fred. I am, if you don't answer my one or two questions."

"Why, you…"

"Now, don't be silly, Fred. It won't do you any good with Lucy, getting in a row with the police and landing in the cells, instead of aboard the *North Star* earning your money for when you set up house with your girl."

Fred paused and scratched his bullet head.

"You think…"

"I don't think anything. I'm no specialist in the ways of women, but you ought to try being a bit less humble with her and take her by storm… Not now, you silly ass. You've your ship to get and my questions to answer. She'll not run away while you're in Iceland. I'll see to that if I've to lock her up till you're back."

Fred actually chuckled.

"Well, I'll be blowed! You're a good sort for a policeman. What did you want to know?"

"You said you were occupied in 'being done' whilst Grebe was being murdered. What does that mean?"

"I picked up with a fellow at the *Arms* the night old John got murdered. He was just passin' through and we had a drink or two. Then we went off for the last ferry together. Len…Leo, or somethin', he was called. I wish I could see him now… By God, I'd…"

He clenched his huge fists.

"As soon as we'd got aboard, he tried to borrow a pound or two. I said nothin' doin'… So he pulls out a little gold lady's

GEORGE BELLAIRS

watch. Said it had been his mother's who was dead. Worth twenty pounds. I could have it for five. And he says straight out, 'I can see you're keen on that girl at the *Arms*...'

"How he knew I don't know. He says how she'll think the world of me if I buy it and give it her. And, just havin' seen her and findin' her not much in my favour, I'm inclined to agree. I've just five pound, three shillings left from my pay and I leave myself with the three bob and take the watch."

Fred's temper was rising, and he had to swallow hard to keep himself in hand. The ferry was coming in again and he had to hurry, for he had suddenly developed a desire to save money in view of Littlejohn's advice, and fourpence on the ferry was a sight different from extravagance on Buzzard's motor launch, privately hired.

"...When I get on the *North Star* and we're under way, I pull out the watch and show it to a pal of mine. He laughs. He'd seen a cheapjack in Falbright sellin' the very same article for a pound in the market and after he'd sold half a dozen, he cleared off before they found out they were brass and wouldn't go proper. This one of mine hasn't gone ever since I got it."

He produced in his huge paw a slightly tarnished little watch, a flashy imitation of a modern style, but made on the cheap.

"I'm sorry, Fred."

"If I could find that Len or Leo, or whatever he calls himself...I'd ram it down his blasted throat."

"But there's one other question. The ferry broke away from her course when old Grebe died and ran down river and lodged on a sandbank. Did everybody leave the ship in the same way? A party from the town hurried down and took them off across the bank."

"Len or Leo didn't wait. He jumped on the bank and off without waitin'. He vanished into the dark. Good job for him, too. If I'd laid me hands..."

"Anything else?"

"Yes. We zigzagged a bit. I was so busy with the watch and payin' for it, that I didn't gather me wits together till it was too late and we were headin' for the bank. But I jumped up then and looked over the side to see where we were. We was headin' first for the Falbright bank of the river; then just as I thought we'd struck, she screwed round her bows again and hit the other bank on the Elmer's Creek side."

"Yes."

Fred scratched his head again as though to stimulate his brain.

"I'm not sure. As I said, I was a bit sort of still bothered about the watch. But I think that as we touched the Elmer's Creek bank, somebody jumped off and on to the sand. There'd be two feet or so on our starboard side. You see, the river shelves sudden. They dredge the channel... You follow... The *Jenny* was in the dredged part, but a foot away was the bank in shallow water. Easy to jump to it and get to land that way. It looked as if whoever jumped got the wind up proper and took the risk. He must have landed all right. I didn't hear no splash."

"Thank you, Fred. That's fine."

But Fred wasn't listening.

Freshly shaved and washed and feeling better for a drop of brandy cadged from his sister, Leo was coming swaggering from the hotel yard, on the look-out for someone from whom to borrow a pound or so. He was posing as one of the principals in the drama of Elmer's Creek. Lucy's brother. The girl who, in spite of his brotherly advice, had got mixed up with a man who got murdered.

Leo didn't see Fred until it was too late. With two quick strides Fred was on him, took him by the throat, jerked his arm, and raised Leo kicking from the ground. Leo tried to shriek but he had no breath. Fred took out the watch and endeavoured to ram it, as promised, down his victim's throat, but Leo bit his thumb. Whereupon Fred raised his massive fist and after throwing Leo in the air, caught his jaw with a punch like a battering ram as he fell to meet it. Leo doubled up, groaned and lay sprawling, stunned, and pretending to be unconscious to prevent another assault.

"You shouldn't have done that, Fred."

Littlejohn took the angry sailor by the arm. He was sorry for Fred with all his problems, but it really couldn't go on.

"What shouldn't I have done? Let him get up an' I'll give him some more. I'll teach him."

"You're doing yourself no good, you know, Fred. Leo's Lucy's brother."

Fred didn't seem to understand plain English at first. He looked at Littlejohn and then at the crowd which had gathered round.

"He's *who?*"

"Lucy's brother."

"Oh. Oh, hell."

Fred didn't even stop to make his peace with Leo or hit him again. They were hauling in the gangway of the ferry, and with three long loping strides Fred reached the gap between the jetty and the boat, leaped over it, gathered himself together on the deck, and ran and hid himself with Joe Webb in the engine room, as though Lucy were in hot pursuit and eager to avenge her brother!

9

THE SARACEN'S HEAD AT PULLAR'S SANDS

The noon ferry had departed taking Cromwell with it. The bar at the *Barlow Arms* was idle and the loungers of the jetty had gone home to lunch. Littlejohn felt at a loose end.

He slowly strolled along the shabby promenade in the direction of the police station. A few late holidaymakers sauntering up and down working up an appetite for lunch. Two elderly men taking the air, shoulders back, breathing deeply, arguing about something. A woman with three children; one carrying a bucket and spade, another a little fishing net, and the third a balloon which suddenly burst, whereat he set up a loud wail. Two more women, one pushing a perambulator, and the other, from all appearances, almost ready to do the same.

The sky was clear blue with a few frothy white clouds riding high. In the distance, the hills north of Balbeck Bay, the close appearance of which, according to certain wiseacres, foretold early rain. The sweep of the coast with the tide out. In the distance Littlejohn could see the narrow estuary of the small river at Pullar's Sands, which could be crossed on foot at the ebb. When the tide was in, you either went over by boat or walked inland to the bridge three miles upriver. On the farther bank, the bulk of the inn stood out clearly. The *Saracen's Head* was the oldest pub in the neighbourhood and originally owed its existence to the ferry.

Dixon was digging in his garden and saluted Littlejohn as he passed.

"Just taking part of my off-time gettin' in the carrots. If it starts to rain, I've had it if I haven't got 'em in."

"The pub at Pullar's Sands, Dixon. Did Jumping Joe spend much time there? He seemed to be making for that direction whenever I saw him."

Dixon put his hands in the small of his back and pressed himself upright. He wasn't as young as he used to be and digging stiffened him up. He looked in the direction of the *Saracen's Head* with an inquiring glance as though he'd never seen it before. At the window behind him, the gallery of infants watched their father with eager expressions.

"Yes, sir. Come winter, he'd sleep in one of the outhouses if it was too bad to stop outside in a hedge or a haystack. He got a lot of his mushrooms and rushes there and gathered samphire if anybody wanted it. He had to come this way to sell his stuff. There's only the pub and an odd house or two at Pullar's Sands."

"Did Captain Grebe ever get that way on his daily walks?"

Dixon nodded.

"Yes, sir. He used to go there quite a bit. But of late, I've not seen him makin' in that direction. The nearest way's along the sands when the tide's out and then was when I'd see him."

"But he's stopped his jaunts there lately?"

"Within the last month or so."

"Why?"

Dixon smiled a bit archly and coughed behind his hand.

"Perhaps he was told to stay away, like. The landlady there, a Mrs Liddell, is a bit of a queer one. She's a widow of not much over forty and a good looker, if you like 'em that way, sir."

"What way?"

Dixon was growing red and Littlejohn felt that somehow the bobby's modesty was bothering him.

"A big, dark woman, like a gipsy. Her husband fell out of a loft and broke his neck. The place is a bit of a farm as well. She runs the farm and the public house. She doesn't say much, but what she does say, she means."

Dixon's mind was working hard to provide a satisfactory description of Mrs Liddell.

"If you was to call there now, sir, you'd as likely as not find 'er dressed in corduroy trousers and a blouse or a jumper with nothin' on underneath it."

He looked round to see if his wife was listening and caught the eyes of the gallery of spectators at the window. He flapped his hand angrily at them and they all vanished.

"Hmm... They do say she's not all she should be...ahem...if you know what I mean, sir."

Dixon's eye caught Littlejohn's in which there was an inquiring twinkle, and the bobby turned a dull red beneath his tan.

"Is that what attracted John Grebe?"

"Some say so. But he wasn't the only one. They do say locally, she didn't object to runnin' two or three men at the same time."

"And then she showed Grebe the door?"

"I don't know, sir. The *Saracen's Head*'s not on my beat, sir. The constable from Reddishaw village, through the woods behind Pullar's Sands, goes there. He's a decent chap and the father of four, but the one before 'im was said to call far too often at the *Saracen* and got himself moved on account of the scandal as went on."

Here Dixon coughed again and looked through the window to satisfy himself that his wife was still occupied at the oven.

"I think I'll take a stroll there, Dixon."

"Like me to come with you, sir?"

It was obvious that Dixon was eager to make a trip of inquiry in the safe company of the Chief Inspector, and he took a step in the direction of his cottage to change from his gardening tunic into his new official rig-out.

"Have you had your lunch?"

"No, sir. But it'll do after. I could regard the time with you as official, like, if you didn't mind, and 'ave my dinner when we get back."

His expression reminded Littlejohn of that of his own dog, begging for her morning constitutional on Hampstead Heath.

"All right, then."

As Littlejohn waited by the gate, he could see Dixon getting the rounds of the kitchen from his missus, who'd cooked hotpot and would now have to keep it warm whilst her spouse went gallivanting to the haunts of a woman who was socially ostracised by the decent matrons of Elmer's Creek and district. They feared her, too, if they'd only been honest with themselves.

Dixon eventually emerged with his ears burning and turned at the gate to wave a pacific hand and make a fawning gesture at his wife who instead nodded to Littlejohn and ignored her bobby.

"Phew! If you don't mind me confessin' it, sir, the very mention of the *Saracen's 'Ead* to the local married ladies is like Solemn and Jommorah. I told 'er I was only goin' in the way of duty, but she carried on as if I might be on some evil purpose, sir…a journey of sejuction, as you might say."

They passed Fothergill, the postman, on his way to empty the boxes and Dixon straightened himself and threw back his shoulders to show he was officially collaborating with Scotland Yard.

"Mornin', Percy."

"How do, Albert. Mornin', Chief Inspector, sir."

Fothergill emphasised his familiarity and disrespect for the bobby.

"Hear you've had another murder, Albert. Comin' to somethin', isn't it? Where were you, Albert, while Jumpin' Joe was being knocked off?"

The exchanges were made on the move and with the protagonists walking in opposite directions. Fothergill was out of earshot before Dixon could think of a suitable shaft in retaliation.

"Gets a bit above himself, does Fothergill, sir. You'd think 'e owned the village since he married a woman fifteen years older than he is, for her money."

Satisfied that he had suitably stabbed the postman in the back, Dixon thereupon descended to the shore and showed Littlejohn the way they would take to Pullar's Sands. It lay for two miles away along the tideline, littered with old cans, corks, spars of wood and seaweed. In the distance rose the squat scattered buildings of the *Saracen's Head*, with smoke rising from one of the chimneys.

They walked in silence for some time, Littlejohn taking in the lie of the surrounding land and the atmosphere of lonely desolation. The fields were flat as far as the eye could see and judging from the vegetation remaining after the autumn crops, yielded corn, potatoes and vegetables of all kinds. Shabby farms rose here and there, many of them surrounded by gaunt, twisted trees to protect them from the wind. Cattle were grazing in some of the pastures and in places large, wired sections held hundreds of chickens.

But it was the feeling of isolation which Littlejohn felt most, as though this part of the country were cut off from the rest of civilisation. A segregated community living its own life away from all the rest, with the ferry at Elmer's Creek as a sort of bottleneck through which one and another of the people there entered the world outside.

"This is a lonely spot, Dixon."

The bobby halted and looked around in the peculiar,

muddled way he had, suggesting that he was seeing something for the first time.

"It was, sir, till the buses came and Elmer's Creek got known for its good air and as a sort of little place for a nice quiet 'oliday."

"How long has the regular ferry been running?"

"About fifty years, sir, but till just before the first war there weren't as many trips across. Before the steam ferry, you 'ad to get a rowing-boat. All this area was called Adder's Moss and was right out of the world. I've 'eard the old people say some of 'em lived and died without ever going across the river. Just stayed here...on and on, forever, as you might say. Peshall was the village and Elmer's Creek only sprung up on account of the river crossin'."

Littlejohn sat on the bank above the shore, a stretch of dry, fine turf with the narrow path they were travelling running along the top. He filled and lit his pipe and offered Dixon a cigarette.

"Go on... Take it, Dixon. You're really off duty."

The bobby helped himself and carefully lit the cigarette to avoid setting his moustache on fire.

"Are you a native of these parts, Dixon?"

"Who? Me, sir? No. I come from Clitheroe way, but I've been here fifteen years. My wife's a native of Peshall. Lived on the little farm you can see over there to the left."

"So, you married and settled here by the grace of the county constabulary."

"Yes."

There was a pause.

"How do you find the people here?"

"I'm still a foreigner to them, sir, though with the wife bein' native, it's a bit easier. A clannish lot. Some of the locals, like Charlie Withers, Fothergill the postman and such, never took to me. Of course, bein' a policeman makes a lot of people sort of reserved with you, doesn't it?"

"Fothergill's a local, then?"

"Oh, yes. Fothergills, Witherses, Bacons, Liddells. They're all names on Adder's Moss and have been 'ere for centuries. Queer folk. Till the district opened up a bit and let in strangers keepin' boardin' houses and pubs and charabancs, they all used to inter-marry and there was a few village idiots and the like around. They married to keep the money in the family, like Fothergill did."

"Did he marry a relative?"

"His cousin. She was a farmer's widow and has plenty of money. Both Fothergill and his missus is past their fifties, so it doesn't make any difference. Too late for children, if you see what I mean, sir."

"And Fothergill resents your intrusion?"

"Yes. The old ones would rather 'ave one of themselves as constable. One of the clan. Fothergill, bein' one of the old fami-lies from the moss, sort o' prides himself on his official position and resents mine. He's mad with pride."

"Sort *of folie de grandeur*, eh?"

Littlejohn, watching Dixon closely, saw his eyes light up at this new and cutting diagnosis of Fothergill's complaint, and then the brightness died away.

"Beg pardon, sir."

"Now, come, Dixon, you knew what I said and what it meant. I'm not one of your official superiors and we're just friends collaborating on a case. You've been decently educated, I can tell. All this playing at being ignorant is just a pose, isn't it? All that about Solemn and Jommorah! You've heard the parson pronounce them at church and I'm sure you went to Sunday School in your younger days. And your dropping aitches and the like. The *tone* of your voice is educated, and your illiteracy is just put on, isn't it? Which school did you go to?"

"Clitheroe Grammar."

Dixon sat with his head down closely concentrating on the glowing end of his cigarette.

"If I'd let on I was educated, they'd have moved me, sir. I'd have got promoted and been shifted elsewhere. They think in the force I finished my education at the elementary school, and I let 'em do it because it suits me."

"Why?"

"My wife won't leave the marsh. She says she'll leave me, or rather I'll have to leave *her* and go in digs if I get moved. That wouldn't do, sir. The constabulary expect a man's wife to go with him."

"Why won't she go?"

"She's just a marshlander, that's all. A lot of them are like trees, rooted here, and they die if they're pulled up. Some can go away and prosper, but Margery, the missus, isn't that sort."

"So you've screwed yourself down to the level of a…almost a peasant?"

"If you like to put it that way. There's the family. I couldn't bear to part with them. Four of them."

"I only saw three."

"The eldest boy is away, training for the sea. He's fifteen."

"You married as soon as you came here, then?"

"Yes."

Dixon blushed and looked out to sea. Littlejohn guessed part of the story, but not all. That came later from Fothergill, in a burst of hilarious spite against his rival. Margery Withers…no near relation of Charlie the Cheat…had decided to become a policeman's wife as soon as Dixon arrived in Peshall, and the girls of the marsh were not backward in getting their own way in the matrimonial direction. Dixon, lonely, an outcast among the natives, living in a damp cottage as lodger of an old woman before the police house was built, found the company of Margery, who kept popping up in various parts of his patrol, very comforting, and then very disturbing. The marsh girls were well known by the vulgar element of Falbright as "'ot stuff".

When Dixon was called to Tim Withers' little tumbledown farm, he thought it was for something constabulary and went with a smile. But he found an ultimatum waiting for him. There was a newcomer on the way and the old man wasn't going to have it called Withers. Dixon or... And the old reprobate had taken a gun down from a hook over the hearth. It was a good job Dixon loved the girl...or thought he did!

"You should read Dr Horrocks's book, sir. *People and Customs of Adder's Moss*. The doctor came here as a youngish man out of the navy. He doesn't seem without money, and a good job, too. The marshlanders don't bother much about doctors. Their old women cure their ailments with recipes handed down. And if they don't cure...well... We've all got to die sometime, sir."

"Horrocks wasn't successful?"

"He might have been, in time, with the new generation as would go to doctors comin' on, and all this agricultural machinery doing people damage that a doctor's needed for. But his book finished all that. They all took a dislike to him. Not that the bulk of 'em read the book, but it got round. There's a doctor in Freckleby comes out here and they send for him, now that they haven't to pay on account of the Health Insurance..."

"What did Horrocks say about them?"

"I won't say he didn't tell the truth for the most part. But it was the way he put it. You can't object to him saying that the marsh people won't mix with the fishermen or their girls marry them. It was and still is, with many families, like marrying a foreigner to marry a seagoin' or a river man. But to say the women of the marsh had easy virtue and chose and seduced the men they wanted to marry...well, if it was true, it was badly put, that's all. He also told how, to be sure they'd have somebody to pass on the money and land they owned, families often insisted on a child bein' on the way before the couple got married. Well, that custom has died out. The doctor's book brought the marsh-landers into bad repute and they resented it."

"So, they used the old women instead of the doctor when they were ill!"

"Yes. Or else sent to Freckleby and paid more."

Littlejohn looked out across the fields and could see the stocky, knotted forms of the men and women, harvesting the late vegetables or ploughing for autumn sowing. Already he'd noticed the twisted, rheumaticky old folk who came from the farms on the marsh, their dark swarthy features, their straight noses, and their black listless eyes which could probably grow passionate with hate or love or resentment. A strange, isolated race, dying out through the encroachment of motor traffic and modern ways. He was reminded of his recent summer holiday, spent with his friend Jerome Dorange, of the *Sarete*, at Nice. Together they had toured the harsh country around Digne and Lurs in Haute Provence, where the French detective had, on the spot, enlightened his English colleague on the Dominici affair.

Isolated passionate people, so near to civilisation, yet so primeval in hatred, love of their soil, contempt for weakness, relentless vengeance, unbreakable family bonds and duties.

"Do you think John Grebe fell foul of any of the marsh folk and brought their revenge on his head, Dixon?"

The bobby paused and frowned.

"I hope not, sir. They protect one another and you'll get nothing out of any of them if they think you're on the trail of one of their kin...and they're all near or distant kin here. You saw how impudent Charlie the Cheat was when we spoke to him."

"What about Jumping Joe? Had he any ties on the marsh?"

"Family ties, you mean? I wouldn't be surprised. He turned up here one day years since and nobody knew where he came from. But some of the old people said he was an illegitimate son of some monied family and had been farmed out far away, and then had returned to his own place. I don't know."

"He mentioned ghosts."

"That's not uncommon here. They believe all kinds of funny things on the marsh. Old things die hard, sir, and this isn't what you'd call Piccadilly Circus after dark. It's lonely and damp and frightening, crawling with life... Rabbits, foxes, stoats, and ferrets gone wild, frogs, rats. Squealing, croaking, terrified, hunting... All going on together. I've had many a bad turn when out on late patrol in winter."

Littlejohn rose and knocked out his pipe on his heel.

"This isn't getting us to Pullar's Sands, is it Dixon? But it's all very interesting. It shows us what we're up against."

They started off again in silence, Dixon wondering if he'd said too much, Littlejohn thinking of this strange little pocket of primitive and declining people among whom he found himself. A plane droned overhead on its way to Ireland.

They reached the little stream which joined the sea at Pullar's Sands. A narrow sheet of fresh water running down a sandy channel and across the sands where, when the tide came in, it would mingle with the sea. And the sea, in turn, would increase the size of the little tidal river beyond walking or wading depth and call for a boat or a journey to the bridge upstream.

They crossed the stream on stepping stones to the far bank where the *Saracen's Head* stood well back from the water. A solid little low-built house, with a group of neglected-looking outbuildings behind it where a few cows were kept and where the bit of produce raised on the few adjoining acres was stored, together with hay and other provender for the livestock.

They had to climb two stone steps to the front door. Dixon casually mentioned that at high tide the sea sometimes reached the first step.

The door was closed. Over it, a sign swinging from a

bracket. *Saracen's Head*, with a crude painting of a black man's head and shoulders almost washed away by the weather. *Esther Liddell, Licensed to sell Intoxicating Liquors and Tobacco.* That almost illegible, too. As Littlejohn raised his head to read it, a curtain at the window over the door moved gently, but he couldn't make out anybody behind it.

Inside there was one large public room with a counter at one end. A shelf behind it with glasses — mostly pint glass mugs — and a few packets of cigarettes. Two large tables and old wooden chairs. A wide iron fireplace with a cheap over-mantel and mirror above. A stone floor, sanded... There were no beer pumps; the barrels, in white padded jackets to keep them cool, stood on trestles behind the counter, with large wooden taps protruding from their bungholes.

The place smelled of beer and stale tobacco smoke. Two spittoons filled with sawdust near the fireplace and a dartboard on the wall beside the bar.

There was nobody about. A large black cat, stretched on one of the padded benches which ran round two sides, rose and fled into the room behind, the door of which stood open. Beyond the door, not a sound, except the loud ticking of a clock.

The two officers crossed the bar and peered in the room behind. The front room was well lighted by three windows; this, the landlady's private retreat, was almost dark. A small casement window let in the sun, which shed rays like a limelight across the room and illuminated a farmers' almanac and the photograph of a man dressed in the private's clothes of the first world war. Tunic, puttees, cap, riding breeches, and an astonished look on the face. A large, dark, puzzled man, perhaps wondering what he was doing in the artillery at all and what he was doing at the photographer's.

The ceiling was low and the walls dark. A rocking chair, a few rush-bottomed ones, a round table with an open work-basket on it, a small fireplace, and the rest of the heavier furni-

DEATH DROPS THE PILOT

ture in the dim periphery. A staircase rose from one corner, enclosed in a wooden casing and with a door at the bottom.

Beyond, the light shone brightly in a small scullery, but before they could reach it, footsteps sounded across the yard behind. Two pairs of footsteps and a man's voice.

"You need a man about the place."

The two seemed surprised when they saw Littlejohn and Dixon. Or rather, the man did. A tall, well-built young fellow dressed in shirt and trousers without collar and with a firm, strong, sunburned neck emerging. Ruddy-cheeked, with a mop of tousled light hair and a countryman's simple face. He had been delivering the beer from the brewery in Falbright and trying to make love in a clumsy way to the woman who accompanied him.

She was dressed, as Dixon had forecast, in corduroy trousers and a yellow jumper drawn over her naked torso and showing the shape of her fine shoulders and breasts. Dark brown hair, almost black, cut short, and a shapely face, large brown eyes and a firm chin. The nose was straight and slightly turned up at the tip.

Difficult to guess her age. It might have been forty or even forty-five. She was tall and well-made and moved with a lazy grace. Although a widow, she wore no wedding ring.

The brewery drayman looked awkward, produced his delivery note, which she signed with the pencil he handed her. Then, without a word, she passed into the bar, drew a pint of beer, and gave it to him. The carrier drank it almost in a single gulp in his hurry to get away.

"Good mornin'. See you next week."

The woman made no reply.

It was as if Littlejohn and Dixon weren't there.

"What do you want?"

She spoke at last. There was no anger or insolence in the tone. No curiosity, either. She didn't seem interested in the sudden appearance of one of the local bobbies accompanied by a stranger. It was all in the day's work.

"Some bread and cheese and beer for the two of us, please."

She went into the back place and soon returned with a plate on which were four hunks of bread, two large pieces of country cheese, and a knife. Then she drew two pints of ale from one of the barrels and placed them on the counter.

"Three and six."

Littlejohn paid. She nodded and put the half-crown and the shilling in the pocket of her trousers. Then she leaned an elbow on the counter and looked through the open door, waiting for them to finish and go.

She must have been a beauty in her youth. Now, although she was striking and doubtless attractive to most men who called there, her whole attitude was one of lassitude, tiredness, as though she expected someone and was weary of waiting or bored with the solitary life she was leading.

"This is good beer."

Littlejohn wanted her to turn her face fully to him and to see it change or lighten as she spoke.

"It comes from Falbright."

She gave Littlejohn a curious, expressionless look.

"You live alone here?"

"Yes. We get a few staying in the spare room in summer. Cyclists or walkers..."

The same flat tone, the same lack of interest.

"You knew John Grebe? He used to come here till quite recently?"

"Yes. He said *he* liked the beer, too."

"Was he a friend of yours?"

She looked at Littlejohn in the same lazy way and now the corners of her lips turned up a bit.

"They're mostly friends who come here. Regular customers who live round about."

She looked at the plate which was now empty and at the two glasses which were empty, too. A suggestion that now they'd been satisfied, it was time to go.

"Two more pints, please."

She took the mugs and filled them from the barrel, with no sign of pleasure or otherwise. Littlejohn put his hand in his pocket.

"That will be?"

"Two and eight."

It was then, as she addressed him, that Littlejohn caught the faint aroma of brandy on her breath. He began to understand. She was keeping her equanimity by drinking, just as some take drugs. He noticed the fine lines round her eyes, the signs of advancing middle age. All the same, her complexion was healthy and tanned and her hands as she manipulated the glasses, quite steady.

"What did Grebe do when he called?"

"He had a drink and a talk with me and his friends."

"Had he friends locally, then?"

"The men from the village, just upstream. One or two retired men who've been to sea…"

Dixon had been silently munching his bread and cheese and drinking his beer. He thought it time to put in a word.

"This used to be a rare retreat for smugglers, sir. Didn't it, Mrs Liddell?"

She made no reply. Dixon regarded her warily, a bit shy of meeting her eyes, like an unsophisticated chap who's heard of a woman's easy virtue and thinks his own private thoughts about how and to whom it is manifest. And then tries to hide the interest he's taking by awkward looks and words which betray him.

Dixon, feeling snubbed, turned his back on the landlady, and continued to address Littlejohn.

"This is the oldest pub round here and all these little creeks used to be used for revenue runnin' in days past. The *Saracen* was a smugglers' retreat, and the cellars are a perfect rabbit warren, aren't they?"

He was going to ask Mrs Liddell to confirm this, but remembering the previous silence, he answered it himself.

"I'll say they are."

"How long have you been here, Mrs Liddell? By the way, my name's Littlejohn. I'm here in connection with the Grebe case."

"Fifteen years."

She showed no interest in Littlejohn himself and merely answered his question.

"You get many regular customers?"

"A few. We do a good summer trade. That and the farm keep me going."

"How long is it since last you saw John Grebe?"

She seemed to reflect a little.

"Three weeks."

"Was he as usual then?"

"I didn't notice him any different."

There was something strange about it all. The brandy, the woman's lack of interest, her tight control of herself. Littlejohn couldn't make it out. She'd either something to hide or she was determined to have as little as possible to do with the police.

The two glasses were empty again and she took them and put them away to be washed without asking if Littlejohn and Dixon wanted more beer.

It was the strangest interview, and she was the oddest woman Littlejohn had ever had to deal with in his career. Here he was at the *Saracen's Head* and didn't really know why he was there. An impulse to take a walk and see the place and then another impulse to have a meal there. He and Dixon were merely a couple of customers, nothing more. They'd no right to press the questions, no right to assume the woman had anything whatever to do with Grebe and his death. And yet, Littlejohn was beginning to feel engaged in a battle of wits with Esther Liddell. She had done nothing, said nothing, but he felt a vague challenge in her attitude.

Littlejohn wondered if Esther Liddell had really loved her late husband and, since his death, little had mattered for her. The brandy...the story of her easy ways...any man would do... the boredom of living alone in an isolated pub...

A newcomer entered. A little chubby man, like an old salt. He wore an old, peaked cap and a reefer jacket.

"I'm late, Esther. Nobody else arrived?"

Then he saw Littlejohn and Dixon, nodded, and sat down.

Mrs Liddell drew him a pint of beer and put it before him on one of the tables. Then she took a box of draughts from under the counter and a board and set them out before him, too.

"He's not come yet, either..."

More steps, and another arrived. Taller and thinner, but the same type as the first. He saw the policemen at once and looked resentful. Strangers weren't welcome; they upset the routine of the old men.

Already Mrs Liddell was setting a pint before the thin man. The pair of them then started to sort out the draughts and put them on the board, all the time watching Littlejohn and Dixon unsociably.

Littlejohn paused and listened. From the room above came a faint sound. He remembered the moving curtain just as the pair of them had arrived and how it had crossed his mind that it might be the landlady. But she had been in the yard all the time.

Mrs Liddell seemed to have heard it, too. She left the bar and with the same lazy grace strolled into the back room. Littlejohn waited a moment, still listening. He heard her open a cupboard and then came the soft plop of a cork being withdrawn. She was taking another bracer. He crossed to the door.

She was just opening the door at the bottom of the staircase, without haste or panic. Just opening it in her usual languid way. Littlejohn entered before she could take a step on the stairs.

"Excuse me."

He was there before her and she made no effort to stop him. Nor did she show anger or fear. She just let him pass.

The stairs were narrow and gave on a small landing with three doors closed and a small bathroom visible at the end of a short corridor. Littlejohn opened the one on the front of the inn.

A man was standing by the bed, apparently disturbed in listening to what was going on below. His attitude of stock-still attention showed no guilt, just curiosity.

A tall, powerfully built man, with broad shoulders and heavy arms and legs. His face narrowed from a wide bald forehead to a firm pointed chin and he was clean shaven and ruddy, with full lips and blue eyes under thick eyebrows. His nose had been broken at some time and had a large irregular hump on the bridge. He was in his shirt and trousers and stockinged feet. He raised his eyes and stood rigid. His glance met Littlejohn's in a frank challenge.

"What do you want?"

Littlejohn didn't quite know himself for a brief second, and then he knew exactly what it was all about.

"Hello, Leo. What are you doing here?"

And from the way the man looked at him, Littlejohn knew he was right. And as if in confirmation, Esther Liddell, who had silently come up behind him, uttered a deep sigh, her only sign of any emotion since the Chief Inspector arrived.

10

THE MAN WHO WOULDN'T TALK

ullo, Leo."

The man in the bedroom smiled faintly. No suggestion of his being cornered or making a bolt for it. Just the smile, half of resignation and half of confidence in his own security.

Leo Fowler, Senior, was at a disadvantage being caught half-dressed, but he managed to keep his dignity. There was a strange calmness about him, and he gave the police a straight look. Obviously a man of character.

There was a faint air of dampness about the room, as though the atmosphere of the marsh had seeped right into the very fabric of the building. In the corners near the ceiling, the paper was starting to peel from the walls.

The room overlooked the front of the inn, and beyond there was a view right across Adder's Moss to Elmer's Creek. An excellent look-out, and it was obvious that Leo Fowler had seen Littlejohn and the constable approaching almost as soon as they'd taken the road along the coast. He'd had plenty of time in which to hide. Instead, he'd remained in his shirt and trousers and without his shoes.

A large double bed dominated the room. The sheets were

clean, but it hadn't been made. The rest of the furniture was old-fashioned and good. The kind which might have been handed down with the inn for generations. The large walnut wardrobe was open, and Littlejohn could see a kitbag on the floor of it and a reefer jacket hanging from a peg.

"You've come for me?"

Fowler looked Littlejohn in the eye and smiled. It might have been a rendezvous for a night out.

"No. In fact, I didn't know you were here, Leo. How comes that? Do you know Mrs Liddell?"

The landlady, still standing silently behind Littlejohn, didn't say a word.

"I just dropped in."

"How long have you been here?"

"A day or two."

Leo was almost as vague as Esther Liddell. It was becoming obvious that the pair of them had arranged exactly how they'd behave if the police arrived.

Littlejohn sat on the bed, pulled out his pipe, and began to fill it.

"That's not quite good enough, Leo. We're on a murder case, and if you don't want to get involved, you'd better be more explicit. How long have you been here?"

Fowler shrugged his shoulders and smiled again.

"I said, a day or two."

Littlejohn lit his pipe, rose, and strolled slowly round the room. Below, he could hear footsteps in the yard, the inn door was opened, and then there was a pause and voices.

"Anybody there?"

Shouting at the foot of the stairs. A customer wanting serving.

"Coming..."

Mrs Liddell turned without a word and slowly went downstairs. The steps creaked as she went. More shouting greeted her as she appeared in the bar.

Littlejohn walked to the wardrobe, took down the jacket from the hook, and turned out the pockets. Fowler watched him quite unperturbed. A pipe and pouch, matches, keys, knife and note-book in the side pockets, and a wallet in the inside one. Littlejohn threw them all on the bed. He knew he'd no right to do it, but he wanted to sting Leo into action. Instead, the sailor only smiled.

There was nothing special in the wallet. Some two-pence half-penny stamps, ten pounds or so in notes, odds and ends of paper bearing addresses and figures, an old photograph of a woman, young, smiling, with an apron on, standing at the door of a cottage in a row.

Littlejohn turned to the coat again and thrust his fingers in the inside match-pocket. There was a thin slip of paper there, which he straightened and examined. A ticket issued at the booking office of the ferry at Falbright. The kind they didn't collect at the end of the trip because you couldn't get on the boat until you'd paid and passed through the turnstile. The slip was dated the day of John Grebe's death.

"So you arrived just in time for Grebe's murder, Leo?"

"If you like to put it that way."

"You'd warned Grebe you were on the way, hadn't you? He expected you."

"You found the postcards I sent?"

"Yes."

Fowler nodded. He looked quite satisfied about it all. Glad, in fact, that the cards had been safely delivered.

"When did you first meet John Grebe?"

"It's so long since, I can't remember."

"You'd better get your shoes on, Leo. You're coming along with us."

"You're arresting me?"

"If you won't answer questions, I can't leave you here. After all, you wrote and threatened Grebe just before he died. Unless you can clear yourself, I'll have to hold you on suspicion."

"Have you got the handcuffs ready?"

Leo looked to be revelling in the situation. Certainly not the cornered criminal. On the contrary. Leo seemed to want to get himself in gaol.

Dixon stood by the door, his eyes wide, trying to take in what was happening. This was something new in his experience.

"By the way, Leo, you don't happen to be married to Mrs Liddell?"

Again the smile. Leo seemed to be enjoying every minute of the whole affair.

"Why?"

Littlejohn indicated the bed with a casual hand. Two people had obviously slept in it. Besides, on the old-fashioned chest with a toilet mirror on top of it, stood a woman's brush and comb, with a hand-mirror and a pin cushion. It was probably Mrs Liddell's own room in normal times. If Fowler were only a casual lodger, Esther Liddell, even if she slept with him, was hardly the type to go through her intimate toilet there as well.

"You honour me, Inspector. She's a fine woman."

"How do you know I'm an Inspector, Leo?"

"Well, there's the bobby there, isn't there? He's police. As for you, I've seen your picture in the paper a time or two."

"You seem to have found your tongue, Leo. Will you answer a few questions now?"

"No."

Just that. It was very awkward. The Chief Constable of Falbright had been on the phone several times already asking Littlejohn how he was getting along with the case. He was one of the aggressive types, one who worked by the book, rule of thumb. He just couldn't understand Littlejohn's methods. If the

Chief Inspector took in Leo Fowler, produced the postcards and the ferry ticket, told him that Leo had been hiding out at the *Saracen's Head* since the night Grebe was killed, the Chief Constable would charge Leo and start building up a case of murder against him, in spite of the fact that Leo wouldn't talk. In fact, Leo's silence would be construed as guilt.

And Littlejohn didn't believe Leo was guilty at all. He was either shielding someone, or...

"You *want* us to lock you up, don't you, Leo?"

The smile was getting on Littlejohn's nerves and yet, he liked Leo. He was a better type than all the rest in the case. Horrocks, Bacon, Chickabiddy, Brett, young Leo, and Tom Grebe. A poor lot... There was something manly and serene about Leo Fowler, Senior. He'd been through the mill somewhere and had come out of it with dignity.

Fowler was gathering his belongings from the bed and putting them in the pocket of his jacket which he then put on.

"I'm ready."

"It's very silly of you, Leo. If you'd answer our questions satisfactorily, you could stay on here, you know, till we need you."

"And if I don't answer them satisfactorily. What then?"

"Come on, then."

"No handcuffs?"

"Not unless you insist."

Dixon began to look awkward. He'd no handcuffs with him. How could anybody expect him to carry all his paraphernalia? He'd only been asked to come out for a bit of a stroll with the Inspector. Now, they'd arrested a man! He wondered if Littlejohn had a pair of handcuffs in his pocket. If Leo insisted, what then?

They went downstairs single file. Littlejohn even let Leo lead the way. And they strolled through the kitchen and bar as though they were pals off for a day's fishing. Esther Liddell was serving beer to some customers who'd arrived in a jeep. Three men with guns, off to shoot duck in the reeds along the bay.

"I'd like a word with you, Mrs Liddell."

She slowly approached Littlejohn again, not even looking curious, and there was no sign between her and Fowler that this was an emotional moment for them. Littlejohn nodded towards the kitchen door and she went in, followed by Leo and the police. All eyes in the bar followed them.

"We're taking Leo with us to Falbright police station. Have you anything to say, Mrs Liddell?"

She looked him full in the face.

"What *should* I say?"

"He's nothing to you, then?"

She didn't answer. It might not have been worth an answer or, on the other hand, she was afraid to betray her feelings for him.

"How long has he been here?"

"You should ask him. It's his business and it's him you're arresting."

"Let's change the tack, then. You knew the tramp called Jumping Joe?"

"Yes. He came here now and then."

"He lived here sometimes, didn't he?"

"When the weather was bad, he'd sleep in the barn."

"Has he been here lately?"

"He was always in and out. He spent his time between us and the *Barlow Arms* getting drunk."

"He was flush with money just before he met his death. Have you any idea where he got it from?"

"I haven't a clue."

Still the same languid way, the same lack of interest, as though nothing in life was new and nothing important anymore.

"He didn't happen to discover that Leo was staying here?"

Leo smiled again.

"And that I gave him the money to keep quiet? Try again, Inspector. Nobody but Esther knew I was here. Hadn't we better be going to the lock-up? I'm hungry and I want my regulation tea."

Esther looked at him with the same kind of smile. They both seemed to be enjoying events immensely.

"I'll get you some bread and cheese."

"You'll do nothing of the kind, Esther. From now on, I'm Her Majesty's guest and the police can find the bread and cheese."

There was nothing more to be said. The whole thing was ridiculous. Leo and Esther obviously acting a part, refusing to speak about anything affecting the Grebe case, behaving as if they'd already spent a long time rehearsing what they would say and do when the police called.

"Come along then, Leo."

Fowler didn't say goodbye to Esther. He just put on his peaked cap and made for the door. The tide was in and Leo even rowed the party over the little estuary in a small boat, moored to the *Saracen*'s side of the water by a long rope which they paid out as they went and which someone on the other side then seized and hauled back the boat.

The three men walked back to Elmer's Creek across the bank on the tideline again. The return journey wasn't as happy. Leo was lost in his own thoughts, smoked his pipe happily, and smiled his aggravating smile now and then. Dixon and Littlejohn didn't seem able to carry on a satisfactory conversation without Leo's joining-in, so there were long painful pauses, which Leo seemed to enjoy. In fact, he seemed elated by the discomfiture of the police and kept talking about the tea they were going to give him when they got him there and how long he was going to be with them at the government's expense.

It was a relief to find Cromwell waiting at the police station at Elmer's Creek.

"This is Leo Fowler, Cromwell. The father of Lily and Leo, Junior."

"Excuse me, Inspector. The stepfather of Lily."

And again the smile.

"Do I put 'im in the cell, sir?"

Dixon was bewildered by the unorthodox turn of events. He didn't know whether Leo had been arrested or simply come with them of his own free will. He wished he could get away for a minute to consult the *Policeman's Vade Mecum* about procedure, but too much was happening all at once. His wife was blazing at him for being away so long and leaving his lunch to spoil. And to add to the confusion, the eldest offspring had been fishing in the river, had accidentally hooked a conger, and been pulled in the water. They'd brought him home wet through.

"Has he to go in the cell, sir?"

Leo seemed more delighted than ever.

"Lead on, Macduff."

"No. We're going over to Falbright. The beds are more comfortable there, Dixon."

Dixon didn't know whether to laugh or cry. In his own cell they gave them a block of wood for a pillow and a rough blanket for comfort. What was there wrong about that, eh?

Cromwell took Littlejohn aside.

"We got through to the Yard and Gravesend, sir. Fowler, Senior, did vanish at the time stated and was presumed dead, later. In 1938, that was. No trace was ever found of him that was recorded. It's quite right about Leo, Junior, and Lily, too. They did live at 13 Tenterden Street, Gravesend. There are people there who still remember them. Nobody seems to know about John Grebe in the old days. Scotland Yard got his picture from Fleet Street. It's been in the papers in connection with the murder and they got a good likeness from the press. Nobody like Grebe was ever connected with Lily's mother. In fact, one old woman who's lived in Tenterden Street for fifty years and refused even to move when four bombs fell round it, said she'd a good idea who Lily's father was, and it wasn't Grebe."

"So perhaps Grebe wasn't her father and he befriended her for some other reason, either conscience or an old man's fancy."

"That's right, sir."

"Very well. We'll take Leo, Senior, over to Falbright and hold him on suspicion. We'd better get moving. Let Dixon stay here now. He's completely bewildered and a few hours on the beat will help him get his thoughts in order."

They took Leo across on the ferry. They might have been returning from a jaunt. Leo seemed to enjoy every minute of it, smoked Littlejohn's tobacco, passed the Chief Inspector his own pouch of shag, and offered to pay for his companions a drink at the *Barlow Arms* as they passed. Littlejohn refused on the strength of their not wanting to encounter Leo's children in the pub.

"Why, Littlejohn? Will it embarrass you?"

The more they were together, the better Leo and Littlejohn got on.

The Chief Constable was annoyed when they arrived.

"Highly irregular, Chief Inspector. You ought to have sent for a police launch. What would you have done if Fowler had tried to bolt? Damned embarrassin' it would have been."

"I knew he wouldn't, though."

"*How* did you know?"

How very trying! How could Colonel Cram, the Chief Constable, understand Littlejohn's ways of working and his dependence on intuition as much as on routine?

Luckily Cram didn't wait for an answer. He was in his element. He almost called a press conference of the two local reporters and told them they'd got their man.

"I wouldn't do that yet, sir."

"Why? The postcards with the threats; the fellah hidin' on the marsh till things blew over; the fact that he's the father, or as good as the father, of the girl at the *Barlow Arms* that old John Grebe was carryin' on with..."

Littlejohn sighed.

"We've no cast-iron proof yet, sir."

Cromwell was meanwhile obeying his chief's instructions. They took a quick photograph of Fowler, who seemed to know what it was all about and smiled so much that they had to tell him to take the smile off his face or they'd knock it off for him. He gave them a good set of fingerprints, too.

"Anything to oblige."

Then the photograph and the prints went off by special messenger to Scotland Yard; fast car to the nearby airport and thence by plane.

The Chief Constable tried his own hand with Leo Fowler, and Superintendent Lecky was as bewildered as Dixon about the whole affair.

"Littlejohn's made the whole ruddy business into a sort of pantomime. We can't do any good with the prisoner. He won't answer questions and seems as pleased as Punch about being arrested at all. It's Littlejohn who's put him up to it."

His staff said he was jealous, of course!

Colonel Cram exhausted himself and his temper on Fowler.

"Anything you say may be used in evidence, of course, but I'd advise you to tell us the truth, my man. It'll be best for you."

"I know it will... But I'm not saying anything to be used in evidence just at present, sir. I'd like to think it over. I'll be quiet in my cell and decide there what to do."

Cram suddenly realised that Leo was laughing at him! "Charge him and put him in the cells."

"What with, sir?"

Littlejohn intervened.

"We'll just hold him on suspicion for the time being. We can't do that for long, though. We'll have to work fast."

"But I'm sure the man did it, Littlejohn. There's guilt, truculent guilt, written all over him. You must get at him, question him severely, press your points. You'll get a confession, I'm sure. I rely on you, Littlejohn."

Colonel Cram placed a confident hand on Littlejohn's shoulder. He did it with difficulty for he was a small man.

"Even if I think he didn't do it, sir?"

"What do you mean?"

"I'm sure Fowler didn't murder Grebe."

"Then why the hell did you pull him in?"

"I didn't pull him in, sir. He *came* in. For some reason, Fowler wants to be arrested. He's either shielding someone or..."

"Or what? This is beyond me, Littlejohn."

"Or else he's afraid lie's marked for the same fate as Grebe and he'd feel safer in a cell."

11

THE HAPPY PRISONER

It was six o'clock in the evening and Littlejohn was waiting for dinner. Cromwell, who had ingratiated himself with a fisherman, had been given a large lobster fresh from the pots and Mrs Braid was cooking it for them. More as an excuse than anything else, Littlejohn put on his raincoat and said he was going out for some tobacco.

The weather had changed. Late in the afternoon a wind had sprung up, it had started to rain, and by nightfall it was blowing a gale. The Irish boat had had a rough passage and when she docked, a passenger who'd fallen from one deck to another, was removed in an ambulance. None of the fishing boats due out that night was putting to sea.

As Littlejohn left the *Barlow Arms*, his hat pulled down and his raincoat collar turned up, he met a small party who had crossed on the ferry. One or two of them had been sick.

The Chief Inspector was a bit fed up. The second murder at Elmer's Creek had raised the case to front-page news and the press had arrived in full force on the afternoon train from London. They were greeted by the excitement of Leo Fowler's arrest and when Littlejohn and Cromwell got back to the *Barlow*

Arms from Falbright, they were almost torn to pieces by anxious reporters.

"Is it true the case is over and you've got your man again?"

Then Leo, Junior, drunk as usual, had taken exception to the remarks of a beefy sailor about his father, and there was a lull in the Grebe Case as they made way for a stretcher bearing Leo to hospital where he remained two days.

All Braid's remaining rooms at the *Barlow Arms* were booked and some of the press had to find accommodation in the village cottages.

Braid complained bitterly to Littlejohn.

"It should be my holidays now that the tourist season's over. Now I can't go, and I've booked my rooms in London. It's not good enough."

"You're wanted on the telephone."

Lucy approached Littlejohn and said it in a dry disinterested voice. She had a crushed, beaten look. Now and then she glanced apprehensively over her shoulder, as though expecting fresh disasters at any minute. First her father's arrest; then her brother making another fool of himself.

The Chief Constable was on the phone, speaking from home in a pained, officious voice.

"I've been thinking about this case. I can't understand you at all, Littlejohn. I suppose you know what you're doing. Here you've arrested a man you say didn't commit the crimes. You must know the risk you're taking, and I hold you responsible. I left him in his cell, as happy as a king, shouting for his food. He wanted kippers and some cheese."

Not a sign of humour in the Chief Constable's voice. Just anxiety and peevishness. Littlejohn almost laughed aloud. Kippers and cheese!

"Are you listening? I was saying, I've rung you up to tell you that I expect a satisfactory explanation before the magistrates sit in the morning."

"Remand him in custody for threatening the life of John Grebe, sir. Anything you like, so long as we keep him in gaol."

"But..."

"I'll be responsible. Good night, sir."

"I warn you, Littlejohn..."

It was a relief to get in the open air, even if it was pouring with rain.

One of the reporters hastily took Littlejohn's place in the telephone box.

"Is that the desk? Take this down, will you? *Relief reigned in the quiet little Homeshire fishing village of Elmer's Creek when I arrived here this afternoon, for Chief Inspector Littlejohn, the famous Scotland Yard detective, had just laid his hand on the shoulder of the murderer who has been terrorising the neighbourhood...*"

The little village store was closed when Littlejohn reached it, but there was a light in the back room, so he knocked on the door.

"Who is it?"

By the tone of the woman's voice, it didn't sound as though relief reigned in Elmer's Creek! She was terrified.

"It's Inspector Littlejohn. Can you let me have some tobacco?"

Bolts, locks and chains, and the woman's frightened face appeared. She didn't invite him in, but took his order, passed out the packets, returned with the change, and then locked up again.

It was the same on the way back. Night had fallen, doors were closed, lamps lit. Now and then, a hurried step from someone anxious to be indoors again. A shadow crossing a blind. A window where they hadn't drawn the curtains revealed a family sitting at an evening meal, a woman suckling a baby, a man changing his shirt.

The Farne Light was lit and the beam flashed steadily, every five seconds, across the untidy little promenade.

Then, suddenly, a loud scream, followed by another, and the village seemed to wake up. A woman rushed into the road, her arms waving, her voice shrill.

"Help! Help! He's hung himself."

It took Littlejohn a second or two to make the woman out, and then he recognised Mrs Tom Grebe. She had come from the side door of the converted chapel, from which a flood of light shone into the alley leading to the house behind.

The promenade became alive with people. It was a wonder where they all came from. Almost like spirits materialising. A ragged knot of men and women followed Littlejohn. There were even children hanging on to their mothers.

"Keep the women and children away. Send them home."

Tom Grebe was hanging from a beam in the wooden shed where they stored the empty bottles and where he kept his battery of hens. He'd even decently covered the batteries with sacks to prevent the hens seeing what he was going to do.

They cut down the body and somebody started to practise artificial respiration, but it was no use. He'd been dead too long.

Mrs Grebe was shouting and wailing all over the place. They could hear her lamentations down at the jetty and more people hurried to join the crowd. Press photographers got busy with their flashlights and reporters started to question the spectators.

One of the fishermen who lived opposite the soft-drinks factory was telling a muddled tale already.

"At first I thought it was another murder, but when I saw the light from Tom Grebe's, I knew what it was. He's been depressed since his brother got killed and this afternoon, I crossed on the ferry from Falbright with him and he looked like death warmed up. Like a man in a dream as didn't know what he was doin'. I can't say I'm surprised at what's happened."

Dixon suddenly appeared and cleared them all away.

"I was just taking the wife and kids to see their aunt on the Moss," he said by way of excuse for his late arrival.

One of the women gently coaxed Mrs Grebe to go home with her. It needed two of them to hold her; she was like somebody in a fit.

"It's that lawyer, Flewker, that did it. He told my husband that his brother had left him not a penny. Just this old buildin' and nothin' to keep it goin' with. All the money to that scarlet woman at the *Arms*. God will punish them all. My Tom made away with himself when he heard of it."

She screamed and repeated it over and over again, until a door closed and shut it off.

It was nine o'clock before they got it all cleared up and the body across in a police boat to the mortuary at Falbright. Littlejohn and Cromwell ate a cold supper on a solitary table by the fire. The usual party had arrived and were sitting in their customary places waiting for Littlejohn to join them. Horrocks, Bacon, Brett, and a stranger; a little man with a bald head, pointed nose, receding chin, and a goatee beard. He was anxious to speak to Littlejohn. Horrocks introduced him as Sir Luke Messiah, the chairman of the Homeshire County Council. His arrival had put Brett in a flurry of toadying and excitement.

"The Chief Constable's been on again, too."

It was obvious that the four men were eager to hear what Littlejohn had to say. Horrocks, his legs crossed, was smoking a cigar and sipping whisky. Bacon was leaning back with his legs and shiny shoes stretched out before him. Sir Luke sat upright, his knees together, and a glass of orangeade at his elbow. Brett couldn't keep still, watching Sir Luke, glaring at Littlejohn for keeping them waiting, mopping his sweating forehead.

Littlejohn laid down his knife and fork, and Lucy, who was hanging about, removed his plate. When he started to help himself to trifle from a dish, it was more than Sir Luke could bear.

"Are you aware, Inspector, that I've come all the way from Freckleby to speak with you?"

He rose and stared about, as though seeking his hat and coat for an exit in a huff, failed to see them, and sat down again.

Littlejohn looked round in surprised good humour.

"Are you wanting to talk to me about the man we've arrested, sir? The happy prisoner…"

Sir Luke boiled over.

"I've been discussing the matter with the Chief Constable."

It was obvious the Chief Constable had rung up Sir Luke and asked for his help. He'd promised to go to Elmer's Creek and put Littlejohn in his place. And here was the Chief Inspector, eating lobster and trifle as though nothing had happened!

"I'm Chairman of the bench at Falbright and I've never heard of such goings-on."

He paused to gather himself together. His words seemed to choke him.

"Captain Bacon and Dr Horrocks are also Justices of the Peace and, I tell you candidly, we shall have something to say in court tomorrow unless you tell a more coherent tale than the one you told Cram this afternoon."

Littlejohn was cutting himself a piece of cheese.

"I'd be grateful if you'd attend to what I'm saying, Chief Inspector. There's panic all over the village. People are scared to go out of doors. You've been here three days and done nothing that I can see. And now you've arrested a man you say isn't guilty. What are we to make of it all? Besides, you haven't played fair by the local police. Kept them in the dark…".

Bacon and Horrocks nodded their heads in assent. It was obvious there'd been a meeting and a decision made before Littlejohn got back.

Littlejohn was eating his cheese and biscuit with apparent relish.

"I warn you, Chief Inspector. We won't be embarrassed on the bench tomorrow. Either…"

Littlejohn wiped his mouth on his napkin, folded it, and put it in a napkin ring marked "2".

"Either what, Sir Luke?"

"Either you give us evidence which will justify our committing him on a charge of murder, or we release him on bail...or even discharge him."

Lucy entered again and made for Littlejohn.

"You're wanted on the phone."

The same dull, flat voice.

"Not the Chief Constable again, I hope."

Sir Luke Messiah gave his two brother JPs a look which almost bordered on triumph. What did I tell you? He's flouting the lot of us. You could almost hear him say it.

"No. It's Inspector Silence. He says he's some information for you."

"Do you mind, Cromwell? Tell him I'm in conference with the local bench of magistrates, will you?"

Lucy started to clear the table.

"The man from the *Daily Trumpet* asked me to tell you he's waiting for a call to London for his morning column and he'll be glad if you'll hurry."

"Tell him to go to..."

The door closing on Cromwell cut off the rest.

Littlejohn drew up a chair in the circle of Justices and lit his pipe.

"You were saying, when we were interrupted, Sir Luke...?"

"We'll release Fowler if you can't produce a cast-iron case for his guilt."

"It's my turn, now, Sir Luke, to tell you I shall hold *you* responsible in such an event. If Fowler is released before I give the word, the bench will be responsible for whatever happens afterwards."

Sir Luke Messiah could hardly contain himself, and it was

only the fact that the Chairman was the local bigwig that kept Bacon quiet. He was obviously seething with rage, as well.

"Listen, Chief Inspector. Today you've arrested a man who's threatened the life of John Grebe. We've got the cards on which he did it. You performed a good piece of work in laying him by the heels. I won't deny it. A good piece of work. And then, you spoil it. You say he didn't murder Grebe at all. In spite of the evidence. Why? *You've* questioned the man. *We've* questioned him. Or rather, the Falbright police have done so. He won't say a word. That's natural. He doesn't want to incriminate himself. Instead, he's as pleased as Punch about it. Truculent, throwing his weight about. Why? Because you, Chief Inspector, have taken his part. He knows you're on his side. Why *are* you?"

"Just a hunch, sir."

"A hunch!"

The three magistrates all said it simultaneously and then, to show how heartily he was in accord with them, Brett said it, too.

"A hunch!"

Cromwell was back, carrying a slip of paper torn from his official notebook. He passed it to Littlejohn, who slowly put on his glasses and read it. You could hear the heavy breathing of the three JPs, and Brett bronchially boiling somewhere inside.

"You'll be interested in this, gentlemen. First, let me explain that today we sent a photograph of Leo Fowler, Senior, together with his fingerprints, to Scotland Yard, and asked if they'd any information about him. This is what they say."

Littlejohn slowly read from the paper.

"Records show that the photograph is that of Walter Mills, not Leo Fowler. Aged 56. Returned to this country September 4th, of this year, from Russia where he had been a prisoner since March 1945, when he was removed from a German concentration camp. According to German files in our possession, Mills was captured and condemned in Germany for smuggling refugees from Germany, September 1938. He was recently released with a batch of English prisoners sentenced in Russia for political offences. Photographs, taken on his arrival in England, follow…"

Littlejohn took off his glasses, slowly folded them, and put them back in his pocket.

Sir Luke Messiah slapped his knee vigorously.

"A traitor…a gaolbird, who's just missed death once. An obvious murderer. Probably a communist, as well. And you say, Chief Inspector, you've got a hunch! It's laughable. Come now, admit, on the face of this new evidence, that he's your man. Mills or Fowler, or whoever he is, came here for the express purpose of murdering Grebe out of revenge. Perhaps Grebe was in this smuggling scheme with Fowler and left him to bear the blame. It's as plain as the nose on your face."

Littlejohn spoke to Cromwell in an undertone and the sergeant went off once more to the telephone.

All three JPs looked cheerful and were obviously waiting for Littlejohn's agreement to make their job of the morrow an easy one.

"Well, Inspector?"

Bacon was almost matey. He leaned across and tapped Littlejohn's knee.

"Well, Inspector? You'll charge him with murder before the court sits and then we'll formally commit him to the assizes. There'll be no bail. He can enjoy himself to his heart's content in prison, then. He seems to like it, from what I've heard."

"I shall do no such thing, gentlemen. We haven't enough evidence to hold him on anything except suspicion. If you release him, it's your own responsibility."

Horrocks, Bacon, and Sir Luke Messiah rose like one man, all talking at once. Cromwell entered quietly, a puzzled look on his face, and spoke a few words to his chief. There was silence as the rest listened, looking more bewildered than Cromwell himself.

"Leo Fowler's greatcoat is still at the *Saracen's Head*, sir. Mrs Liddell says it wasn't in the wardrobe with the rest of his gear because she'd got it downstairs in the cupboard. She'd been cleaning it and putting on a button."

Sir Luke Messiah was the first to explode.

"What *is* this nonsense? Greatcoats... *Saracen's Head*... Putting buttons on... Are we all going mad!"

He tore at his goatee beard and gurgled deep in his throat.

"It means, sir, that I'm more convinced than ever that Fowler's not guilty and I can't charge him with the Grebe murder."

"In that case, we've nothing more to say. We shall know what to do in the court tomorrow."

"Very well, sir."

The four men stamped out without a good night and Little-john and Cromwell could hear them talking outside under the window and then Sir Luke and Bacon shunting their cars about in the dark.

Lucy was back.

"You're wanted on the phone, sir."

She'd got to saying it like a weary gramophone.

Littlejohn followed her out passing on the way the group of impatient pressmen, eager to telephone their latest stories to their papers.

It was the Chief Constable again.

"Any news? Anything further to report?"

Littlejohn seized the elbow of one of the reporters outside the box, pulled him in, and handed over the instrument. Then he lit his pipe and listened with a smile as the pair of them sorted it all out.

12

THE BUSINESS OF THE EURYANTHE

Saturday morning. It was just past seven and Littlejohn, after having a bath, was shaving as best he could in front of the large mirror on his dressing table. Damp and sea air had affected the quicksilver which gave a distorted image like one in a sideshow on a fairground.

The weather had improved. The rain had ceased, and the gale had blown itself out. High clouds scudded across a blue sky and all the buildings and the road down the quay had a spring-cleaned appearance.

There were a few people about: Cromwell returning from a constitutional; a couple of reporters talking with some old salts at the head of the jetty; five-day-week men going off with lines and bait for a day's fishing; others on their way to the ferry. The tide was coming in and the smoke of the departing Irish Mail was just visible on the skyline.

Littlejohn and Cromwell ate a good breakfast, which Lucy served. She still looked tired and worried.

"Would it be all right, sir, if I came to court this morning to see father? It might cheer him up. He seems to have nobody..."

"I wouldn't worry, if I were you, Lucy. He's quite cheerful and comfortable. It will all end up all right."

"I wish I could be sure."

The two detectives crossed the ferry and not far from the pier head on the Falbright side, found the police station. The sergeant in charge looked surprised to see them. Business was quiet. Leo in his cell; the body of Tom Grebe in the morgue; and a man who'd been celebrating the last night of his holidays, got drunk, and broken a shop window. He'd been sick in his cell.

"I'd like to see Fowler. Is he all right?"

"Yes, sir. Two kippers, bacon and eggs, toast and jam for breakfast. He asked for more. Slept well."

"You're doing him well, aren't you? Any visitors?"

"The Super and the Chief Constable. He seemed to rile them. The Chief was proper put out when he came back from the cells. I'll come with you and open the door, sir."

Cromwell stayed behind in the office to ring-up Scotland Yard for fuller details of Leo's wartime offence.

Leo was lying on his bed digesting his meal. His hands were clasped behind his head and he was settled comfortably on his back gazing at the ceiling. He smiled as Littlejohn entered and scrambled upright to greet him.

"Morning, Leo."

"Morning, Inspector. Good of you to call. Things are busy this morning. I've had two already. You look a bit more cheerful than the others."

Littlejohn drew up the solitary wooden chair and sat astride it. He filled his pipe and offered his pouch to Leo, who took it eagerly.

"A smoke's a godsend. I've run out of tobacco and they say smoking's against the regulations."

"You'll soon be out now. The magistrates are determined to release you on bail if you can fix up sureties."

"I thought I was in on a murder charge."

"Hardly."

Leo sat up and looked puzzled.

"What's going on? Why did you bring me in, then?"

"Because you're safer here."

"That's just what Esther said when she saw you coming to the *Saracen*. She wanted me to give myself up."

"Don't you think you'd better tell me the whole story, Leo? I know a lot of it, but it will help me if you fill in the gaps."

Fowler gave the Chief Inspector a shrewd look.

"How much *do* you know?"

"I know you were once a lot nearer execution than you are at present, Leo, and that you just missed death by hanging by the skin of your teeth."

Leo passed back Littlejohn's pouch and slowly lighted his short briar. He puffed the smoke in great voluptuous gulps and then nodded affably to the Inspector.

"That's right."

You couldn't help liking Leo, and Littlejohn felt a warm feeling for him. He was a man who had evidently suffered a lot of hardship and who'd come through it on the strength of his ironical sense of humour and strange, smiling invulnerability.

"All this good-humoured acceptance of arrest, Leo... You're enjoying yourself, with your kippers and your bacon and eggs, because you're safer in here than rambling about at liberty. Just as Mrs Liddell told you. Aren't you? You're afraid you might go the same way as John Grebe if you don't watch yourself."

Fowler removed his pipe and gave Littlejohn a look of admiration.

"I've got to hand it to you, Inspector. You know your business. How did you get on to that?"

"A hunch, that's all. And I almost shudder to utter the word because the whole bench of justices slapped me down last night for using it. However, let's say, for a start, that you went down to the jetty at Elmer's Creek to find John Grebe when the last boat came in on the night the old man died."

"Right again. I came quietly to Elmer's Creek, by night. I wasn't going to advertise my arrival by using the day ferry where everybody sees you. I got in after dark. Half-past seven, in fact. I was on my way to the *Saracen* where I know the landlady, and she'll do me a good turn any time."

"How did you come to know Esther Liddell?"

"All in good time, Inspector. I'll tell you one day. It's no concern of yours at present."

"We'll not argue about it. Get on with your tale, Leo."

"I returned for the last ferry intending to take Grebe by surprise. I'd warned him I was coming, but I thought if I faced him when the boat came in, it would shake him up a bit."

"Did you meet anybody you knew?"

"No. I saw my son, Leo, half-seas over, making for the last ferry, and I saw Lily, my stepdaughter, come to the door of the *Barlow Arms* and see him safely off with a sailor who seemed to be looking after him and who was nearly as drunk as Leo."

"You knew Lily was at the *Arms?*"

"Yes. I had my way of finding out. I'll tell you later. I guessed Leo would fetch up there, too, trying to get money out of her when he knew where she was."

"Go on. You went down to meet Grebe."

"Yes. But I was frustrated about springing a surprise. He came off the boat with another fellow I didn't know, of course, and I wouldn't know him if I saw him again. I knew John by his uniform."

"The same as your own? Officer's cap, uniform greatcoat?"

"Yes."

Leo shot another admiring glance at Littlejohn, who looked back at him blandly.

"That's right. Grebe walked a little way with the man I

mentioned; almost as far as the *Arms*. I followed them. They said good night and the little fellow went on."

"Wait a minute, Leo. Did you follow on their heels or otherwise?"

"No. They were in the middle of the jetty walking on the asphalt; I was on the footpath, level with them. It was dark. I couldn't be recognised."

"Go on."

Littlejohn pulled another pipe from his pocket, filled it, put the old one away, and lit the new one. He handed his pouch to Leo again who rammed tobacco in his pipe as he spoke, after knocking out the dottle on the iron leg of his bed.

"Grebe crossed to the *Arms* and instead of going in by the front door, went in through the side gate which leads to the yard where there's a garage made from the old stables. There's also a door there leads into the public bar behind. If you want a quick one, that's the best place to go, I hear. So I gathered that Grebe might be wanting a drink to keep out the cold without any fuss, because the ferry was due off in a few minutes."

Leo stopped to light his pipe, got to his feet, and started to pace up and down the cell presumably to stretch his legs, for he showed no excitement as his tale went on.

"I followed him. I thought, this is just the place to give him a surprise. It was pitch dark in the yard, except for the light from an upstairs room which had the blind down. The other windows overlook the sea which is just at the back of the pub. For a minute or two, the pair of us must have been in the yard together in the dark. I thought, as soon as he opens the side door and lets out the light, I'll bid him good evening and see what he has to say to that."

Leo paused in his pacing and faced Littlejohn with a challenging smile as if to say, 'You know everything; take it up from there.'

And Littlejohn did.

"But he didn't open the door!"

"No, he didn't."

"He wasn't going for a drink at all. There's a gentlemen's lavatory in that yard just at the side of the house. John Grebe always took his drink slowly. He wasn't in the habit of having a quick one between ferry crossings. Was he stabbed as he came out of the lavatory?"

"Yes. When the door didn't open, I crossed as softly as I could and saw the reason. He was inside, so I waited to greet him when he came out. Then, I realised there was somebody else there. I could have cursed at being done again, but I waited. I heard Grebe come into the open air, and then I heard a scuffle and a grunt, and one of them fell. That's all. I beat it hell for leather. I knew that with the postcards and my record, I was as good as hanged if I was caught. I hoofed it like mad to the *Saracen*. Esther put me up, and there I planned to stay a day or two till the heat was off, and then make off. But tell me this…"

He paused and this time his face assumed a serious, puzzled look.

"Tell me this… Grebe died and was found in the river. Did he somehow make his way to the ferry and get her half over the river and then fall overboard? How in blazes did he manage to do it, and why?"

"He didn't. He didn't take over the ferry. He was dead in the yard of the hotel. Somebody carried him and threw him into the river just off the point behind the *Arms*, and somebody put on his cap and greatcoat, took the ferry half over, ran her into a sandbank, climbed overboard, and got away across the bank on this side."

"Why take over the ferry? Why not leave the body and beat it? It was a shocking risk."

"Not at all. It was dark, the murderer or his accomplice was Grebe's build. All he had to do was put on Grebe's uniform cap and coat. Grebe's body was found without them and it puzzled us a lot at the start. He put on the clothes, went to the ferry in the dark, climbed the bridge, and..."

"And Bob's your uncle!"

"Exactly! Anybody intelligent could handle the ferry after seeing her navigated for a bit. The reason why the murderer acted as he did was to get an alibi. Either he wanted it to look as if Grebe had been killed on the way over, or else after he landed on the other side. In the latter event, the murderer's navigation went all haywire and he hit the bank. If Grebe hadn't turned up at the ferry time, there'd have been a hue and cry, they'd have gone straight to the *Arms* to see if he'd had a drink and might have found the body. By acting as he did, the criminal confused Grebe's trail and gave himself a good hour to put things straight at Elmer's Creek."

"But aren't we forgetting something, Inspector?"

"I'm coming to that, Leo. You mean, that whoever the murderer was, he was after *you*, not John Grebe. You were both of a size, wore the same uniform and, in the dark of the hotel yard, you got mixed up and the killer got the wrong man."

"That's it. And you and Esther think he'll have another go at me, and I'm safer in gaol."

"Right again. Now, who could be anxious to see you dead and silenced, Leo? What secrets do you hold about people round here?"

Leo sat down and, for the first time, looked excited.

"The only one I can think of is Grebe. Yet there must be somebody else here who thinks I know a lot, which I don't. I don't know a thing, except that Grebe and I were in a racket together before the war and I'm sure Grebe was acting for somebody else. In other words, there was a gang of them and, although I didn't know any member of it except John Grebe, who was their mouthpiece, they can't be sure."

"You must have been followed from the moment you arrived in Elmer's Creek. They were on the look-out for you because you'd sent the postcards and warned Grebe you were on the way. When they found they'd got the wrong man, they acted quickly. The first thing to do was to get the ferry off to time and, by Jove, they did it! What was between you and Grebe?"

"It's a long story. During the first war, Grebe was captain of a trooper in the Mediterranean and I was a junior officer. We got on very well together, but he drank heavily at the time and ran her aground off the North African coast. We tried to keep him off the bridge, because he wasn't fit to navigate her, but he was stupid. There was an enemy raider about, and our ship was a sitting target, stuck in the mud. The raider just shot us to kingdom come. Luckily, there weren't many troops aboard, but about fifty men lost their lives and the ship was blown to smithereens. It affected Grebe's mind a bit. He packed up after the inquiry and the fearful row that followed and vanished. It turned out later that he came here, out of the way, and started afresh on a cockeyed sort of ferry job."

"You didn't know where he was when you returned to England?"

"No. I was anxious to see Grebe again and square accounts, and he was perhaps as anxious to hide himself in case I turned up one day. Meantime, his conscience must have bothered him about the way he'd treated me, because he started trying to find my children. He might have wanted to make amends to them. He found Lily, down-and-out in Southwark, brought her here, and did his best for her, little thinking I'd try to find them both if I ever came home. Or, maybe, he thought I was dead. I don't know. I went to Gravesend when I got to this country, and the few people I knew left in Tenterden Street thought they'd seen a ghost when I appeared on the scene. They said somebody had been there inquiring about my family. I guessed it was Grebe. There was an old girl whom Lily visited from time to time. She knew Lily's last job was at a cheap little cafe in Southwark. I went straight there, and they told me Lily had packed up and gone to a place called Elmer's Creek, where a man who'd been to see her at the cafe had got her a job. They gave me the address she'd left. I found out that way where Grebe was living."

"You changed your name when you changed your job?"

"Yes. I even bought forged identity papers and master's ticket. I didn't want my family to know if I got into trouble in my risky exploits. You see, Lily thought I was a little tin god. Somehow, I didn't fancy disappointing her."

"Walter Mills?"

"You've worked quickly."

"I've got to work quickly. If I don't solve this case over the weekend, my name will be mud. The local police think I'm making a real bloomer of it."

Leo threw back his head and laughed.

"They want to hang *me*, no doubt."

"I wouldn't put it past them. Well, do we get on with the remainder of your story, or do we wait till the rest of it arrives from Scotland Yard? My colleague's waiting patiently for it over the phone just now. It should be here any minute."

"I might as well tell you first-hand, then. After the first war, I gave up the sea and trained as a Thames pilot. I was there till 1935, when Grebe turned up at my house and put a proposal to me. It was very hush-hush, and nobody was to know. So I told the family I was still piloting on the Thames, when all the time I'd taken on a new job. It was a profitable one, believe me."

Leo lit his dead pipe again and Littlejohn refilled and lit his own.

"Grebe had got the use of a private yacht; a beauty called the *Euryanthe*. He said he'd hired it, but it looks to me now that it belonged to a syndicate. How else did he get the money for the enterprise? We used to cross to the Continent. Germany, and there, at Hamburg, Bremen, and some other small ports on the Baltic, we picked up wealthy Jewish and other political refugees from the Nazis. They were people who couldn't get exit papers and we smuggled them aboard. They paid well. But that was chicken feed. Some of the refugees had been granted exit papers but weren't allowed to bring their money out. A lot of them were wealthy. That's where we came in."

A tap on the cell door and the constable was there.

"The sergeant said to warn you, sir, that the court sits in half an hour and that the Chief Constable and magistrates will be here any time."

"Thanks, constable. We've nearly finished."

"You've got to make it short, Leo."

"Not much more, sir. You never saw such a ship as the *Euryanthe*. Grebe said she'd been used in America for liquor-running under prohibition. Hidey-holes everywhere. In places you'd never think of. The furnishings, doors, everything…they were all thin wood or sheet steel, with cavities. They held a fortune and we put gold in them. Gold in specially cast bars. There was quite a secret trade in them in Germany at the time. Grebe had picked the crew and they were a sound lot. He did the deal and took the money, I presume. I was master, I got my wages, and they were lavish. Later, I found out when it was too late, they made most of the money smuggling dope. The rest was a profitable little side-line which covered the main traffic. I was properly taken in! Served me right! We did half a dozen or more trips before the Germans grew wise to what we were doing."

"What happened?"

"The Jerries must have smelled a rat for quite a long time. We'd turn up in port like a pleasure yacht with 'the owner' on board, who wasn't the owner at all. He was Jack Liddell, and to make matters more real, he'd his wife with him. They were a good-looking pair and looked the part. That was how I first met Esther Liddell, and I don't mind telling you we took a fancy to one another right away. Got up as the owner's missus, she looked swell, I can tell you. And in those days, I reckon I wasn't a bad-looking chap, either. The Russians and Germans between them have spoiled my beauty."

He chuckled as though it were a joke.

"How did you know she kept the *Saracen's Head*? Was it sheer luck you found her?"

"No. During the yachting stunt, I got to know she lived at Pullar's Sands, and was a native of the place. All those years I was a prisoner, I thought a lot of Esther. We'd plenty of time, you see, for brooding, and I swore if ever I got away, I'd find her again. A bit silly, perhaps, but you get that way in concentration camps. I set out to find her as soon as I got home and settled properly. I'd not the foggiest notion when I set out after Lily and Grebe, that Pullar's Sands was the next village. I saw the signpost and you could have knocked me down with a feather. But it was quite understandable. Esther and Jack were locals whom Grebe took on to play the part of owners of the yacht, and with the rake-off they bought the pub. Then Jack got killed and Esther carried on. She'd got browned off and was hitting the bottle good and square when I found her. But we'll soon put that right. When all this is over, I feel like settling down in a little country pub myself, with the sea right at the front door."

"And Esther minding the house?"

"You've said it. She never forgot me, and I must say, that after the time we had on the *Euryanthe*, I never forgot her or wanted another."

"Finish the tale, Leo. The JPs will be here any minute."

"As I was saying, the Germans began to rumble our game, and one night, the Gestapo stopped me in the street in Hamburg. I was taken to headquarters for questioning. Somebody had blown the gaff on me. I don't know who did it, but I've a good idea. I shall keep my suspicions to myself till I've found out properly and then knock the living daylights out of him. If I tell you, you'll only stop me."

"You'd better, you know. This is murder and we'll deal with it."

Fowler didn't seem to hear but went on with his tale.

"The *Euryanthe* was under way and off at the very time I was being questioned and knocked about. They were mad at missing getting the ship and they took it out of me. They half killed me. I can still show you the marks. The mate took the *Euryanthe* away and left me to stew, and I finished in a concentration camp. Hell on earth till the end of the war. But that wasn't the end for me. I'd got friendly with another prisoner in the camp, and when the Russians invaded Germany and took over, it seems *they* wanted my pal for something, too. They took us both off and I think they must have murdered him; I never saw him again. I was shipped to another camp and I became one of the lost men till a couple of months ago, when the Russians suddenly started to be nice to me. I wondered what they were after. It seems they were trying to be friendly with England again. I didn't do as badly as some prisoners in Russia. I was in a logging camp. It was hard, but we got our food and a proper bed, even if it *was* bug-ridden. I managed to keep healthy and that pleased me, because I was keen to get back one day and sort out things, especially who'd betrayed me. I started off by inquiring about the *Euryanthe*. She'd gone down at Dunkirk with her owner aboard. So that was a dead end."

"Her owner lived here... In Peshall."

"So, it *was* a syndicate then?"

"Probably."

"To cut a long story short, I came after Lily, but I wrote to her first from London. She wrote back and, as innocent as the day, told me all about Grebe. So I set off north in slow stages and sent Grebe postcards on the way. I didn't want to kill him. That seemed just silly, after I'd just got free from a hell on earth. I wanted to pester him and make his life a misery, to haunt him and upset him, till in sheer desperation, he'd chuck himself in the river to end it. Somebody stepped in and did it for me."

"Who *did* betray you, Leo?"

"The mate who took the *Euryanthe* away under my very nose, died in the war when his ship was torpedoed. But there were others. Esther said she and her husband were dead against leaving me in the lurch, but some of the crew were eager to get off, and they locked the pair of them in their cabin till the ship was well out at sea. I believe her. If I didn't, I'd just as soon throw myself in the river and end up like Grebe."

The bobby was back.

"May I interrupt again, sir? Court's sitting."

Leo looked questioningly at Littlejohn.

"Where do we go from here, sir?"

"I'll insist on a remand in custody, and you won't say a word. You'll probably come up again on Monday, and I hope for your sake and mine, we're in the clear then."

"Okay. And thanks for everything. By the way, look after Esther till I'm in circulation again, will you? If someone's so keen on curtains for me, they might, knowing I fetched up at her place, think she's better out of the way, as well."

"I'd thought of that one, too. I'll see to it."

And they both followed the constable into the courthouse.

13

CHICKABIDDY

W e shall hold you responsible."
Littlejohn was sick of hearing it. The Elmer's
Creek magistrates didn't turn up on the bench after all, and Sir
Luke Messiah and a lady JP in tweeds, with a face like a horse,
dealt with Leo Fowler. Littlejohn insisted on holding Leo on
suspicion without bail. The Chief Constable was bound to
support him, so Leo went back to his cell, where he immediately
called for his lunch. Roast beef, carrots, and fried potatoes, with
Yorkshire pudding and horseradish sauce! And apple fritters to
follow. He insisted on the fritters.

After lunch, Littlejohn left for *Solitude*.

The water was choppy in the river and waves were lapping
round the stone head of the jetty. Some sailing boats were
tacking their way out into the Farne Deep. From the village he
could see breakers beating the lighthouse and covering it
halfway up with spray.

It was Saturday half-holiday, and the ferries were full of trippers from Falbright. Young men and girls taking an afternoon
out and men who owned little boats coming over to fish.

The road through Peshall was busy. Motorists were enjoying

the bright afternoon and cyclists were abroad. A stack of bicycles in front of the two cafes in the village and, inside, barelegged men and girls were drinking soft drinks and buying ice cream. Fothergill waved to Littlejohn from the door of the post office where he was handing over the noon collections.

Between the village and *Solitude*, Littlejohn noticed a board, "Houses for Sale", and another, "Desirable Building Plots", with the name of an estate agent in Falbright. Roads and drains had apparently been laid out and then the venture had fallen flat. Heaps of old sand and concrete and a rusty mortar-mixer stood beside a shanty with a window broken. This must be the building estate started by Grebe and his friends and then they'd either struck a snag or buyers had fallen off.

A man leaning over the gate watched Littlejohn as he examined the place from the road.

"It's the water stopped them," he said, anxious to find somebody to talk to. "Quicksand and water under that land. When they dug the drains, the pipes sunk in the sand."

So the scheme was a flop and the little gang lost money. The Chief Inspector wondered whose idea it was and how the rest had reacted when it failed.

The gates were shut at *Solitude*, but Littlejohn edged one of them open and closing it after him, made for the big house along the neat gravel drive. There was nobody about in the grounds; all the staff were on half-holiday. A thick hedge of tortured bushes on the sea side sheltered the garden which sprouted palms, eucalyptus and bamboos. Behind the house stood greenhouses in good condition and a summer house made of logs.

The place was completely isolated and built on the model of a small French chateau, even to the flight of steps leading to the broad front door. Littlejohn tugged the chain and could hear a bell ring indoors.

An elderly maid took his hat and vanished to announce him.

Then she returned and led him into the library. A beautifully panelled room with oak beams in the ceiling and hundreds of uniformly bound books on the shelves. The kind you buy wholesale from a bookseller and never open again. The rest of the house was silent.

There was a log fire in the hearth and Mrs Iremonger was sitting in front of it, taking tea from a small table. A silver service and fine china. She rose to meet Littlejohn.

Although Chickabiddy's life had hitherto been gay and fast, she still looked well-preserved and handsome. She was wearing a light-grey tweed costume with a white nylon blouse fastened at the neck by the same single stone diamond brooch Littlejohn had seen before. As she walked towards him, Littlejohn could see she'd been drinking something stronger than tea before the cups arrived. There was a decanter and glasses on the sideboard and one of the glasses was half full of what looked like whisky.

"You called then, Inspector. I thought you'd forgotten."

A pleasant, husky voice, too, and a rather coy smile. She shook hands with a firm grip.

"Is this a social call, or professional?"

"Mainly professional, madam."

"Tea? Or would you prefer…?"

"Tea, if you please."

She poured a cup, handed it to him, and offered him an armchair near her own. *Petit fours?* Or perhaps a cigar? There seemed to be nothing lacking. Over the fireplace, a very fine oil painting of a yacht, the *Euryanthe*. And on the opposite wall, a large oil portrait of a man who must have been Iremonger himself. A smallish, portly man in a reefer jacket and yachting cap, with a sea-blue background. A face of character, full, pink, with a little sharp nose and very blue eyes. There was something about the picture which surprised Littlejohn. The artist had skilfully captured a look of despair in the smile and general attitude. The look of a man who smiles when he's lost faith and hope.

"That was my late husband, Inspector. A very fine man."

Littlejohn remembered how Iremonger and Chickabiddy had got so drunk in the yacht, that they'd left their guests and walked over the side and into the river.

"I heard so, madam. He was lost with his yacht at Dunkirk, I believe."

"So you've heard that. Yes. That's the yacht, the dear *Euryanthe*."

She was playing at drinking tea. Obviously she'd take to the whisky if Littlejohn would join her, but he stuck to his cup. In fact, he said he'd have another when she asked him. He took a cigar, too, which Chickabiddy produced from a cabinet, and lit it from the lighter she handed him.

"And now... You said this was a professional call."

She sat down and played with the two rings on her wedding finger. A plain one in platinum and another with five large diamonds together worth a fortune. Strong, square hands and steady, apart from the nervous movements of the fingers.

"I called to ask about the *Euryanthe* really. Before the war, did you hire her to anyone?"

She gave him a searching, suspicious look, trying to fathom what he was getting at. Somewhere in the house behind, a large dog began to bay. Littlejohn wondered what Mrs Iremonger did with herself after dark when the outdoor staff had gone and the servants had retired. A large silent house, surrounded by the marshes and the sea, with one solitary woman alone living with pictures of a man and a yacht.

"Hire her? No. She was too precious to us. Perfect in every way."

"And yet, in the late thirties, I believe she appeared many times in German ports without her owners. Did you lend her, then?"

She tried to look relieved, but it was a poor effort.

"Oh, that. We lent her to John Grebe. He was a master mariner, cooped up here for a quiet life, yet interested in ships. In fact, my husband offered to make him master of the *Euryanthe*, but he refused. We lent her to him, however, several times. Better that than putting her up in the river when we didn't want her."

"That must have been on many occasions according to my information."

She shrugged her shoulders as though it was too long ago to remember.

"She came from America originally, I hear."

"Yes. A friend of my husband had her built. Then he fell ill, too ill to sail her, so he sold her to us."

"She'd been engaged in the liquor traffic?"

"Who told you that?"

Littlejohn didn't reply. He was busy knocking the ash from his cigar into a silver bowl which reminded him of a surgical dish.

"The friend who built her was the sort who wouldn't tolerate curtailment of his liberties. What right had they to inflict prohibition? He made his yacht with a view to..."

"Smuggling liquor? And other things? Did you know Grebe used her for sneaking valuables out of Germany for wealthy exiles?"

He said nothing about the dope. He was feeling his way.

"He told me something of the kind. My husband and I didn't object. She was being used in a good cause."

"Did you and your husband finance any of those ventures? They certainly needed money to run the ship and man it, and Grebe presumably wasn't rich."

She couldn't wait any longer but made for the decanter eagerly and poured herself a stiff whisky and filled it up with soda. Then she repeated the process and handed Littlejohn the glass.

"I'm sure you'd like a drink, Inspector. Good health."

"Good health, madam."

He sipped his drink and she drank hers almost in a single gulp, like a man who finds water after a thirsty agony of waiting.

"Where is all this leading? John Grebe is dead, murdered. Is this helping to find who killed him?"

"I hope so. We've arrested Leo Fowler, the man who was captain of the *Euryanthe* when she was running treasure from Germany. He had a grievance against Grebe and traced him here to get even with him. I don't think he intended to kill Grebe; perhaps just to blackmail him. This captain was betrayed into the hands of the Gestapo and ended up in a concentration camp and then in a Russian prison camp. He's very sore about it, naturally, and he's now anxious to know who informed against him. It must have been somebody who either bore him a grudge or thought he knew more than was good for him."

"Very interesting. So he killed Grebe, after all, and now he has to pay the price."

She set down her empty glass and then picked it up nervously and held it between the palms of her hands as though trying to warm it.

Littlejohn was watching her face. Her eyes were wide, and he could see a little flame of fear lighting them. She couldn't restrain herself and rose to help herself to more whisky.

"You're not drinking, Inspector."

"I'm all right, thank you, madam."

"Why tell *me* all about this captain and his smuggling? Why bring me into it at all? It makes a good story, but what has it to do with me?"

"I had an idea that you and your husband were financially interested in those trips. After all, it was your yacht."

A silence. Littlejohn expected to be shown the door. But Chickabiddy was of different mettle. She wanted to know just how much Littlejohn knew.

"If you've got the man who killed John Grebe, you've surely finished the case. This would be very nice as a social call, Inspector, but it obviously isn't. You're here trying to find out something from me. Just as though you weren't satisfied at having a man in prison but wanted somebody else. As though the case wasn't solved, after all."

"I'm seeking further information because the *Euryanthe* belonged to you, as I've said before."

"Well, I can't help you. That was all in the past. This murder is in the present. I don't see the connection."

"Don't you? Where were you on the night Grebe died, Mrs Iremonger?"

She laughed harshly. The whisky was taking effect and she was losing control.

"Whatever for? I didn't kill Grebe. He was a friend of mine, and of my husband when he was alive. I'd no reason..."

"All the same, will you tell me, please?"

"I was here, as I usually am after dark. I've few friends to visit and sometimes I read and sometimes I play cards with my French maid, Henriette. She will tell you I haven't been abroad after dark for more than a fortnight. She's out at present, but you can call to see her any time."

"You are friendly with Dr Horrocks and Captain Bacon?"

"Yes. They're neighbours and they frequently call here. But rarely after dark, if that's what you're getting at. I think they foregather every night at the *Barlow Arms*."

"They used to call together, with Grebe, I believe. You were a syndicate running the building estate down the road."

"How clever you are, Inspector! Yes, and you've found it out. Simply...just like that."

She snapped her fingers in his face.

GEORGE BELLAIRS

"I wish you were in the local force. We could be good friends. You must have lived a very interesting life and could tell many stories of crime and horror. I like stories of crime and horror. What about John Grebe? Give me some details."

She helped herself to another drink and frowned at Little-john's half-filled glass.

"You're a poor drinker, Inspector."

"I'm on duty, madam."

"Don't keep calling me *madam*. To my friends I'm known as Chickabiddy. A name my husband invented and everybody in our set calls me that. I insist... You may call me Chickabiddy. We're friends, aren't we?"

They said Iremonger had picked her out of the gutter and given her a veneer of manners and culture. Now, she was shedding the case-hardening as the whisky did its work.

"Details of John Grebe... Details... Details..."

"He was murdered by mistake."

Her eyes opened wide.

"Who told you that? Who told you? Didn't you just say Leo Fowler did it?"

"No. Someone out to kill Fowler mistook Grebe for him in the dark and knifed the wrong man. They both dressed alike, in uniform, and they were both the same build."

"But Grebe died on the ferry. I tell you, he died on the ferry."

"No, he didn't. He died long before the ferry left Elmer's Creek. He died and was thrown in the river and the murderer took the *Falbright Jenny* halfway over the river himself and then grounded her and ran ashore across the sandbank."

She was on her feet, rocking from side to side.

"This is incre'ble. You must be a magic'n."

"You mean, you know what happened? How did you know?"

Suddenly she pulled herself together, sat down, and passed her hand across her forehead in a tired gesture.

"I didn't say I knew. I don't know a thing about it. All I said

170

was, you were wonderful to think out such an idea. Why have you arrest'd the other man then...the old captain of the *Euryanthe*? What's his name...Leo Mills...Leo...? Walter Mills, that's it. You got it all wrong, Inspector."

"Walter Mills. You're right, Mrs Iremonger. But how did you know his name? I told you Leo Fowler."

"You're trying to trap me. *You* said Walter Mills. That's how I got the name. I don't know any Walter Millses. It was you who said Mills. And stop calling me Mrs Iremonger. *Call me Chickabiddy.* We're friends, aren't we?"

She was drunk now, utterly drunk. The sort of thing that probably went on night after night as she sat in her lonely house, bored to death, missing the man who'd given it all to her, probably in a moment of drunken folly. And then he'd lost faith and hope and gone and got himself killed in a last heroic sacrifice at Dunkirk and gone down with his beloved *Euryanthe*.

"Did your husband know about the money you made on the *Euryanthe*?"

"No! He thought it was charity. That Grebe was rescuing them out of pity. We never told him."

"Who's *we*?"

"I don' know what you're talking about."

She curled up in her chair and fell asleep. Short of shaking her violently and then trying again, there was nothing more to be done.

Footsteps outside, the front door opened and closed, and then a dark, slightly built woman entered the library. She was dressed in a smart black costume and a little hat to match. She looked at Littlejohn standing rather stupidly beside the sleeping form of Chickabiddy, and then at her mistress, curled up in the chair.

"*Comment?*"

The French maid, Henriette!

"I called on your mistress and in the middle of our conversation, she just curled up and fell asleep. Will you please look after her?"

"Look after her?"

The French girl seemed tickled about it. She gave a tinkling, ironical laugh, seized Mrs Iremonger by the shoulders and, with amazing strength for one so small and slim, jerked her from the chair. Mrs Iremonger tottered and half opened her eyes.

"Your guest is going, madame. You must say goodbye."

As Chickabiddy showed an inclination to return to the chair, the maid shook her roughly again.

"Say goodbye, I tell you, say goodbye."

"Goo'bye. Call again. Call me Chickabiddy."

She sank back in the chair and was fast asleep in a moment. The maid shrugged her shoulders, showed Littlejohn to the door, and gave him his hat.

"Is she often like that?"

"No, sir. She doesn't get drunk until later as a rule. And then not too often. It is when she gets lonely and afraid of people, or memories, or this house. Did you frighten her? It is unusual for her."

"Perhaps I did. However, she'll sleep it off, won't she?"

It was growing dark outside. On the road, men passed with fishing rods and fish on strings. Cyclists were hurrying home, their lamps lit. Windows lighted here and there across the marsh. A cat crept along the road and its eyes glowed like little lamps in the beams of a passing car. The Farne Light was throwing its fingers across the open country and out to sea.

Cromwell was waiting for him at the *Barlow Arms*. It was a relief to see his rugged friendly face.

"I arranged about Mrs Liddell. I called and told her I'd fixed it for the police to send a man to keep an eye on the place and give her protection. It's one of the Falbright men, a new chap from the county force who isn't well known. They've got him up as a cyclist and he's pedalled to the *Saracen's Head* and he'll stay there for a few days."

"Good. What did Mrs Liddell say to it all?"

"Not a thing. A funny woman. She'd been drinking a bit. She listened to what I had to say about Leo wanting somebody to protect her while he was away. She took it without moving a muscle. The detective we sent seems a bit baffled and scared about her, but he'll do his job. He's a decent sort."

"Thanks, old man. Let's get something to eat, now. And I hope it's something good."

Lucy was waiting for them in the dining room and she even gave Littlejohn a smile.

14

A HAIRCUT AND A SHAVE

B efore he left Falbright police station after the appearance
of Leo Fowler in the magistrates' court, Littlejohn told the
Chief Constable and Superintendent Lecky a story which at
first left them incredulous. Then, after the Chief Inspector had
detailed the steps by which he'd deduced it, they expressed
approval and went so far as to apologise half-heartedly for their
rather cavalier treatment of him in the case of Leo Fowler.

John Grebe hadn't taken the *Falbright Jenny* into the river and
beached her on the night he died! Someone who looked like him
had done it, whilst Grebe's body was floating about in the water
behind the *Barlow Arms.*

The identity of the unknown pilot, the murderer, now
assumed top-rank importance and the whole of the police
machine in Falbright was geared up and put in motion to obtain
more information. Joe Webb, the stoker, and everyone known
to have crossed to Elmer's Creek on Grebe's last trip or
returned to Falbright with the murderous pilot, was questioned.
The Women's Guild and the Methodist parson were very closely
grilled. O Beulah Land! Whenever the Rev John Thomas

174

Jingling, BA, heard or saw those lovely hymnal verses afterwards, he felt slightly sick.

Not a thing came to light from all the constabulary work, which started as Littlejohn made his way to see Chickabiddy at *Solitude* and continued long after.

Whilst he was away, Littlejohn left Cromwell to his own devices. They had worked together for so long and understood each other so well, that short of definite orders and a fixed object in view, the Chief Inspector always gave his colleague a free hand. He knew full well this meant that Cromwell would return with a considerable contribution to the case.

Left alone at the *Barlow Arms*, Cromwell ran his long fingers through the thinning hair at the crown of his head and the shaggy fringe which was beginning to hang over his collar at the back and nodded.

"Is there a barber on this side of the river, Lucy?"

"Yes, sir, in a manner of speaking."

And she gave him all the information she could about it.

Cromwell firmly settled his bowler on his head, lit his pipe, which was a replica of Littlejohn's, and sailed out, smiling to himself. He was almost in Peshall village when he met Fothergill, unhurriedly and uninterruptedly making his way down the road. The postman was on the afternoon delivery. He always walked steadily to the *Barlow Arms*, his bag full and arousing the curiosity of those he passed on the way, but he never started to distribute its contents until he had turned about at the *Arms*. This was his first port of call and there he took a drink to speed him on his labours.

As a rule, Fothergill, the responsibility of Her Majesty's mails heavy upon him, never halted until he reached the starting post. He already knew the contents of every article in his bag. Post-cards he read shamelessly; circulars and routine bills, he passed on with contempt; regular letters he weighed carefully in his hand as he sorted them and, like a psychometric practitioner, imagined, with a fair amount of accuracy, what they contained. The new, interesting, or intriguing ones he read over in the post office lavatory, for he always took a cup of tea before starting on his rounds and it was a shame to waste the steam from the kettle.

On this occasion, Fothergill honoured Cromwell by halting and bidding him good afternoon. Since the game of darts in which Cromwell had licked him, Fothergill had developed a morbid interest in the sergeant. He was like a dog, sizing up and sniffing round a rival who had caught him unawares and beaten him. Fothergill was preparing for round number two, by which he hoped to restore his lost prestige.

"Good afternoon, Mr Cromwell. A bit blustery."

"Good afternoon, Mr Fothergill. Feeling better?"

"Yes. More meself again. It was that pork upset me. And did I give Porter, the butcher, the rounds of the kitching about it! I told 'im he was lucky I didn't take 'im to court and sue him for damages. He gave me two pounds of sausages as a peace offerin'."

Fothergill had a dishevelled look. He was never elegant at the best of times, with his overgrowth of eyebrows and his heavy moustache, but the last delivery always saw him at his worst. He washed himself once a day after breakfast and slowly deteriorated as the sweat of toil and the dust of his rounds accumulated. He removed them in the evening with a damp towel before leaving to play darts.

"I've got a letter for you, Mr Cromwell."

Fothergill fished in his bag and handed over an envelope addressed in childish handwriting. Passers-by and those peeping round curtains in nearby cottages felt their blood boil at this deviation from routine, this currying of official favour.

"Looks as if it might be from your best girl."

Cromwell stared right into the cunning eyes regarding him from under their ambush of eyebrows and put the letter in his pocket. It *was* from his best girl; his eldest daughter, aged six, who always kept up a regular and loving correspondence with him when he was away from home. Cromwell looked at Fothergill's dirty tobacco-stained fingers with their cruel nails and felt like socking the postman on the jaw for daring to handle the precious letter at all.

"Any news?"

"About the murder, you mean?"

"Of course."

"You'll have heard about Fowler, the man we took across to Falbright gaol?"

"Yes. 'As he confessed?"

"No. They never do. The magistrates remanded him in custody till Monday. They'll have to decide then whether or not to commit him for trial, I suppose."

Fothergill leered.

"That will, o' course, depend on what you and your boss find out in the meantime, eh?"

He took the remnants of a fag from between his cap and his ear, lit it, and puffed the smoke through his moustache which made it look like a miniature moorland fire.

"Yes, I suppose so."

Fothergill gave Cromwell another crafty look. This was developing into a battle of wits. One trying to find out something new and perhaps confidential, the other wondering how much his antagonist really knew.

"You're a native of these parts, Mr Fothergill?"

"Yes. Born in Peshall, on the Moss. My family's one of the oldest hereabouts, if not *the* oldest."

"You must know a lot about what goes on in the locality. Do you know Mrs Liddell at the *Saracen's Head*?"

Fothergill's grin was almost malevolent. Cromwell could have sworn that the very name he'd just uttered was like a breath on the grey embers of a fire. A flame of either hatred or desire was kindled in the eyes intently regarding him from under the heavy unkempt brows.

"Huh... Yes, I know her. You arrested Fowler there, I hear."

"Yes."

"In her bedroom."

"Yes."

Cromwell felt like someone blowing on the ashes from which sparks would soon appear.

"She's a bad lot. A bad lot. I could tell you a thing or two about Esther Liddell."

"Could you now, Mr Fothergill. What is it?"

"Not just about the *Saracen's* being a disorderly house... You and your boss aren't interested in such things. Wot you might call chicken feed for big chaps from Scotland Yard like you two. But more serious things... Yes. It's all dead and done with now, I suppose. But when her husband was alive, I did hear they was mixed up in smugglin'."

Fothergill closed one eye and nodded.

"I was told that in confidence, but as there's murder about now, I wouldn't be doin' my duty as a public servant if I didn't inform you, Mr Cromwell."

Cromwell didn't press for the source of Fothergill's information. Already, in his pocket, his fingers, lovingly caressing the letter from his daughter, had found the answer. The flap of the envelope was almost loose. His little girl always relished sticking down the flap, licking the gum, rubbing it in, putting all her weight on it to keep the messages she sent secret. And now, the letter had obviously been steamed. Cromwell could hardly keep his fist from Fothergill's stubbly chin. The postman had apparently not thought a thorough resealing of such childish messages important. But he oughtn't to have fancied he could deceive Cromwell.

Fothergill's little eyes were fixed on Cromwell's face as he tried to find out the impression he was making. "It's so long since. Before the last war, in fact. You couldn't pin it on 'em now, if you tried, Mr Cromwell. But I tell you just to show you the type of woman she is. All that lazy, couldn't-care-less attitude of hers. It's all put on. Still waters run deep, Mr Cromwell."

"This is serious, Mr Fothergill. We'd better have another talk, in private."

"Yes. I've me deliveries to make. You'll be at the *Arms* tonight, won't you? We'll have a drink together, shall we?"

"Right."

"So long, then, Mr Cromwell."

Fothergill wiped the back of his neck by passing his grubby hand to and fro across it and then he raised his peaked cap and mopped his brow.

"Hot, isn't it?"

Cromwell didn't find it so, but then, Fothergill had obviously been labouring under some emotion. Cromwell noticed that. And it must have been deep emotion, too, for the marshland folk, as far as Cromwell could see, weren't the kind who wore their feelings on their sleeves. It needed a lot to make them show them.

"Good afternoon, Mr Fothergill. I'll be seeing you."

The postman pulled himself together and resumed his jaunty, self-opinionated strutting to the point where he began to deliver his letters. He turned round once to see what Cromwell was doing and they waved to one another.

Frank Trott ran the newsagent's shop in Peshall, and his premises also housed the post office, where a paid girl clerk did the official work. Trott did a good business with his papers, journals, stationery, lending library, and tobacco licence. But that wasn't enough. Frank was a marshlander, too, and thrifty at that. So he added to his other duties the one of village barber. Two nights a week and Saturday afternoons until six was long enough in which to serve the farmers and fishermen who couldn't come in the day, and Frank made two or three extra pounds a week thereby. His little saloon was at the back of the newspaper shop and when it was not in use professionally, he and his wife made it into a small dining room.

Cromwell turned in there. Two yokels and a man who looked like a sailor of some kind were sitting in the shop itself waiting their turns, and in the little room behind, Mr Trott was just wiping off a farmer he'd been shaving.

"Come in, Mr Cromwell."

Everybody in the village knew Cromwell as the man who'd beaten Fothergill at darts. He was almost a freeman of Adder's Moss.

Mr Trott came into the shop to greet his distinguished new client. He was a little, bald, lightly built man, with a smooth clean shaven face and very white, small hands. His pale blue eyes missed nothing. He was in his shirt sleeves and he wore a large white apron.

The barber turned to the waiting clients and addressed them. "I'll take this gentleman next, if you don't mind. You've plenty of time, it being your afternoon off."

The customers looked daggers but didn't say anything. They just sat and listened.

"Mr Cromwell is of the London police and his time is, in consequence, very valuable. You see that don't you?"

The customers nodded or grunted a reluctant assent. But they had to agree. Otherwise, it meant the return fare across the ferry added to their bills and the fag of finding a barber in Falbright.

"So come right in, Mr Cromwell."

Reluctantly, for he liked fair play, Cromwell allowed himself to be led to the inner room, like a patient entering for a major operation. Mr Trott respectfully pressed him into a chair.

"Haircut and shave, please."

Mr Trott eased the chair into a semi-reclining posture, covered Cromwell with a cloth, and started to strop a razor with deft strokes.

"I hear you beat Mr Fothergill at darts the other night, sir."

There was triumph in the barber's voice.

"Yes. I think I caught him on one foot, though. He wasn't very well at the time."

"Rubbish, if I might say so, sir. He's a bad loser. A lot of us are very gratified at the beating you gave 'im. He wants taking down a peg. He's far too uppish."

Mr Trott tested the razor, took up a brush, poured powder on it, passed his fingers over Cromwell's cheeks, and began to lather them.

Cromwell shuddered. The barber's fingers were like those of a corpse. Cold, soft, clinging. They had a pneumatic feel about them.

"You a native of these parts?" said Cromwell from the side of his mouth, for Mr Trott had just laid the other side free from lather in a long surgical sweep.

"Yes. Born here. Fothergill, you know, has a natural dislike for all newcomers. He thinks he owns the village, and you ought to ask his permission before you settle."

Another sweep and the other cheek was bare of soap.

"Do *you* know Fowler, the man we arrested?"

"No. But I know the woman who keeps the place where you found him. The *Saracen's Head*. Her husband, Liddell, was a regular customer of mine before he died."

A pause, for Mr Trott with a series of short, chopping shots, was now on Cromwell's long upper lip.

"Yes. I knew Liddell. Pity he died so young. His wife's a beauty, although from what I hear, her morals aren't too good.

Between you and me, sir, Fothergill's always been a bit sweet on her. He was after her before she married. Not that she'd look at a freak like him. He still hangs around the *Saracen* from time to time. He married a relative older than himself for money; so I guess he still fancies the old love."

Mr Trott wiped Cromwell's face with an old sponge and dried it.

"There! I think that'll suit you, sir. How do you like the 'air?"

"Trim back and sides and not too much off the top."

Mr Trott felt Cromwell's cranium like a phrenologist, stood back a few feet to examine it in perspective, and then started to snip round it.

"Did you ever hear anything about Liddell and his missus being engaged in smuggling?"

"Not exactly, sir. But before the last war, they'd go off for days, sometimes weeks at a time. They didn't keep the pub then; he was a clerk on the railway — a local man. What they did, nobody seemed to know. Did Fothergill tell you that?"

"Confidentially, yes."

Mr Trott eased the clippers round Cromwell's ears and neck.

"Well, Fothergill ought to know. Everybody knows that he reads letters before delivering 'em. He's never been caught, mind you. Too clever for that. But he can't stop talking and showing off and he lets something out of the bag now and then that he couldn't possibly know if he hadn't steamed a letter open and read it."

Cromwell looked anxiously at his reflection and the course of the operation through the mirror before him. Trott seemed to be shearing off a lot of hair!

"I wonder how he got hold of that smuggling tale."

"You can bet, being keen on Mrs Liddell, he'd open all *her* letters."

"Is Pullar's Sands on his round?"

"No. But we get the mail here with ours, sort it, and the

postman from there bikes over for it and delivers it. Fothergill handles it all."

"Are you postmaster here?"

"Sub-postmaster. Been twenty years at it. I've been at it longer than Fothergill. He only took over in 1939. He was at sea before then; a deckhand on a cargo boat. Then he got scared or fed up with the sea when war broke out. If you ask me, he did it to keep out of the war. He said he'd only one lung. Funny, he only found it out when war came."

"So, he was a sailor. That's interesting...very interesting. And do you mean to tell me that he can open letters and you can't catch him at it?"

"He's too cunnin'."

"You're a bit slow, aren't you?"

Mr Trott looked pained and bit his lip as though holding back his tears.

"We aren't all detectives, Mr Cromwell."

"And his mention of the Liddells' smuggling might be another of Fothergill's indiscretions, the ones you mentioned he commits for swank?"

"Yes. Anythin' on the 'air, sir?"

"There's enough on it as it is, I think."

Cromwell's hair was put in ship-shape with the greasy communal hairbrush before he could prevent it. He put on his hat, which fell over his ears, and he had to pack it with bus tickets to make it fit. Outside, he met Fothergill just back from his rounds.

"Been havin' an 'aircut, sir?"

"Yes."

"Not much of a barber and too much of a gasbag, is Trott. All the same, he's the on'y one, so beggars can't be choosers."

Mr Fothergill leaned against the pillar box in front of the post office, took another fag from between his ear and his cap, and lit it.

"How did you know about the Liddells' trafficking in drugs, if I might ask, Mr Fothergill?"

Fothergill took out his cigarette and regarded the lighted end for a second. Then he raised his cunning eyes.

"I tramp this village more than anybody else. More than Dixon...more than anybody. And I hear a bit 'ere and a bit there in the course of my rounds. Putting two and two together, I offen get a full tale. Let's just walk down the road a bit. I'm off juty now and I see Trott keep lookin' through the window at us."

They set off slowly strolling in the direction of *Solitude*.

"'Ow is the case going, if I might be so bold, Mr Cromwell?"

"Not at all. We're still quite in the dark."

"I'm sorry, Mr Cromwell. I'd like to 'elp if I can."

Fothergill wore a bothered look as though his own reputation were somehow at stake.

"Isn't the man Fowler you've laid hands on, the guilty party, then?"

"It doesn't seem so. The Chief Inspector doesn't think he's our man."

Mr Fothergill paused in his walk and faced Cromwell.

"Why? I don't know much about these things, but I'd say Mister Leo Fowler was as likely a culprit as most. And for why? 'E sent those postcards threatenin' the life of Captain Grebe, didn't 'e? And 'e was hidin' out at the *Saracen* out of the way of you fellows, wasn't 'e?"

"Yes. That's true. But what motive could he have?"

"Lucy, the girl at the *Arms*. Grebe took 'er away from London, and Leo Fowler was 'er stepfather. She's told me so this very day. Fowler came 'ere to settle accounts with Grebe about 'er. Take my word. There's more there than meets the eye."

"But how did Grebe, after being stabbed, take the ferry halfway over?"

"He didn't. Fowler did that after he'd killed Grebe and shoved him in the water from behind the *Arms*. Then he took the ferry half over, ditched her, jumped off because the bank was near, and beat it over the sands to Pullar's Sands where you picked him up, hiding at the *Saracen*, where he'd slept with the landlady meanwhile."

"How do you know all that?"

Fothergill tapped his forehead.

"Thought it out. No other way. Grebe was dead. 'Ow could 'e ferry the boat over? And another thing... What about Jumpin' Joe? Tell me that."

"What about him?"

"Right from the time Grebe was killed, Joe had money and to spare. He was drunk all the time. And talkin' about seein' ghosts. Why did he do that?"

"You tell me."

"He saw somebody 'e thought was Grebe walkin' across the marsh and after, when he 'eard Grebe was dead all the time, 'e thought 'e'd seen a ghost. But somebody who didn't want Joe to talk kept him drunk by givin' him cash for booze, till they realised they couldn't keep Joe drunk forever. Then they killed 'im before 'e sobered up and put two and two together and guessed who it was an' started talkin' sense round the village. Joe knew too much. That's why he died. Poor Joe..."

"And you think it was Leo he saw going to the *Saracen* after he'd killed Grebe and escaped from the ferry after beaching her?"

"Exactly. And you try any other theory and you won't find it better than mine."

"It sounds to hold water."

"Of course, it does. Don't let that chap Fowler fox you. He's a cunnin' chap, is Fowler. Don't let 'im get away with it. Well, our ways part 'ere, Mr Cromwell. That's my place."

Fothergill pointed across the fields to the right, where stood a large, whitewashed cottage in a garden, surrounded by fields.

185

"It used to be a farm, but we let off the fields. See you tonight at the *Arms*, I 'ope. S'long."

Cromwell bade him goodbye and slowly made his way back to Elmer's Creek. He was lost in thought and his pipe was cold. He was at the door of the *Barlow Arms* before he came to himself and looked surprised to find himself there.

15

EARLY IN THE MORNING

There was a sharp knock on the bedroom door.

"Seven o'clock, sir."

"Right, thanks."

The mattress creaked as Littlejohn pulled himself into a sitting posture in the bed. Next door, he could hear Lucy getting Cromwell up as well.

The night before, they'd asked Lucy to call them at seven and she'd seemed a bit surprised. It was Sunday morning and most folk stayed a bit longer in bed.

"Are you both going to early communion?"

As he shaved, Littlejohn could hear the bell clanging in the church at Peshall for early service and it was punctuated by the rhythmic bumps of Cromwell doing his morning exercises in the next room.

The day was clear and chilly and from where he stood the Chief Inspector could see the estuary, with the tide ebbing and leaving the sandbanks jutting into the river like great brown whales. At that early hour, the weekend sailors were already taking out their yachts for the day. The stiff breeze filled their sails as they tacked to and fro between the banks of the river. In the creek behind the *Barlow Arms* the receding tide was leaving a mass of mud, dotted with tin cans, barrel hoops, broken crockery and rubber tyres. All the rubbish from the hotel seemed to find its way there and was renewed as quickly as the tide rotted, rusted, ground it up, and washed it away.

A few women on the road which led to the church and two men in jerseys making their way to the waterfront to fish.

Cromwell joined Littlejohn in the dining room. He was carrying his tin of Strengtho and handed it to Lucy. He religiously drank a brew of it first thing every morning. Lucy took it dutifully and shortly returned with a beaker of it looking like thick brown soup. Cromwell drank it with relish as Littlejohn finished his porridge and then they went on to the ham and eggs.

The room still smelled of stale cigar smoke from the night before. Horrocks, Bacon and Brett had then been there as usual. The atmosphere had been a bit strained and after dinner, Littlejohn and Cromwell had joined the locals in the bar, where Cromwell had again beaten Fothergill at darts. This time before a larger audience, for the place was crowded on Saturday night. Fothergill, a poor loser, had again made excuses. He'd pleaded he'd drunk too much and made himself unsteady before the contest.

Now they were making an early trip to Pullar's Sands. The Chief Inspector was anxious to talk to Esther Liddell again. She knew a lot more than he'd thought.

Cromwell put on his cap. Since his haircut his bowler had bothered him, and he'd had difficulty keeping it on in the wind. They followed the road to the signpost and then took the path along the shore. Half the blinds of the village were drawn and as they passed the police station, they saw Dixon carrying coal from the woodshed. From the chimney ascended the smoke of a wood fire waiting to be built up. Indoors, the children were being washed and made ready for Sunday School. They were in their Sunday clothes and were subdued and afraid to play in them. Dixon was so busy that he didn't see Littlejohn and Cromwell.

Smoking their pipes, the two Scotland Yard men walked along the tideline. There must have been a storm or a wreck somewhere, for the beach was strewn with rusty cans full of pineapple chunks and peaches and old sodden sugar bags. Two men were busy rooting among the rubbish, piling up driftwood and examining the other flotsam and jetsam of the night tide.

The sky was clear, and they could see the whole length of Balbeck Bay with the hills beyond. The cattle from the fields on the landward side had been taken in for milking. Smoke was rising from the farmhouses — low buildings squatting in the flat fields — and the mass of chickens in the runs of the poultry farms rushed here and there like white clouds in the distance.

The water at Pullar's Sands was low enough to allow the pair of them to walk over the stream across the large stepping stones. The *Saracen's Head* was quiet and ready for the day's rush of trippers. Smoke rising from the chimney here as well and, as the detectives landed on the bank before the door, Esther Liddell appeared with a broom brushing out the dust, matches and fag ends of the previous night. She wore riding breeches and a knitted yellow jumper and, as usual, had little else on beneath it. This time, she nodded and gave the new arrivals a ghost of a smile.

The detective from the county force was dressed as a cyclist in khaki shorts and shirt and was sitting on a box on the bank just above the inn, fishing in the river. Two little trout on the grass beside him. He looked proud of them. He tried to be discreet and, whilst showing no familiarity, merely said good morning and, when he deemed himself safe from prying eyes, he winked at Cromwell.

Littlejohn and Cromwell entered the inn. It was out of hours for beer, so Littlejohn asked Mrs Liddell for some coffee.

"It's a bit chilly and coffee will warm us up."

She acknowledged the order with a nod and another faint smile and retired to the kitchen. They could hear her putting pans on the stove and then grinding coffee at a little mill. The appetising aroma of the drink itself soon came drifting through the doorway.

There was nobody else about. The clock somewhere in the back room chimed a quarter past nine.

Finally, Esther Liddell entered with coffee. This time she seemed to have kept away from the brandy bottle. She was quite sober but, as usual, languid, moving about with a silent grace, like a cat.

"Join us, Mrs Liddell?"

She didn't answer but returned to the kitchen and emerged with three large blue cups and saucers, filled the cups, placed them on a table near the door, and then went away again for a plate of lumps of shortbread. She sat down with the two men.

"I've got to talk to you, Mrs Liddell, and you've got to talk to me. It's important…vital for Leo Fowler."

She raised her eyebrows and looked Littlejohn full in the face. For her age she was a very handsome woman, and Littlejohn could understand Fowler wishing to settle down as landlord of the *Saracen's Head* after all his wanderings and troubles. A nice easy life and a good looking, sensible woman to look after him. He'd be good for her, and she'd be good for him.

"I can't see what good I can be to Leo Fowler. He was only lodging here for two or three days."

And that was the answer to Littlejohn's imaginings!

"And yet, he slept in your bed and was entirely at home."

Littlejohn had to say it, shocking though it must have sounded, judging from Cromwell's surprised expression. This was the first real coherent thing Esther Liddell had yet said to him, and here she was trying to wash her hands of the whole affair.

"I've had a long talk with Leo, and I know quite a lot about the days when you and your late husband were the so-called owners of the *Euryanthe*. Now, let's settle down and talk sensibly."

She sipped the hot coffee, her eyes fixed on Littlejohn's face. He wondered if the faint smile was a challenge, or impudence, or perhaps just a hint that she was friendly.

She behaved with the same indifference as when he was there before. For the most part, when you look or speak to anyone, a kind of rapport is established for better or worse. You like or dislike them; wish to remain with them or get quickly away. But with Esther Liddell, Littlejohn felt no reaction at all. It was just a blank! She spoke and responded with no apparent emotion. Fear, interest, like, or dislike were not there. Littlejohn felt *not there*, as well, as far as Esther Liddell was concerned. And such a state could only, as a rule, arise from idiocy or mental trouble, alcohol, drugs, or some paralysing emotion which wiped out all other feelings.

It wasn't mania. That was obvious. The woman was as sane as Littlejohn or Cromwell. And she was as sober as a judge. She bore no trace of drugs, either. Littlejohn knew that kind only too well. And then he understood. It was despair. Sheer, paralysing despair which held Esther Liddell in its grip. She was utterly drugged by it.

As he sipped his drink and met her eyes from time to time, Littlejohn tried to imagine what it could all be about. The death of her husband? Or some tragic love affair? Misery, loneliness, or the return of some dreaded enemy to spoil her life — the cosy, comfortable existence at the *Saracen's Head*? Or...blackmail?

They had scarcely spoken a word over the coffee and any remark, casual or otherwise, Littlejohn or Cromwell made either received no answer or a mere monosyllable.

Finally, Esther Liddell rose.

"More coffee?"

"Please."

She went into the kitchen to refill the earthenware jugs which held the coffee and the milk.

Hastily Littlejohn touched Cromwell on the elbow.

"Get a report from the policeman who's fishing. Ask him if anyone's been here…a full report. What's she been doing since he arrived? And then, go across to Falbright, get into the newspaper files about the death of Jack Liddell. You may have to get someone to open the office. It's Sunday, but bring me a full account of all that happened and everyone concerned… Take a taxi or borrow a car. But please be quick, old chap. Make an excuse to get away…"

Mrs Liddell returned as they were speaking together. She betrayed not the slightest interest in their whispering but poured out two more cups of coffee.

"Not for me, please, Mrs Liddell," said Cromwell, holding up his hand as she drew his cup towards her. "I've got to get back to meet a colleague who's arriving on the morning train."

Cromwell didn't know if there *was* a morning train, and he hoped Mrs Liddell was as ignorant. She appeared to be.

"Well, sir, I'll see you for lunch at Elmer's Creek. Till then, goodbye. And goodbye to you, too, Mrs Liddell. Lovely coffee. I'll be seeing you."

He rose, put on his cap, and made an awkward exit. Mrs Liddell didn't seem to mind. Littlejohn could see from where he sat his sergeant stroll to the river, pick up one of the fish the disguised constable had caught, and enter into apparently casual conversation with him.

Littlejohn took a piece of shortcake, broke it, and ate it. Then he took out his pipe, lit it, and drank the rest of his coffee. Mrs Liddell gathered up the cups.

"Don't go."

She looked at him, without interest, like an automaton obeying an order.

"What's the matter with you, Mrs Liddell? Are you ill, or unhappy, or is anyone or anything bothering you? Because, if so, I'd like to help."

"I'm all right. I can look after myself. What made you think...?"

It was Littlejohn's turn to avoid an answer.

"I want to ask you one or two questions. You knew Leo Fowler — Mills, as he was called then — before he came a few days ago?"

A pause.

"Yes. I met him years ago when my husband was alive."

"On the *Euryanthe*?"

"Yes."

The same flat uninterested tone. She didn't even seem to wonder how Littlejohn had found it out.

"Are you in love with him?"

"No. He's just a friend."

That wasn't how Leo regarded it, but it didn't matter for the time being.

"Before the war, you and your husband were employed by John Grebe as 'owners' of the *Euryanthe* in the business of making trips to German ports and smuggling refugees and their money away?"

"Yes."

"Fowler, or Mills, was skipper. Forgive my plain speaking, but it's necessary. Was there an affair between you and Fowler during those trips?"

Even that didn't shake her. No surprise, no excitement, not even revulsion at the thought of it.

"No. My husband was there with me."

"Who else was aboard? You see, I hear that Grebe signed on a crew and many of them were local men."

"Yes, that's right. The mate was a Londoner and I heard he was killed in the war."

"Who else was there?"

She seemed just too lethargic to think but vanished into the back room. Littlejohn could hear her opening and closing drawers and then she returned with a bunch of papers. She handed them over without even looking at them. A sheet of shabby notepaper, two photographs, and some newspaper cuttings.

The photographs were faded and dog-eared, too. One was a plain print of the *Euryanthe*, just as Littlejohn had imagined her from the painting in Mrs Iremonger's house. The other showed a group of men, obviously part of the crew. A snapshot taken in port somewhere. Mrs Liddell and a young man, tall and well-built, with a smiling round face and a short moustache, with his arm through hers.

"Was this your late husband?"

"Yes."

The man wore the semi-nautical suit of a yacht owner, yachting cap and all. Esther Liddell was dressed like a lady and wore her clothes like an aristocrat. Even in that old photograph, Littlejohn knew she was the kind who drove men mad. Or some men, at least, who liked them that way. Difficult to imagine the lethargic woman sitting opposite and the beautiful, vivacious animal in the picture were the same. Even the way she looked at the camera was a challenge to the photographer. The full lips, the flashing teeth and smile, the intriguing cock of the head, and the invitation in the eyes came out over all the years the photo-graph had been taken. And, by the looks of it, her husband was the same. Unless he had found the wife who could hold him in thrall for good, here was a man who would wreak havoc among the women.

"And is this Fothergill?"

It was an anti-climax. The entrance of the slapstick comedian right in the middle of the melodrama!

"Yes."

A younger Fothergill, but the same moustache, the same buck teeth, the cocky nose, slightly turned up, and the head a little on one side, as though questioning, nosing into all that went on.

Littlejohn put down the photograph and took up the piece of soiled notepaper. It was a list of the officers and crew.

Mills, Catterall, Moore, Keith, Fothergill, Rimer, Battersby, Snyde, King.

"Where are they all now?"

"I don't know. Moore, Fothergill, Rimer and Snyde, were local men. Catterall died, as I said. Moore joined the RAF and was killed, too. Rimer went away. I don't know where. Snyde is in Falbright, I think, on a fishing boat. The rest got other jobs and we lost trace of them."

"And you put to sea when the alarm was given about the Gestapo, and left Fowler to pay the piper?"

"Catterall did. Jack and I were against it. The rest of the crew were with Catterall and we were locked below till we were miles from Hamburg."

"And Fowler came back to find you and thank you?"

"You know he didn't. He knew where we lived at the time we were running the *Euryanthe* and he came here because he'd none of his old friends left."

"He also came to find Grebe. What was Grebe's part in all this?"

"He arranged all the trips to Germany and ran the outfit."

She still answered without spirit. The memories of those days of adventure ought to have roused some enthusiasm, but they didn't.

"Did he represent some other parties? He couldn't have financed all that himself."

"Mr Iremonger lent the ship. Mr Iremonger was a Jew and he did it out of charity for his own people suffering under Hitler. Jack told me that more than once. But his wife and Grebe and some others — I don't know who they were — took advantage of it."

Another silence. It was all told in a matter-of-fact way, but now, as Esther Liddell forgot her own troubles, whatever they were, she warmed up a little. But only in a word or two. Then she lapsed into her old lethargy.

"In other words, Grebe, Mrs Iremonger and their friends started shipping dope as well as refugees."

"I heard so. I never saw any dope. Catterall and Snyde looked after the hiding places for the gold they said we carried. They must have hidden the drugs, if there were any."

"How did you know about the drugs, then?"

"Fothergill once told me, a long time after. He has ways of getting to know things. He simply said we'd been smuggling drugs and that when Mr Iremonger found out, he never spoke to his wife again. He said he didn't mind a keen or risky deal with anyone, but he resented anybody borrowing his yacht for dope smuggling, especially unknown to him and under the guise of helping his own people in their trouble."

"And he went to Dunkirk and atoned by losing his own life and the ship he loved in a good cause?"

"He never looked up after he heard of the drug racket. He was never the same again. I think it was because his wife had let him down as much as anything."

"How long have you been here on your own?"

She returned to her old mood of couldn't-care-less.

"My husband died nine years since."

"And you don't intend marrying again?"

It was very pointed, but she didn't mind.

"No."

She rose and collected the cups together. Some cyclists were gathered outside the inn. Four men with spidery machines and dressed in small shorts and thin shirts. Tousled hair, naked hairy legs, dusty and thirsty. And three half-dressed women also with cycles like skeletons. Two of them looked like men except for their figures and the third was fat and bulging out of her tight clothing.

"Anything to drink?"

They all poured in the *Saracen* and the men strutted round, showing off, two of them obviously after the same girl.

Littlejohn rose, paid his bill, and thanked Mrs Liddell. She made no reply, but just nodded and gave him the faint enigmatical smile again. One of the cyclists eyed her over and made a noise half between a hiss and a whistle as her beauty struck him. Outside, the detective was still fishing. Two more little trout. Littlejohn asked him about the sport, and he said it wasn't so bad.

"You reported everything to my colleague? Right. Carry on. You're doing good work."

The policeman smiled proudly and forthwith hooked another trout. It was smaller than the rest.

Nothing like encouraging a fellow on a boring job. Talk about the policeman's holiday! The man looked every inch a bobby in spite of his cycling get-up.

Littlejohn strolled into the village of Pullar's Sands. A few houses, two of them thatched and whitewashed and obviously 'improved' by somebody who'd retired there. Then one or two more cottages, a pond with ducks swimming on it, a large stone cross, and what looked like a maypole on the village green. Two old men sitting on a wooden seat on the edge of the pond, gossiping and watching the ducks.

"Nice morning."

The two looked up and made a place for Littlejohn on the seat. He sat down, took off his hat, and passed the men his cigarette case.

"Thankee, thankee."

"Don't mind if I do, though I'm a pipe smoker myself."

"Have a fill of mine, then."

They all started to smoke.

"I've just walked in along the foreshore. Is there a way back inland?"

"Oh, ah. Down the lane there and you'll strike the main road to Elmer's Creek. Been 'ere long?"

"A few days. Nice place. I'm at the *Barlow Arms* for a day or two."

"Oh, ah. Mrs Braid's place. She's sister-in-law to Ben here, ain't she, Ben? Remember 'er husband. 'Im and me was at school together. Sixty years since, that was."

"Nice life for a policeman and a postman. Open air and the sea..."

"'Cept when the winter comes and the winds is a-blowin'. Don't envy 'em their jobs then."

"I suppose they don't stay long. They'll think it too dead-alive here if they want promotion."

The two men eyed him and wondered what he was getting at. But Littlejohn's eyes were innocent enough and he seemed just to be gossiping out of politeness.

"They were telling me the other night at the *Barlow Arms* about the constable who got moved because he was too smitten on the landlady of the local pub."

He said it as if to himself. The elder of the two men, who was almost toothless and held his pipe with his gums, cackled round the stem of it.

"Har. Luke Boddy, that were. A married man, too, but Mrs Liddell got proper in his blood. All roads of his beat ended at the *Saracen*. She could jest twist 'im round 'er little finger. I did 'ear he war moved on account of closing his eyes to drinkin' after hours. Then Jack Liddell met his accident and war killed. Fell out of the loft over the barn right on 'is 'ead. Dead when they picked 'im up. Boddy was busy on that, too, I can tell ye. Never away. We all thought he'd 'ave left his own wife at Reddishaw village and come to live with Mrs Liddell, who didn' discourage 'im, like. Then they moved 'im to the other end of the county. Seemed to pull 'im up, like. Nobody ever saw 'im again. A proper tellin'-off he must 'ave got."

"Well, you can't say Mrs Liddell's not attractive."

The gummy old man cackled again and pointed his pipe at Littlejohn and dug his pal in the ribs.

"Another of 'em! Another! They all fall for Mrs Liddell. She's 'ad a few in 'er time. After the constable, it war the doctor as looked after the death of Jack. 'E got callin' reg'lar, too."

"The police doctor?"

"Ar... Doctor Horrocks o' Elmer's Creek. A gentleman, 'e was. But 'e's like me an' Ben 'ere..."

The old man dug Ben, his stooge, in the ribs again.

"Past it. That's wot Ben and me and Dr 'Orrocks is. Past it. But we've still an eye for a good looker, 'aven't we, Ben? That's about all, ain't it, Ben?"

Ben said "AT", and wrestled to get the last puff from his cigarette.

"Ar... She's a good looker an' she wears well. You gotta give it to Esther. She wears well."

Littlejohn left them and made his way home by the inland road.

Tall hedges sheltered the fields and the cattle from the winds of the coast. Flat land, still, stretching for miles out of sight, with stocky little farmhouses and shanties dotting it. Here and there a few new bungalows and smallholdings.

People were returning from church and men were still cycling with fishing rods and tackle in the direction of the sea. Near Peshall, Littlejohn met Fothergill walking home after his weekly Sunday parade to the *Barlow Arms* and back. He was hardly recognisable in his light-grey, ready-made tweed suit and cloth cap.

"Mornin', h'Inspector."

"Good morning, Mr Fothergill."

"Jest takin' the h'air? Nice day for a walk."

He eyed Littlejohn inquisitively, almost asking him what he'd be doing all the morning.

"Yes. Been to Pullar's Sands, gossiping with two old natives, a fellow called Ben and another without teeth."

"Oh… Biles and Ben Braid. Ben's the uncle of Braid at the *Barlow*, but young Braid is ashamed of 'is uncle. The old man used to be a hawker in these parts and the family thought themselves a bit above 'im. Decent old chap, for all that."

"By the way, you never told me you'd been to sea in your young days."

Fothergill's cunning little eyes glinted under their shaggy ambush of eyebrows. Funny how with his overgrowth of hair, you couldn't tell quite what was going on in the postman's mind. It hid his eyes and their emotions like the bushy topknot of a shaggy dog.

"Oh, yes; served before the mast, in a manner o' speakin', in my early days."

"The *Euryanthe*…"

"'Ere, 'ere. You 'ave been gossipin', Mr Littlejohn. You 'ave been gossipin'… Yes, yo're right there."

"Smuggling. Refugees and dope…"

"Now, now, h'Inspector. 'Ave an 'eart. Rescuin' refugees, but dope…dope, sir. We was all taken for a ride there. We knew nothin' of that till the owner, Mr Iremonger, found out and played 'ell. Broke 'is heart, that did, because being a good Jew, he lent the boat to 'elp his own people in their distress, in a manner o' speakin'. Grebe and Mrs Iremonger and the rest just took advantage…"

"The *rest*… Who?"

"Well... It's all over and past harmin' now. I did hear that Dr Horrocks and Captain Bacon found the money for the fittin' and takin' of extra hands, includin' yores truly. Whether or not those two gents *knew* of the dope, I wouldn't be prepared to say. I might be slanderin' their good name. It was Grebe arranged it all. I suppose they all drew their dividends. We was paid well for the risk. Then, the Germans got wise and it was all off."

"And poor Leo Fowler — or Mills, as he called himself — took the rap."

"The mate gave orders to put to sea and leave 'im. We was under orders and with the captain in gaol, in a manner o' speakin', and us likely to follow if we didn't beat it 'ell for leather, you can't blame him. Now can you, Mr Littlejohn?"

Again the hooded eyes and the whine in the voice which held a hidden threat in it.

"Did Horrocks and Bacon never make a trip...or Grebe?"

"The doctor did. Twice. He was a rare sailor in his young days. Been a ship's surgeon and ought to 'ave been a mariner proper. Loves his boat and the sea, still..."

"The two old boys at Pullar's Sands said he was sweet on Mrs Liddell at the time."

Fothergill coughed and leered from behind his camouflage of eyebrows.

"And 'oo can blame 'im? She was, and is, a rare beauty. The number of men in these parts 'as has gone off their heads about 'er! Crazy for her! The doctor was among the rest, I guess. I wouldn't take away any man's good name wilfully, sir. But the doctor and Mrs Liddell was both sweet on one another for a long time. Even before Jack died. But then, the doctor 'ad a wife of his own."

The purring, malevolent tone seemed to bode no good for the doctor, however much Fothergill admired his seamanship.

"But we get older, don't we, Inspector, sir? We get past luve's young dream and even a beauty like Mrs Liddell, in time, doesn't stir our passions anymore. Don't you find it so, Mr Littlejohn?"

Littlejohn grinned at Fothergill and the postman recoiled an inch or two. The Inspector's smile had more in it than mirth. It somehow accused Fothergill of dark feelings which the hooded, hidden eyes concealed from the light of day.

"I heard Jack Liddell was rather a one for the ladies, too."

A pause. Littlejohn had only guessed it and, as if by an extra sense, Fothergill seemed on his guard for a minute. Then it passed off.

"You're tellin' me, Mr Littlejohn! 'Ow a man could be such a fool with a woman like Esther to share 'is bed, if you'll excuse the way I put it, sir... A long while before he died, no good lookin' girl on the marsh was safe from his blandishments. A wonder many an angry father or sweetheart didn't pepper his backside with a shotgun. Caused bad blood between him and Esther, I can tell you. I did 'ear she grew to 'ate the sight of 'im, because it was only nacherall that some of the many fellows of the neighbourhood who fancied Esther for themselves should tell her of her husband's goings-on, just to strengthen their own case, isn't it, sir?"

Fothergill removed his cap and mopped his sweating brow. It was a habit of his when his emotions got the better of him. Just one of those things which betrayed him, in spite of his ambushed eyes.

"I'll bet she hated the sight of Jack before he died."

"Was this going on at the time you were on the *Euryanthe*?"

"Everybody knew Jack had women in Hamburg. He used to say when we was all together in the fo'c's'le that he liked the luscious German blondes... Ah, he was a one for the ladies."

Fothergill never missed a soul passing by on the road and greeted them stiffly or genially according to their sex and station.

"Well, it's dinner time, sir, and the joint won't wait. So, I'll bid you good mornin', or rather *aw revwar*, till we meet again. I'll be down at the *Arms* tonight and I hope to get me own back from yo're colleague, sir. He's a good darts player. Gets more practice than me. I'm a busy man with little time to practice."

And with that shaft, Fothergill turned down the path to his farm, now and then looking back, as was his custom, to see how Littlejohn was getting along and who he might meet next.

Littlejohn was thinking hard.

Fothergill. A sailor of the *Euryanthe*. Fothergill, the man reputed still to be sweet on Esther Liddell and in the habit of hanging round the *Saracen's Head* every hour he could decently spare. Fothergill, the liar, the letter-opener, the purveyor of gossip and tall tales just to swank and improve his prestige. Fothergill the...

Littlejohn turned and saw Fothergill waving to him and then the postman removed his cap again and mopped his brow, although the weather was full of the chill of autumn.

16

OLD NEWS

C romwell strolled from the *Saracen's Head* after his excuses to Mrs Liddell and tried to make his encounter with the man fishing in the stream as casual as possible. The county detective was called Powdermaker, Detective Constable Powdermaker, and he came in for a fair share of ragging from his colleagues on account of the explosive sound of his name and the length of it. At first he had objected, as far as discipline allowed, to disporting himself as a cyclist in the appropriate get-up, for he was a muscular man and looked more like a weightlifter. However, assured that he was enjoying the unusual honour of collaborating with Scotland Yard, he agreed with a good grace and when he arrived at the *Saracen's Head* he hid his bicycle and borrowed some fishing tackle.

"Morning," said Cromwell.

"Morning," said Powdermaker, trying to look as standoffish as possible. He had been given to understand that river fishermen were a peculiar lot who resented intrusion when hot on the job, and being a member of the County Police Dramatic Society, he tried to put his heart in the part he was performing.

"Fish biting well, this morning...? *Anything to report?*"

Cromwell picked up a fish, didn't know what to do with it, and put it on the grass again.

"Not bad. Just caught enough for my lunch... *Not much. There's nothing doing here and the landlady's the rummest woman I've met for many a long day. She never says a word; seems lost in her own thoughts all the time.*"

Cromwell picked up the fish again and tried to look as though they were discussing it.

"You're not fly-fishing, then? That's regarded as a bit *infra dig* for trout, isn't it?... *Anybody particular called or been hanging about?*"

"Give us a chance. I've never fished with fly in my life. I borrowed this line and some bait in the village. I bet the chap who lent it me's a poacher... *The regulars call here and a few of 'em are a bit sweet on the landlady. She's a smasher, you must admit. The only thing of note is that Fothergill, the postman from Peshall, comes regularly every day.*"

The angler hereupon landed another fish, a large one this time, and he and Cromwell detached it from the hook and admired it together.

"You're quite a fisherman, Powdermaker... *What's Fothergill want?*"

"I'll just bait my hook again."

Cromwell took a piece of bait, sniffed it, and rolled it in his fingers.

"I thought you used worms for trout when the water's dirty like it is now and you're not fishing according to rule. This stuff smells of alcohol. Is the idea to get the fish tight first?... *What does Fothergill want? Come on, I've not got all day.*"

The fisherman flung his line and watched it drift.

"That's right... *I don't know. You'd think he owned the place. Chucks his weight about, calls the landlady Esther, and has a drink or two of short stuff or even a meal whenever he comes.*"

"Well, I must be on my way. Good hunting... *Is Fothergill sweet on the landlady, too?*"

"*I wouldn't say so. No. He seems more like somebody who holds a mortgage on the house, the way he carries on.*"

Cromwell picked up the big fish again and weighed it in his hand. Then he put it down and wiped his fingers on his handkerchief.

"Well, keep up the good work, Powdermaker... *You the only one staying here?*"

"*Since I came, there's always been a casual walker or a cyclist stayed the night.*"

"Good job. Bit dangerous in the house alone with a woman like Mrs Liddell."

"Here. Look here. There's nothing like that about me. I'm a married man."

"They all say that. So long."

Cromwell left him roaring with laughter. He thought it looked very natural and free and easy. Later, when it didn't matter anymore, Littlejohn told him the pair of them had looked like a couple of conspirators.

There was no taxi available in the village and the next bus didn't leave for an hour. So Cromwell put his hand up to a passing motorist, a young man with a handlebar moustache, a sleek blonde companion, and a fast, little car.

"Can you give me a lift to Elmer's Creek? I'm in a hurry for the ferry."

"You police?"

Cromwell felt a bit chagrined but admitted it.

"Your photograph was in the *Falbright Trumpet* yesterday. I must say you look a bit different in that cap. Jump in."

Cromwell wished he'd chosen another car. Squeezed up against the flashing blonde young lady, he was too terrified to experience any other emotions, and when they poured him out at the head of the jetty, he felt a bit sick. The presence of the police didn't seem to deter the young man at all from a steady seventy miles an hour.

"Glad to give you a lift any time, Inspector. Cheerio!"

"Thanks. I'm a mere sergeant, but I'm grateful."

The ferry was almost empty, as it was noon, and most of the traffic consisting of people out for the day, was going in the other direction. There was a queue for the *Falbright Jenny*, now in commission again, at the Falbright landing stage.

Cromwell asked his way to the offices of the *Falbright Trumpet*. The place was an old shop with the windows obscured by moth-eaten green curtains and there was a printing works behind. The door was locked. The sergeant was standing wondering what to do next when a young man in a sports coat and soiled flannel trousers crossed the road to him.

"Can I help, sergeant?"

"You seem to know me."

"I do. Name's Cobbett and I'm on the staff of the *Trumpet*. I'm also local correspondent for the *London Daily Cry* and I've been at the *Barlow* on and off, ever since old Grebe pushed off. Funny you've never seen me."

"Sorry. How do I get in here?"

"Why? Got a scoop? Be a sport, sergeant."

"I want to look at some old files. Nine years back."

"That'll be a pleasure. Some fresh development? If so, give me a *quid pro quo* if I help you."

"Agreed. But you're not to assume anything or print anything on the strength of what I'm after now. I want the files about the death of Jack Liddell, late landlord of the *Saracen's Head* at Pullar's Sands."

"Ah. I wondered when..."

"What's that?"

"Come in."

The reporter, a young chap in his early thirties with a fresh round face and curly fair hair, took a key from his pocket and unlocked the door.

"Take a pew."

Cromwell sat on an old wooden chair behind the counter of what looked like the advertisement office. Little boxes on the wall for answers to advertisements, and copies of the last two weeks' *Trumpet* in wooden frames. The young man disappeared down a trapdoor and pattered on the wooden stairs to the cellar. In a minute or two he reappeared carrying a large, dusty bound cover containing *Trumpets* of nine years ago. These he banged on the counter, filled the room with their dust, and then opened them at the appropriate pages after rummaging about a bit between the binding.

"There you are. But before you start, I might be able to tell you a thing or two. I was an apprentice then and covered the case in the coroner's court until it grew a bit interesting, then a senior man went. But I still followed it. What do you want, sir?"

Cromwell was a bit reticent. He'd been caught that way before and since a suspect had once disappeared and taken a fortnight to find through a little remark to a reporter, he'd been cautious.

"Come on. I won't spill until you say so."

"All right, then. Was there anything funny about the death of Jack Liddell?"

The young man, Cobbett, took out a cigarette from a battered packet, offered Cromwell one, lit them both with an old brass lighter made from a cartridge case, and sprayed the smoke in the air.

"Funny you should ask that after all this time. Yes, there was. Or, at least, I thought so. The Coroner found a verdict of death from misadventure. Liddell fell from the loft above his barn, right on his head, and died instantly. It was in the morning, early, about ten, and the pub was closed for drink at the time. Let me briefly put the case."

Cromwell took out his notebook.

"You needn't bother. I'll lend you the copies of the *Trumpet*, if you'll promise to let us have them back, and you can read them at your leisure. Meanwhile if you just jot down these four points."

Cobbett ticked them off on his fingers.

"One: Liddell was lowering a bale of hay from the loft to the yard. His wife said she was in the barn below, raking together the last bits of hay to find a place for the bale. She said her husband seemed to catch his foot in the rope of the hand-hoist he was using, tripped, and fell. Got that?"

Cromwell took it down in a mixture of scribble and a private shorthand which was his own invention.

"Yes."

"Two: The time was given as ten-thirty. Check it later from the news report. But at ten-thirty, a man passing the *Saracen* on his way from digging for bait on the shore, said he saw Mrs Liddell *with her husband* in the loft. That was got over at the inquest by her saying she'd given the time by their clock, which was five minutes slow, and she'd just heard it strike the half-hour from where she was in the barn below. Her explanation was readily, I might say eagerly, accepted by the Coroner. She's a damn good looker, you know, and at the inquest she pulled out all the stops. She was in black and most striking."

Cromwell wrote it down.

"Three: She was in the village five minutes later, asking for help and breaking the news. She telephoned from the *Saracen* for a doctor and the bobby at Reddishaw... Now... The doctor was a chap called Horrocks..."

"I know him."

"Yes, he's still there, on the retired list. He was also police surgeon, so his evidence was important at the inquiry. He said the post mortem bore out all Mrs Liddell had said. The body had been left just as it fell, except that Mrs Liddell said she had raised her husband's head in an effort to help and found that his neck seemed broken and he was dead. But this is note three: Horrocks was a friend of Mrs Liddell, and also her family doctor. There was gossip about him and her. He was a married man, but he spent a lot of time at the *Saracen* and was sometimes there out of hours and when Liddell was away. Take that for what it's worth."

"I understand."

"Four: The local constable stationed at Reddishaw village and in charge of Pullar's Sands, was a chap called Boddy. He was another of Mrs Liddell's admirers and was always calling at the *Saracen* on his beat. In fact, the locals made a joke of it. Boddy had a wife and kids, too, and his conduct during the inquiry and inquest called for comment. He behaved like a man bemused and his routine work, to say the least of it, was juvenile. The man who passed the pub at half-past ten came forward of his own accord. Boddy just took Mrs Liddell's tale as gospel, reported exactly what she said, and did no independent investigation at all. He and Dr Horrocks smoothed it all over, you'd nearly say hushed it up, and Mrs Liddell went home with the Coroner's sympathy, buried Jack, and carried on as before."

Cromwell looked Cobbett steadily in the eye.

"And you think she might either have pushed him through the door of the loft, or hit him on the head and thrown him down?"

Cobbett lit another cigarette.

"Now, don't put me down as saying that, sir. All I said was, it was a damned funny business. I fancied myself an amateur sleuth at the time. I wanted to be a London crime reporter. I've married since and I have three kids and I've put all those follies away. But, as I say, I was interested in crime at the time and I thought it all a bit fishy and followed my own lines of inquiry. They led nowhere, of course. Boddy was moved almost at once and put on traffic control or something in a town at the other end of the county. That showed the constabulary powers-that-be thought he'd fallen short. I think he fell short deliberately to protect Mrs Liddell. Horrocks was a power in the land, and he's now a JP. What he said at the inquest was just lapped up like holy writ."

"And that's just your theory? You'd no proof?"

"None whatever. I don't suppose I was the only one who thought things. But it all died down and things were as before. The idea was purely circumstantial on my part. But look at it..."

He held up his hand and ticked off his fingers.

"Jack Liddell and his wife didn't get on. He was all over the shop after women. She was decidedly easy on the virtue, too. They'll tell you that in Pullar's Sands. It's a wonder the women there don't tar and feather her and run her out of town. But the men like her. She's a good looker and has the reputation for being a good sport. Perhaps Jack's philandering made her that way. Why didn't they get a divorce, you say? They were Catholics. There's quite a number on the marsh and there's a church at Reddishaw where the lord of the manor's also Catholic. The only way was for one of them to die..."

Cobbett ticked another point off on his finger.

"...Mrs Liddell had plenty of good chances and Jack stood in the way. Finally, she had in Horrocks and Boddy a couple of men who'd swear black was white if she said so. They seemed absolutely infatuated. And they happened to be the local police doctor and the Liddell's doctor at the same time, and the village bobby who was supposed to investigate the catastrophe..."

Cromwell shut his book and snapped the elastic band. Cobbett made a neat bundle of the old copies of the *Trumpet* and handed them to him.

"Thanks, Mr Cobbett. I'll not forget this."

"Don't let on that I told you. You'll have to base your own theories on what you read in the paper and it'll be the official account and the official verdict. I've not said a word, remember. It's as much as my job's worth."

"I'll see you aren't involved. But, in turn, don't say or report a word of this line I'm following in your paper. I'll let you know any developments and you'll get the first news."

"It's a bargain. Can I give you a lift to the ferry?"

"Thanks."

It was an easier ride than the one to the ferry over the water. Cobbett's was an old family car and took things quietly.

All the way to the landing stage Cromwell brooded on the information he'd just received. This was a new line with a vengeance. Lucky Littlejohn had concentrated on the *Saracen's Head* angle. Suppose Mrs Liddell had killed her husband. How did it affect the death of John Grebe?

As they drove in the car, there nagged at Cromwell's mind a question he'd forgotten to ask Cobbett and he couldn't think what it was. It worried him, and twice he opened his mouth to speak, and closed it again each time.

"What is it, sir?" asked the reporter after the second attempt.

"Something I wanted to ask you and I've forgotten what it was. It'll come to me and I can ring you up. Perhaps it's not important."

But Cromwell knew, deep down, that it was.

He thanked Cobbett again as they parted at the turnstiles of the ferry and Cobbett gave him his card in case the elusive question definitely arose in the sergeant's mind. Cobbett waved as the ferry cast off and returned to his old car.

Hooting warnings to the Sunday shipping weaving about in the river, the ferry described a long arc. There was a festive air about the shipload. This was the one-thirty boat and excursionists to Elmer's Creek and beyond filled it. Men with their wives and sweethearts, lads of the town in parties out for a spree, members of families off for a reunion, and a group of old men and women from the Falbright Old Folk's Home out on leave with free ferry tickets to spend half a day with their own people over the river. One of them was talking to Cromwell when, suddenly, the lost question rose in the sergeant's mind.

Who was the man returning from the shore who said he saw Mrs Liddell on the upper floor of the barn with her husband?

Cromwell hastily excused himself and retired to the little saloon which was usually full in winter and on wet days, but today was empty on account of the cold sunshine and the sights of the yachts and fishing boats on the river. He took the bundle of old newspapers from his pocket and turned them over and over until he found the account of the inquest. He read it hastily, a line at a time.

The Coroner asked the witness, Jonathan Snyde, to tell his story in his own words. Snyde said...

And then the account already given of how Snyde had passed the *Saracen's Head* at half-past ten and seen Mrs Liddell in the loft with her husband.

How did he know the time? Why, by the ferry bell at Elmer's Creek, of course. It was a still morning and it was plain to be heard.

Then, Mrs Liddell had explained it all, about the clock being slow, and the Coroner seemed satisfied.

Cromwell turned back to read another part of Snyde's statement.

Coroner asked, was there nobody else about at the time? Mr Snyde replied there was nobody on the shore. Only a small boat rowing ashore on the tide...

Cromwell looked at the date of the death of Jack Liddell. June 1st, 1946...

He wondered who and where Jonathan Snyde might be and could hardly wait for the ferry to tie up before he was off and hurrying to the *Barlow Arms* to find Littlejohn.

Their late lunch stood neglected as Cromwell told his chief all that he knew and all that he thought about it.

17

THE LOST WITNESS

A nd now for Jonathan Snyde..."

Littlejohn and Cromwell had finished lunch and taken little interest in it on account of the turn of events and the way the case was taking.

Braid was hanging about the dining room, pretending to tidy up after the meals served to trippers. He was trying to overhear what was being said, too. It was almost opening time at the *Barlow Arms* and excursionists from inland and from the ferry were gathering round the door waiting for beer.

"Do you know a man called Jonathan Snyde, Mr Braid?"

Braid almost ran to the table in his anxiety to get hold of more gossip to purvey with his beer.

"Snyde? Of course, I do. Regular customer 'ere. Likely as not he'll be over tonight on his way to the ferry with his wife. He comes over reg'lar to see his old dad who lives just along the river. You can see his cottage from here."

Braid ran to the window and pointed. Nobody followed him so he ran back.

"Did you want 'im? You'll find 'im at his dad's. He's a native of these parts, who moved over to Falbright when he got a job on the docks."

The riverbank on the Elmer's Creek side was alive with people enjoying the fine day. Fishermen, walkers, whole families promenading, children playing on the mud of the tideline, hunting out treasures brought up by the river and left behind on the ebb. Old Snyde's cottage lay about a mile from the ferry, a single storeyed, tarred little place where he lived himself, a retired fisherman watching the river traffic pass his door. In front, on the bank itself, an old rowing boat, overturned, served as a shelter for coal and lumber.

The front door was open, and Mrs Jonathan Snyde was standing there taking the air and nursing her grandchild. A fat, shapeless woman, rocking the infant to and fro and making strange noises to keep it good.

"Is Mr Jonathan Snyde in?"

The woman eyed the two detectives up and down.

She'd seen their pictures in the local paper and had a terror of the police. She clutched the child to her heavy rolling bosom as though they were about to kidnap it.

"What's it all about? He's respectable."

Having given her husband this testimonial, she wobbled indoors and called him loudly.

Snyde appeared quickly. He'd been helping his father dig his little bit of back garden. A family man was Jonathan Snyde, and he was often heard to say how much he admired his dad: "Eighty, and as sprightly as a chap of forty. Puts it down to eating raw onions straight out o' the earth... Says they disinfect the innards."

"Here I am."

A burly man of fifty, with a walrus moustache, a round red face, hair clipped close to his skull, and a mouth full of false teeth which didn't fit properly and made his speech sibilant.

"Yes, Mr Snyde. Sorry to disturb your Sunday, but we need a bit of help."

"Oh."

Mr Snyde looked round for his wife to hear this. A bit of help for the famous Littlejohn, the present talk of the town. Mrs Snyde was there, all right, listening as hard as she could. She proudly imagined reading all about it in next Friday's *Trumpet*. *"Johnny Snyde, the popular local bowler, assists Scotland Yard."* Oh, yes. Johnny was a champion bowler when the crown greens were at their best. Mrs Snyde also imagined Scotland Yard as a vast flagged court somewhere in the highlands, a remote headquarters where mysteries were practised.

"Can you throw your mind back, Mr Snyde, to the inquest on Jack Liddell? You were a principal witness, I think."

"S'right," whistled Jonathan through his teeth. The face of his father appeared round the curtains like an old apple framed in a shaggy ring of white whiskers.

"You passed the place just before Jack's death…"

"S'right. Five minutes afore. She wuz with Jack in the loft. I'll alwiz stick to that. Swore it on me Bible oath."

"I think you said there was someone else about. Somebody rowing a boat in from the sea."

"S'right. Jest beaching the boat as I got past the *Saracen*."

"They'd pass the inn about five minutes after you?"

"If they came that way. They might 'ave gone to Peshall along the shore… Likely they did."

"*They*? Who were they?"

"Mrs Iremonger from the big 'ouse and a man a-rowing of her. She always goes there every June first. Went this year. Takes a wreath and chucks it in the deep water. 'As herself rowed out."

"Why?"

"Dunkirk Day, o' course. Her old man died June first at Dunkirk. Went down with the *Euryanthe*. Many's the time I've sailed in 'er."

"Yes. We know."

Snyde's mouth opened. He wondered if he'd put his foot in it. However, Littlejohn's bland smile comforted him.

"S'right."

Cromwell couldn't resist it.

"S'right," he said, and Mr Snyde looked at him as if he'd gone mad. "The chap in the cap's a bit potty," he later told his dad.

"Did you see who the man was?"

"No. Too far away. She generally gets the gardener to row out the boat. They 'ave a rowin' boat at the big 'ouse, you know. Motorboat, too... Used to 'ave a yacht..."

"Yes, the *Euryanthe.*"

"S'right."

"Well, thanks, Mr Snyde. Sorry we butted in on your Sunday peace."

"S'quite all right."

And he bade them good afternoon and went straight to tell his dad all about it and take his advice as to what he ought to do next.

"We'll have to call and see Chickabiddy again. This is an awful nuisance, Cromwell. I hope she's not drunk."

She wasn't. Just half-seas over, and she welcomed Littlejohn and Cromwell like two invited guests.

"Come right in, Inspector. And bring your friend."

She was sitting in the garden, drinking her own mint julep, and reading *Fox's Book of Martyrs.*

"I just love these old plates showing how they spiked and fried and roasted people they didn't like. Don't you think they're interest'n? I found this book in the attic and I'm sorry I never read it before."

Just bored. Bored to death and in search of anything to relieve the tedium.

"Have one of my mint juleps... Recipe given to me by a friend from the Old South."

She poured two glasses.

"Go on, drink."

Cromwell's face was a study at first, and then he looked relieved, and then delighted as the drink went down.

"You can both call me Chickabiddy. All my friends do."

"We're in rather a hurry...ahem...Mrs..."

"Ah-ah. Call me..."

"We're in rather a hurry...ahem...Chickabiddy..."

Littlejohn daren't look at Cromwell or there'd be one of those explosions of Cromwellian mirth which would spoil everything.

"...We just want to ask you if you remember Dunkirk Day... the day Jack Liddell fell and killed himself?"

Mrs Iremonger rolled her head from side to side and sniffed.

"Shall I ever forget that day? My heart went down with the *Euryanthe*, the day I lost my dear... Shall I ever forget?"

"Yes. Do you remember that particular day? You rowed out to put your beautiful flowers on the sea."

"Yes. I grew them in the greenhouses. Red, white and blue, they were. I remember the day very well... What did you say your name was?"

"Littlejohn, madam."

"Ah-ah... Call me... Your *first* name..."

"Thomas."

"Well, Thomas, I remember that day because Williams, the gardener, gathering the flowers knocked over my beeautf'l hydrangea... 'And for that, I shan' let you row me out to sea,' I told him, an' I didn'."

"Who did?"

"You'll never guess. Why, Fothergill. He was jus' delivering the letters and arrived providesh'ly... You shall row me, my good Fothergill, I told him. And he did..."

"And you both returned here?"

"Oh, no. I came home on the shore, but poor Fothergill got

so hot rowin' the boat, I gave him five shillings. 'Go and getta drink, my good Fothergill,' I said, and I sent him off to the *Saracen's Head* to quench his thirsht... By the way, Thomas, another julep to quench *your* thirst? And that of your good friend...Mr...?"

"Cromwell."

"What's your real name? Don't joke about it."

"It *is* Cromwell, madam. Robert Cromwell."

"Well, Robert, have a mint julep and call me Chickabiddy."

Just then, and providentially, the telephone rang indoors, the maid came out to get Mrs Iremonger, and the pair of detectives were able to get away, although she told them to wait.

"It's too bad to drink her julep and then sneak off at the first chance. But I just can't stand any more of it, Cromwell."

"She's got a nerve, anyway. Thomas, Robert, Chickabiddy. Who does she think she is?"

"I don't know. But she won't last long at this rate. Solitary drinking... She's obviously tottering on the verge of DT's. And nobody can do anything about it. I guess she realised what she owed to old Iremonger when it was too late."

"What do we do now?"

"I've never had a word with Captain Bacon alone. Let's try the hall. It's only a few minutes from here. He was a buddy of Grebe's and put up some cash for the smuggling on the *Euryanthe*. I wonder how far he's mixed up in all this. At any rate, we want a proper alibi from him."

"You don't suspect...?"

"No. I don't know who killed Grebe, but I soon will. This day's work should bring it to light. Thanks mainly to you, old chap."

Old chap! Cromwell glowed. He'd rather have that than all the medals in the world and all the tea in China!

"But where do we go from here, sir?"

"To the hall."

They were there already. The main gates were closed. The lions rampant looked ready to fall upon the heavy metal gates and tear them apart. The lodge seemed lifeless, too. The door shut, and not a sound to be heard. Charlie the Cheat was probably somewhere with his dog, hunting rabbits for the pot or else with his pals drinking.

Littlejohn opened the gate and he and Cromwell went through. He felt as he bent to fasten the latch that someone was watching him and, turning quickly, saw that the dark, handsome woman whom he'd previously assumed was Charlie's daughter was staring at them through the window of the cottage. Her thick hair was dishevelled, and her eyes fixed and hunted looking. Suddenly she withdrew and the Chief Inspector imagined her on the house telephone, ringing up the hall to tell them strangers were approaching.

The drive with its double line of old trees was untidy. Moss growing over the gravel; tall, unkempt rhododendrons in shaggy clumps; sour earth; dead leaves; rank grass...all the way to the house, which suddenly came in view.

The building wasn't unattractive from the front and, at one time, must have been a fine place. Stone-built, low and flanked by two ugly towers obviously added later, it looked poverty-stricken and desolate. The lawn in front was neglected, the flower beds overgrown with weeds and grass, the roses gone wild.

They rang the bell and, after a time, Captain Bacon himself answered the door. He didn't speak at first, but his looks were enough. His jaw dropped and his purple cheeks flushed.

"Good afternoon, sir. Could we have a few words with you?"

"Couldn't it have waited till I came to the village tonight?"

"It's urgent."

"Come in, then. You can hardly stand there on the doorstep."

He made way for them to enter. The air of the place smelled musty. Like carpets and hangings riddled with moths and dust.

The hall was too big for its contents. Old furniture which seemed too small, a carpet which didn't fit, shabby antiques out of keeping, and anything old and graceful already far-gone in decay. The paint had almost disappeared from the walls and woodwork. There were patches more vivid than the rest where large pieces of furniture or pictures had been removed. The unmistakable odour of dry rot hung about.

Bacon, in his pride, had bought the home of his forefathers, and then he hadn't been able to keep it up.

They entered the living room, which might have been the only habitable one in the place, for it contained everything needed for day-to-day existence. Books, a writing desk too full of old papers to close properly, a dining table with the remnants of a hasty lunch still on a tray, a sideboard cluttered up with bottles, dirty glasses, apples lying in a pile without a dish, a banana... The furniture was heavy and ugly, the pattern of the frayed carpet had completely disappeared, the rug was in ribbons, and the fireplace in which a small wood fire was smouldering, obviously hadn't been cleared out for days. In one corner stood a large brass oil lamp: in another a harp. Littlejohn wondered about the harp...

"Well?"

Bacon was smoking his pipe. He neither asked his visitors to sit down nor offered them tobacco or drinks.

"Well..."

"We're just checking events again on the night Captain Grebe met his death, sir. You were at the *Barlow Arms*."

"I've already told you all I know. Horrocks and I left at ten o'clock. Horrocks walked with me part way and we parted at his door about ten past ten. I came straight on home. Nobody saw me after I left Horrocks, so I've no alibi. But I didn't kill Grebe. Why should I?"

"You were involved in rather risky business with him just before the war, weren't you, Captain Bacon?"

Bacon grew dull purple again.

"I don't like the word risky, Littlejohn. It has an unpleasant sound."

"But it *was* risky. You financed the running of the *Euryanthe* between England and Germany, ostensibly helping refugees but actually bringing dope."

"Who's told you that? Because it's a damn lie!"

"Mr Iremonger didn't know his ship was being used for the drug racket, but his wife, Grebe, and their partners did. You and Dr Horrocks were partners."

"We didn't know about the dope till after. It must have been Grebe's side-line. I tell you, there was no quarrel between Grebe and me on that score and I'll trouble you to keep my name out of it. Or else I'll..."

"You'll what, sir?"

"Don't try to make me lose my temper, Littlejohn. I'm not the only one who thinks we'd have done far better without Scotland Yard interferin' in this case. Our own police would have solved it long ago."

"In what way, may I ask?"

"Plain as the nose on your face. That fellow Fowler... He was master of the *Euryanthe* when Grebe was runnin' her. He nursed a grievance against Grebe because he, Fowler, got caught by the German police and spent a long term in gaol. He came here to settle with Grebe, and *he* did it. I don't understand you, Littlejohn. Why haven't you charged Fowler with the murder? What's holding you back?"

"I have good reasons."

"A hunch."

Bacon sneered and laughed a mocking laugh. He was trying to make Littlejohn lose his temper and was enjoying trying to humiliate him.

"You seem to know all about the case, Captain Bacon. You've learned all the facts from somewhere and you've got it all cut and dried. Why weren't you at court the morning Fowler came before the magistrates? Would it have embarrassed you to meet him?"

"How dare you? I'll..."

"Or were you afraid? You and your friends are too eager to have Leo Fowler charged and hanged. Far too eager. I almost think you're hiding something. You're either implicated in this crime, or else you're covering up. Let me go on! All this crowd of villagers here... The postman, the landlord of the *Barlow Arms*, the local barber, Mrs Liddell of the *Saracen's Head*, your gatekeeper at the lodge, the sulky natives of the place. All hanging together in a conspiracy of silence led by their decayed gentry... Dr Horrocks, Mrs Iremonger, and you, sir. Even the bench of magistrates knows more than it will tell and fears to sit in court because of it."

Bacon bounded across the room and drew himself up in front of Littlejohn. He was at a disadvantage, because he lacked the necessary inches and had to stand on tiptoes to thrust his face in the Inspector's.

"I'll break you for this. I've never had such impudence from an under strapper before. You're behaving like a hooligan, Littlejohn. Yes, a hooligan. And now, I'll trouble you to leave. I've no more to say to you and unless you withdraw what you've already said, I'll report the whole matter to the Home Office. In which case, I presume you'll deny you ever said it."

Littlejohn regarded the angry captain with a faint smile and looked down at him like a schoolmaster patiently waiting for a yelling pupil to shut up.

"And now, sir, if you've quite finished abusing me, I'll tell you one of the reasons for my call. I wanted you, as a magistrate, to sign a warrant for the arrest. But after your exhibition, I wouldn't ask you in any circumstances. *You* don't think I'm fit to hold my office as Chief Inspector. I, in turn, think you quite unworthy to hold the Commission of the Peace. I'll go so far as to say, sir, you ought to be struck off the panel. Good afternoon."

Before Bacon could gather himself together, the detectives marched out of the room, down the shabby hall, and out of the front door. Behind them Bacon started to bellow.

"I'll set the dogs on you... Damned scoundrel. I'll help you out of the grounds with a hound at your heels."

He flew in the direction of the kennels, waving his arms, shouting incoherently.

But Charlie the Cheat had taken the dogs for a walk! Cromwell was the most indignant of the two.

"For two pins I'd go back and beat the old swine up."

"Really, old chap. And you an officer of the law. Let's go and find Fothergill. We're in for another exciting time there, I think."

From the main road, they could see the postman, still in his ill-fitting mufti, leaning over the wooden palings of his cottage in the field, talking to a man who looked like a farmer. His far-seeing eyes spotted the police officers, and he waved his hand. Cromwell in reply made beckoning motions with the whole of his arm.

"Let him come to us, sir. We've had enough of going after people."

"Have it your own way, Cromwell."

Fothergill showed no reluctance. He dismissed the farmer with gesticulations and strolled along the by-road to meet his visitors.

"Once again, gents. Afternoon, Mr Cromwell. Goin' to give me my revenge tonight at the dartboard?"

"We'll see. The Chief Inspector wants a word with you."

Fothergill turned to Littlejohn with a smile on his face, but they couldn't see whether his hidden eyes were smiling or not.

"Only too pleased, sir. Any 'elp I can give?"

"Yes."

There was no smile on Littlejohn's face. His grey eyes were stone cold and seemed to bore right into Fothergill's mind.

"Yes, Mr Fothergill. How long have you been blackmailing Mrs Liddell?"

Fothergill's smile grew sickly and he looked hurt.

"Me? Me, Mr Littlejohn? Now, really..."

"Don't bandy words, Fothergill. Talk straight and quickly. Or else I'll arrest you here and now as an accessory in the murder of John Grebe."

Fothergill removed his cap and mopped his sweating brows, and then all his swank and bounce left him. He even went at the knees and looked ready to collapse.

"I didn't do it, Mr Littlejohn. I swear I didn't."

"You didn't do what, Fothergill?"

"I didn't kill Captain Grebe!"

"Nobody's accusing you of it, but you know a lot about it you haven't told me. But first of all, what happened the day Jack Liddell died? You passed the *Saracen's Head* just at the time Liddell met his death. You'd been rowing Mrs Iremonger out to sea to put a wreath on the water and you left her on the shore to get a drink."

Fothergill's jaw fell and his buck teeth protruded.

"Who told you that, sir, because...?"

"Never mind the excuses. What did you see? I want the truth, this time. I know you were there."

"I was on my way for a drink and just as I came in sight of the *Saracen*, I saw Jack Liddell and 'is wife standin' at the open door of the loft. Jack was movin' a bale of hay and she was creepin' up behind him. I stopped and watched."

"Were you hidden?"

"Well... They couldn't see me from where I was, because of the hedge between."

"You were hidden and spying on them. That's enough. Go on."

"Next thing, Jack had vanished, and when I got to the inn there he was, lyin' in the yard."

"Did you go for help?"

"No, sir. I was goin' to go, but as I was on my way to the village for assistance, I saw the policeman and some others comin' down to the *Saracen*."

"So you cleared off and did nothing. You even kept quiet at the inquest."

"What could I say, sir? I ask you. What could I say? Snyde 'ad told all he knew. I didn't see Mrs Liddell actually push Jack."

"You kept it all to yourself and later went to Mrs Liddell and told her you knew everything, and you got her properly in your clutches. In fact, you've since behaved as though you owned the *Saracen's Head*, sponging on Mrs Liddell and throwing your weight about."

Fothergill tried to look indignant but failed.

"I've never been anythin' but friendly, Mr Littlejohn. If I'd told what I saw, I might 'ave got Esther Liddell in trouble, and after all, I didn't see 'er push him."

"You told us that before. But you blackmailed her on the strength of it."

"I...I..."

"Let's leave that for the time being. What happened when Leo Fowler arrived? You were there or turned up and started to throw your weight around as usual, I suppose. What did Leo say to that?"

"I don't know what you mean."

"You do, Fothergill, and I warn you..."

"All I can say is that Fowler turned up, cheeky as you please, an' started to bully Esther around. I 'appened to be there."

"I'm sure you did. Go on."

"You seem to 'ave got your knife in me for some reason, Mr Littlejohn. I don't know why. I haven't done you any 'arm."

"I want to know what happened between Fowler and you."

"He assaulted me, Mr Littlejohn. I'm not a violent man, sir, and I like to be left in peace. He nearly throttled me. He's a terror when he's roused and as strong as an ox."

"He asked you what you were doing there. Did you tell him the whole story?"

"Certainly not. He asked me wot I was doin' there as if he owned the place. I trust I be'aved with dignity. I told 'im I was a friend of the landlady."

"To which she replied?"

"She wasn't there at the time."

"But she entered into the argument later. What did she say? I want the truth, Fothergill, if you're keeping out of grave trouble."

"She got nasty and accused me of takin' advantage of her state of widowhood and 'avin' no man about the place to protect her."

"Go on."

"It all came out."

Fothergill looked as if he wanted the earth to open and swallow him. People passing kept eyeing the conversing group and by evening news had flown round the village that Fothergill had been arrested.

"*What* all came out?"

Fothergill started to breathe heavily and roll his head from side to side.

"It's difficult to talk about some things, Mr Littlejohn. I've per'aps been a bit free and easy at the *Saracen's Head*, but I never wished any 'arm to Mrs Liddell. As I said, all's been done friendly, like. It was wicked of her to say it wasn't..."

"She told Fowler about your blackmailing her?"

"Well... In a manner of speakin'."

"What do you mean by that?"

"Fowler just went berserk. He kicked up a 'ell of a row. There was nobody else there at the time, an' a good job, too.

Fowler raved and stormed and it was then he tried to strangle me."

"In other words, he wrung from you a confession about the kind of hold you had over Mrs Liddell."

"You could call it that, but she joined in and got excited, too. After all the things we said to one another in the course of the 'orrible row, Fowler seemed to know everythin'."

"And then did he kick you out?"

"Well, he didn't exac'ly kick, but I went. I was glad to go, Mr Littlejohn. As you know, I'm a man of peace."

"Did you get the impression that Fowler and Mrs Liddell were in love or good friends?"

Fothergill's bushy eyebrows rose and he sighed with relief. The limelight had left his own misdeeds and now he was eager to betray anybody to save his own skin.

"Love? Friends? On the contr'y, Mr Littlejohn. Leo seemed quite content to settle there, but not out of love. He actually said as...as I left, that he'd now take up where I'd left off. And he laughed a loud laugh."

"In other words, he'd make himself master and throw his weight about and sponge, just as you'd done before?"

"You are 'arsh on me, sir, very 'arsh. But I've no ill feelin's. I'm anxious to aid the law all I can."

"You'd better be, Fothergill. When was all this?"

"The day before Grebe died. It was about four o'clock when I was at the *Saracen*, makin' one of my usual friendly calls, and suddenly Leo turned up. He might 'ave owned the place. 'Oho, Fothergill,' 'e says. 'I've a bone to pick with you and a few more...' I told 'im I was glad to see 'im again, returned from the dead, in a manner o' speakin', and I told 'im point blank, that it was no wish of mine that he was left to 'is fate. Funny thing, but after all he'd gone through, he didn't look much different. Thinner and sort of colder and bloodthirsty in manner, but you'd easy have reckernised him. He asked Esther, too, if she'd been on his side when the *Euryanthe* left 'im behind. She said, yes, of course."

"And you left him there in possession?"

"You'd have thought so."

"How did Esther Liddell take it?"

"That's what I was goin' to say when you mentioned them bein' in love. As I was ready to leave, she told 'im he could stay there a day or two and then he must go. But Leo answered cold-blooded like, 'I've been lookin' for a place like this, dreamin' of it, while I been away. A place where I can spend the rest of me days in peace. After all, you owe me that after the *Euryanthe*...' and he laughed as if it was a yewge joke."

"Is that all?"

Fothergill nodded gravely.

"Except that in my opinion, Fowler murdered Grebe, as I said before to Mr Cromwell. Fowler 'ad what the Yanks call a chip on 'is shoulder. He believed all of us aboard the *Euryanthe* had agreed to sail away and leave 'im, and he seemed to hold Grebe responsible more than all the rest. He said when he'd 'ad a meal and a drink and a bit of Esther's company...as cheeky as you like he said that...when he'd 'ad a drink, he'd got a thing or two to say to Grebe. It's my view he went off an' killed 'im the next night."

"You can leave opinions to us, Fothergill. Meanwhile, I want you to come along to the *Barlow Arms* with us. We want you in sight, instead of running round to your friends and warning them that we know far too much. Come along."

"But... What will people say and what are you goin' to do with me there?"

"Never mind what people say. Far too much has been said already and a little more won't do any harm. As for what you're going to do... Until we need you, you can play darts with Sergeant Cromwell."

Fothergill bowed his head. The last straw!

18

THE JOLLY BLACKMAILER

L ittlejohn had decided on second thoughts to place Fothergill in the custody of Dixon at the Elmer's Creek police station. It left him and Cromwell free to pursue their inquiries, but it overwhelmed Dixon. The village bobby had, in his dreams, triumphed over his official enemy, Fothergill, in many ways, but he had never in his wildest imaginings, held him under lock and key in the parish cell.

"Have I to lock him up?"

"Yes, but make him comfortable. He won't be any trouble."

Dixon was in mufti, too, for it was Sunday afternoon. He wore a dark blue suit and a black tie. His wife's Aunt Maria was with them to tea. She had buried her second and favourite husband five years ago, but still retained perpetual widow's weeds for him. When she visited the Dixons, she expected them to join her in signs of mourning. She was reputed to have a tidy bit put away and Dixon and his missus believed in keeping on the right side of her.

Even as he discussed official matters with the Chief Inspector, Dixon could hear Aunt Maria slapping his kids for being noisy. He had even to put up with that!

"I'll want Fothergill tonight and I'll telephone you later what to do with him. Give him a good tea."

That wasn't difficult either, for much was laid on in the way of eatables when Auntie called. A tall thin woman, she had an insatiable appetite. Already she was shouting that she was hungry.

As Littlejohn and Cromwell left the police station a small knot of villagers had formed at the gate. The news that Fothergill was in the lock-up was staggering and unbelievable. Both church and chapel were full later that night as people foregathered to discuss the latest developments.

Littlejohn crossed to Falbright and saw Leo in gaol.

"Well, Leo. Still enjoying yourself?"

The cell was full of smoke, for with Littlejohn's permission, the attendant policeman had sent out for tobacco for Leo's pipe, and he was lying comfortably in his favourite posture, flat on his back on his bed. Smoke curled up to the ceiling.

"Yes, sir. Having a grand weekend, and thanks for the tobacco. My only complaint is there's no religious service here on a Sunday. I feel I ought to go to chapel."

He raised himself to a sitting position and eyed Littlejohn with the usual good-humoured twinkle.

"For a blackmailer, Leo, you're a very jolly man."

Leo paused with his pipe halfway to his mouth.

"Say that again, Inspector."

"You heard me, Leo."

Leo slapped his thigh and laughed.

"Well, Inspector, you beat the band! What have you been finding out since last I met you? You look full of it."

Littlejohn lit his pipe and puffed out the smoke to join that of Leo's pipe, curling all over the shop.

"Let's stop this cross-talk for a bit, Leo. This is serious. You gave me to understand that you proposed marrying Mrs Liddell and settling down to keeping a pub. What you really meant was, you know so much about Esther Liddell, that you intend to live on her earnings at the *Saracen's Head* for the rest of your life. Fothergill's talked, so I know all about it."

Fowler didn't turn a hair. He seemed as pleased as ever.

"Why did you try to mislead me, or at least keep me off the trail? Your own neck was in danger at one time, you know."

"Let's forget that. I arrived at the *Saracen's Head* and I liked the look of it. I also liked the look of Esther. I told the truth when I said I *always* liked the look of her. But she didn't like the looks of me apparently. To be quite candid, she's got more refined and fastidious since the days when I first knew her. Now, Inspector, who could have made her that way? Surely, not Fothergill!"

"No. I've a good idea, though. So she wouldn't take you on as landlord then?"

"No. On the contrary. She seemed to dislike me for some reason. And judging from the uneasy way she and Fothergill received me, they'd both had something to do with leaving me behind to the tender mercies of the Gestapo in 1938. However, I'd got over that. On the other hand, there was Fothergill lording it in the place as if he owned it. I couldn't understand that. So, I got it out of him. After all I've been through, I'm a past master in the art of getting things out of people. I don't suppose Fothergill has told you that I locked him in a room, tied him to a chair, put a bucket over his head, asked him to explain his privileged position, and every time he said no or even hesitated, I gave the bucket a damned good beating with a poker. It didn't raise even a black eye, but it made Fothergill most eager to confide after two or three drum solos."

"No. He didn't tell me that, but I guessed you'd put him through some sort of third degree."

"It seems all wasn't well with the way Jack Liddell died. Of course, any woman would get fed up with a human tomcat like

Jack. He'd try any loving wife's patience. I don't blame Esther, even if she did do it, which guilt is based purely on Fothergill's evidence. But I did say, that if Esther didn't behave, I'd see the case was reopened, *with* another witness — Fothergill — this time."

"Why didn't you tell me all this before?"

Fowler grinned.

"Really, Inspector. I wasn't going to help you solve the case and deprive me of a nice cosy retreat for the rest of my life. You would have reopened the Jack Liddell affair if I'd spoken..."

"And why are you talking about it now?"

"Because when I saw you on your way to the *Saracen's Head*, I put a proposition to Esther. I said unless she sent word to me before noon today that she'd marry me, I'd tell you what I knew. You see, don't you, that we'd got to be married. If anything happened to her and I was a mere lodger at the inn, I'd be out on my neck. Even if she left the place to me in her will, there'd have been investigations and the limelight might have made it very uncomfortable for me. I'd no intention, as I said, of losing a nice little billet dropped in my lap. Besides, Esther must share the responsibility for what I've been through. She and her late husband could have warned me or helped me to escape or held up the ship a bit. She'd got to make it up to me. Also, my being always there would just remind her that people don't play dirty tricks and get away with it."

Leo wasn't smiling any longer. His face was grim and drawn. He was in the grip of an obsession he'd nursed for years.

"It pleased me to think of always being around in the snug little village Grebe and Bacon and Horrocks and Mrs Iremonger had settled in. I just wanted to haunt them. All of them must have hated my guts when I appeared like the voice of conscience and I think any one of them would have murdered me. One of them did try and got Grebe instead."

"Have you never thought it might be Esther?"

"Never entered my head. She couldn't have taken the boat half over the river and beached her the way someone did. She hated boats. Has done ever since the *Euryanthe* episode."

"Who is it, then?"

"Have you thought of Fothergill? He was one of the *Euryanthe* gang. I'd given him the one big hell of his life with his head in that bucket at the *Saracen's Head* and I'd taken his place at the inn as, shall we say, a privileged guest. Also, I knew his part in the Jack Liddell case, and I'd only to say the word and his high-and-mightiness the village postman would be unfrocked and disgraced. He'd every reason..."

"He's in gaol in Elmer's Creek right now."

Leo smiled again and slapped his leg.

"Well, I'll be damned! You do work quickly, Inspector. You're one ahead of me all the time."

Littlejohn rose and knocked out his pipe on the heel of his shoe.

"I'll be off now, Leo, but you're coming over to join us in a little meeting of the *Euryanthe Old Boys' Association* at eight tonight at the *Barlow Arms*."

"I can't wait!"

Littlejohn sailed back over the river on the ferry after making arrangements with the police for Leo's appearance at Elmer's Creek that evening.

"I'll hold you responsible for him."

The Chief Constable speaking over the phone sounded as if he thought Littlejohn had gone mad again.

Dusk was falling as Littlejohn arrived at the hotel. The lights of Falbright were coming on and the Farne Light and the navigation buoys of the channel were flickering intermittently. A cold wind sprang up and filled the sails of the boats returning to harbour after the day's good sport.

The last call of the day. Littlejohn knocked at the door of Dr

Horrocks's house near the police station. An elderly grey house-keeper answered.

"Is the doctor in?"

"There's no surgery on Sunday."

"I thought he wasn't in practice anymore."

The woman eyed him up and down and as good as told him not to be impertinent.

"He's still a doctor and in emergencies never says no. But on Sundays it has to be…"

"I'd like to see him."

He handed her his card. She screwed up her eyes to read it.

The house was a detached one surrounded by a fair-sized garden. Mainly neat lawns with here and there a geranium bed and some rose bushes, the last flowers of which were hanging sadly in the autumn cold. Quite different from Bacon's shabby place.

Indoors it was the same. The housekeeper, having taken Littlejohn's card and invited him in, left him in a wide square hall, beautifully panelled with pictures which must have cost a small fortune on the walls. A Corot and a Cezanne, and genuine by the looks of them. Antique furniture, well kept, worth its weight in pound notes. A deep carpet… Nothing out of keeping, nothing ostentatious. Everything in good taste.

The doctor received him in the library. The place was full of books, but clean, well-arranged, tastefully decorated, carefully ordered. A large, gilded Louis XV desk with medallions on a blue ground, bergère chairs in brocade, a boule clock over a marble Adam fireplace. A room to make a collector's mouth water.

"Good evening, Chief Inspector. You wanted to see me? It must be urgent."

Horrocks was standing on the rug waiting for him, Little-john's card in his hand. As he removed his cigarette, Littlejohn casually observed that the large signet ring was missing from his finger.

The doctor was in tweeds and wore leather carpet slippers.

"I've been having an easy day. I usually take out my boat, but I didn't feel like it... A drink?"

The same languid, kindly manner, the grace of a perfect gentleman, in keeping with the lovely things with which he had surrounded himself.

"I won't drink at present, if you don't mind, sir."

"You've not seen my house before. Pity. Come again. I've one or two things you might be interested in."

"I'm sorry to disturb you, sir, but I just wanted to check your alibi for the night of Grebe's death. Let me see..." Littlejohn consulted his notebook.

"You left the *Barlow Arms* at ten, walked as far as your home with Captain Bacon, who left you at the door. You then discovered you'd left your stick at the *Arms* and returned for it. That would be about...?"

"I daresay I got back there at just after half-past ten."

"And you neither saw nor heard anything unusual?"

"I can't say that I did, Chief Inspector. Why?"

"I wondered."

"Are you any nearer solving the case?"

"A little, sir. We're following one or two lines of inquiry."

"Including alibis again?"

The doctor smiled a tired smile. He looked fed up with the whole business.

"You must excuse the apparent ill-temper some of us have shown over this case. We treated you badly the other night, I must admit. We're old men now and settled in our ways. This business has shaken us up quite a lot. Grebe was one of our little party of cronies and a murder here is most disturbing. Especially as some of us are magistrates, too. You must confess that fellow Fowler has rather tried to flout us. Bacon, in particular, thinks you've encouraged Fowler a little. But don't think harshly of us. We didn't intend to be discourteous or unhelpful."

"I quite understand. My colleague and I are on edge, too. We haven't had much help locally. The whole village seems to have ganged-up against us in a sort of pact to say nothing to help. It's made things difficult."

"I see."

Horrocks rubbed his chin.

"Anything I can do?"

"Not at the moment, sir, but after dinner at the *Arms* tonight, I want to see you all again. We might be able to talk it over and arrive at some useful conclusions."

"A good idea."

"Well, thank you, doctor, for your kindly interest. I'll get along now and see about an evening meal. My colleague must be famished."

The housekeeper let him out. She seemed better tempered now, almost apologetic for the reception she'd given Littlejohn when he arrived.

"The doctor's not getting any younger, sir. I have to see that he doesn't overdo it. He's still at everybody's beck and call, even if he has retired. The nearest doctor in practice is four miles away and they still send for Dr Horrocks in urgent cases and he never refuses. I get cross sometimes."

"In the night, too, I suppose."

"Yes, sometimes."

"Did they call him out the night Captain Grebe died?"

She looked at Littlejohn in her most kindly manner, grateful for his interest.

"Not late on... I suppose the police doctor did that. But earlier that evening, in fact not long after he'd got in, somebody telephoned and out he went in a hurry. I was in bed, but after all these years with him, I've come to imagine all that goes on. The telephone, the rush for his bag, his hat and coat, and out into the night. A perfect gentleman is the doctor."

"It's good to get such an excellent report from one's intimate servant."

They hadn't heard Horrocks open the library door. He stood there, smoking his pipe. He eyed them both benevolently, smiling gently, as though pleased with what he'd heard.

19

THE COWARD

The Chief Constable was the first to arrive.
"I don't know what all this is about, Littlejohn. It's a very strange way of conducting an inquiry. I've brought the blank warrant form, too. It's not even signed. What you're going to do with it, I don't know. I hold you responsible."

"There'll be a number of magistrates present at the meeting, sir. One of them can sign it, if and when required."

"This is a nightmare."

The Chief Constable mopped his brow, left Littlejohn, and made straight for the bar for a drink.

It was a quarter to eight. The two Scotland Yard officers had had dinner and now Cromwell was on his way to Pullar's Sands to bring Mrs Liddell to the gathering. Littlejohn smiled to himself at the thought of the motley crew which would assemble in the dining room at eight.

Braid had protested when Littlejohn had insisted on the privacy of the room.

"It's Sunday and it's our busiest day. This murder's caused a record crowd and we'll need all our accommodation to cope with them. It's most inconvenient."

Leo's arrival caused a sensation. Everybody recognised him as he passed through the hall into the dining room.

"That's the murderer. I wonder what's going on."

Leo was accompanied by a policeman and the crowd round the bar were vastly intrigued.

"He ought to be handcuffed. It's not fair. If he breaks away, it'll be some other poor devil as'll get stabbed. The way the police carry on these days…"

"What do we pay rates for, anyhow?"

Bacon and Horrocks were the next in. By this time Littlejohn had sent for a pint of beer for Leo, who said he hadn't had a drink for two days.

"What's that fellow doin' here?"

"He's been invited like the rest, sir."

Bacon glared at Littlejohn. He was still sore about the interview at the hall. Horrocks was smoking a cigar already. Littlejohn noticed he hadn't brought his stick this time.

The bobby who'd escorted Leo from Falbright was ready to return. Littlejohn had told him they didn't need him. Now the Chief Inspector took him into the hall.

"You know where Dr Horrocks lives? Well, just go round to his housekeeper and ask her to give you his stick. He's forgotten it and wants it. Then bring it to me, but don't come in the room. Send Lucy in for me and I'll come and take it from you here."

"How long is this going on?"

Bacon and the Chief Constable had ganged-up against Littlejohn. They thought the whole business an officious sort of farce. Horrocks, on the other hand, seemed very amused and drank his whisky with obvious enjoyment.

Littlejohn hadn't time to answer. Fothergill had arrived with his red-faced, self-conscious bodyguard. As they passed through the hall, there was another commotion from the crowd round the bar.

"Wot, another arrest? Fothergill! What next?"

The postman tried to stop and harangue the crowd. He just wanted to tell them he was a police witness, not a suspect.

"It's all right, chaps... I'm just..."

Dixon then jostled him out of earshot. Their arrival in the dining room caused another fuss. Bacon, who seemed to be objecting to everyone and everything, raised his voice again.

"This is the limit! Fothergill, if you please, this time. What's *he* doing here? The fellah'll be arrestin' the whole village next."

Fothergill smiled a sickly smile.

"Jest givin' the police a bit of ready 'elp, sir. I've come of my own volution, I can assure you."

"What are you doin' accompanied by a bobby, then? Hey, you, Littlejohn. How long are we to be kept waitin' here?"

Littlejohn gave Bacon a bland smile.

"Not long. Just till Mrs Liddell arrives."

That made them all sit up, even Leo. The thought of Esther joining the party had added a little stimulus... Bacon even felt his tie to see if it was straight.

Finally Cromwell and Esther. As they entered the front door, they were greeted by the flashbulbs of the press photographers who, tired of hanging about without much to do for days, were now really going to town. Leo, Fothergill, and now Esther. A page-full of pictures for tomorrow.

"Anybody else due?" one of the photographers asked Cromwell.

"You might even see John Grebe before the night's out."

"Who's he?"

Esther Liddell caused a mild sensation. She was dressed like a woman this time, instead of in the usual trousers and shirt. A black costume, a little black hat, make-up, lipstick... There was even a faint aroma of expensive scent.

All the men except Leo rose. Leo just sat in his corner, smiling, enjoying it all. Esther didn't seem impressed. She still wore the same blasé, almost baffled look the police had come to know

241

so well. She didn't even flinch when she saw Leo. Fothergill tried giving her a smile, but she didn't seem to see him.

"Will you all please sit down?"

Bacon looked ready to say something but followed the rest. Rather a rickety-rackety crew. The Chief Constable, red, puffing, quite out of countenance and inwardly objecting to being pushed around, as he thought, by a mere Chief Inspector. Bacon, the lord of the seedy manor, seeking an opportunity of asserting himself, especially now that Esther had arrived. Bacon in his shabby suit and highly polished shoes, drinking a lot of whisky he couldn't afford, even trying to cadge a glass or two from Horrocks who paid for three rounds in succession. Horrocks, deep in his chair, smiling, trying to look like a man of the world, contemptuous of the whole business. And then the comic turns, Leo and Fothergill. Leo was slumped beside the fire with his feet on the mantelpiece, lounging as if he didn't care a damn. And Fothergill, out of his element among the shabby local gentry.

"Where's Brett?"

Littlejohn smiled at Bacon again.

"I think he's in the other room, sir. We've enough here as it is."

"But I object. He's usually one of our party."

Nobody took any notice.

"I did invite Mrs Iremonger to come, as well. You called on your way to Pullar's Sands, Cromwell?"

"Yes, sir. The maid said she wasn't well enough..."

Nobody asked what was the matter with her. They all knew.

"You left somebody in charge at the *Saracen's Head*, I suppose?"

Esther Liddell didn't answer. It was left to Cromwell. "Yes, sir. A man called Folland, from the village, stands-in for Mrs Liddell when she takes a few hours off."

"And when did he last stand in?"

"On the night Captain Grebe died, he said. He was there from nine till closing time at ten-thirty. Then he locked up and left. Mrs Liddell hadn't got back by then."

Everybody sat up and listened. Except Esther Liddell, herself. To her it was just old news, not worth getting excited about.

Littlejohn looked at Mrs Liddell. She was very striking in her black suit, with a white blouse, and a solitary gold brooch holding it together at the neck. No other finery, except the wedding ring which she'd never worn when he'd seen her before. She was playing nervously with the ring as Littlejohn's glance fell upon it. He looked at it for a second, paused, and then went on.

"You might take notes, will you, Cromwell?"

"Certainly, sir." Out came the big black book and the ball-pointed pen which Littlejohn had given him last Christmas.

"Tell us about the death of Jack Liddell, Fothergill."

They all looked up again, even Esther Liddell this time. Bacon looked ready to explode. Littlejohn filled his pipe and lit it.

Fothergill's voice wag dry and hoarse. He had to make two efforts before the words would come.

"What must I tell?"

"Right from when you left Mrs Iremonger's boat."

"Get him a drink, first. Ring the bell, Leo."

Lucy came at once, Leo waved to her familiarly, and at his order she went off and brought Fothergill a tankard of beer, which the postman drained eagerly. He wiped his mouth and moustache on the back of his hand.

"Go on, Fothergill."

"There wasn't much to it, sir. I was passin' just at the time Jack was killed. Snyde had said Jack and his missus was together in the loft. She said at the inquest, she left her 'usband just after that, an' wasn't there when he fell an' broke 'is neck. I passed five minutes later, and she was still there. So her evidenks at the inquest wasn't quite true."

He paused.

"Well, Mrs Liddell? What have you to say ?"

She had been given a glass of whisky at Bacon's order and she took a sip very listlessly and spoke in the same monotonous tone as ever. As though she didn't care what happened.

"I'm tired of it all. Tired of being bullied and harrowed to death. Yes, I was with him when he fell. I didn't want to kill him. I hated him, but I'd enough to live for without him. *He* wanted *me* out of the way. There was a wealthy widow at Parth he took a fancy to, but she wouldn't have anything but marriage. He wanted a divorce, but I wouldn't. I was brought up Catholic and so was he. I clung to the bit of old-time decency that was left in us. So, he tried to trip me out of the loft. Crept up behind me and I just turned as he reached me. I pushed him away, he staggered, and fell through himself. That's all. I've told it now and I'll take what's coming."

She took another deep drink and lapsed into her semi-stupor again, just as if she'd never spoken. She was neither excited nor concerned about what the rest thought.

"And on the strength of what Fothergill saw, he blackmailed you ever after."

Fothergill was going to protest when she spoke again.

"I'd said one thing in court and couldn't go back on it without looking as if I'd murdered Jack. So I put up with Fothergill. Everything except his loathsome efforts at lovemaking."

"'Ere, I never..."

Leo laughed outright and then drowned it in a good swig of his beer.

"Oh, oh, oh. Fothergill, the local Don Juan."

Then silence. As though they were all thinking about what was to come next. Nobody even rebuked Leo.

"And then Leo arrived, wrung the truth out of Fothergill, and took his place as blackmailer."

"Call it that if you like. I don't care."

She looked as if she didn't, too. She didn't even glance in the direction of the two men.

Littlejohn turned to the postman.

"Tell me, Fothergill, were you never afraid that someone... say, Mrs Liddell, might do you violence to rid themselves of your presence?"

Fothergill perked up. A chance to show how clever he was.

"I left a note, signed, in me own hand, in my cash box at home, sayin' that if ever violence was done to me, it was likely to be Mrs Liddell, because of what I knew about her. And I wrote down the whole story..."

Bacon couldn't hold it anymore.

"You damn cad, Fothergill. Horse-whippin's too good for you. By gad, for two pins..."

"That will do, Bacon. Let Littlejohn get on with it. We're going to be here all night."

Horrocks seemed to be the only one capable of controlling Bacon, who took it like a child, without protest or anger.

"Leo wasn't as prudent, were you Leo?"

Fowler cocked one eye.

"I'm listening, sir. Most interesting."

"Leo took over Fothergill's place without thinking that Mrs Liddell might be heartily sick of the blackmail, of the perpetual presence and pestering of men she didn't like or want about the place. He didn't write a protective letter like our friend the postman. He just went out into the dark and almost got knifed in the back."

Everybody looked up again. Things were getting warm now and there was a noise in the room. The murmur of several voices, not in spoken words, but in exclamations and catches of

the breath, which all together sounded like the alarm of spectators as a climax is arrived at in a melodrama.

"You were followed in the night, Fowler. You were followed
all the way from Pullar's Sands. You were too intent on giving
your old enemy, Grebe, a shock as he landed from his ferry, to
notice. And when he did land, there was someone with him, so
you had to wait. You followed him into the dark yard of this
hotel. There was someone there waiting for you, someone
who'd dogged you with a knife."

For the first time, Horrocks showed keen interest. His face
had changed. Still composed, but pale and drawn, and his hands
tightened on the arms of his chair.

A knock on the door. Littlejohn sprang up to answer it. It
was the constable from Falbright with Horrocks's stick.

"We'd a job to find it, sir. It wasn't in the hall stand where his
housekeeper says he usually keeps it. We found it on the top of
the bookshelves. She remembered seein' it there when she
dusted the place."

"Thanks. Please stay here with it for a minute."

Littlejohn returned and sat down again. There were no
comments this time from Bacon or the Chief Constable.

Colonel Cram was beginning to see that soon he'd have to
eat humble pie. This was the end of the Elmer's Creek affair,
and he knew it now.

Littlejohn looked round at them all and his face was stern.

"From the very beginning of this case, we've had no help
whatever from anyone. Only Dixon has shown any inclination,
and he's been half afraid of the local powers-that-be."

There was a commotion as Bacon and Cram tried to speak at
the same time.

"Someone *must* have had an idea what happened, but nobody
gave us even a hint. All that the upper classes, Captain Bacon,
Dr Horrocks, Mrs Iremonger, Sir Luke Messiah, even you,
Chief Constable, wanted was for us to pin the crime on Leo

DEATH DROPS THE PILOT

Fowler, arrest and charge him, and go back to Scotland Yard. And in that you were all helped by the local inhabitants, none of whom came forward, although someone must have seen strange things happening on the night of Grebe's death. The only one who got talkative was poor Jumping Joe, and he got killed for it."

"I do assure you, Littlejohn..."

"May I go on, please, doctor? In the dead darkness of the inn yard, Grebe went in the gentlemen's lavatory and Fowler waited for him to surprise him when he came out, hoping the light of an opening door would light up his face. They were men of the same build, wearing naval caps and greatcoats. The murderer got the wrong man. Grebe was stabbed in the back and killed. Fowler, knowing himself in trouble if they caught him, fled to the *Saracen's Head*. He went back there fortified by the knowledge that he'd seen the murderer of John Grebe...or he thought he had."

Leo never said a word. He just smiled again, a cocksure smile, as though he knew more than Littlejohn.

"We can imagine the murderer's thoughts when, as Grebe fell, he recognised he'd killed the wrong man. In five minutes, the ferry was due out, and if Grebe didn't arrive to take her over, there'd be a search and a hue and cry. The murderer therefore acted quickly, carried the body to the point behind the inn, and flung it in the sea. Unfortunately, the tide was coming in, the body was swept into the river, and instead of drifting out to sea and giving the murderer time to cover his tracks and think things out, the current took and left the corpse under the pier at Falbright, where it was found the same night. The killer might even have hoped the body would never come back here but vanish forever."

Cromwell was jotting down notes with his ball-pointed pen. Mere scribbles; he knew it all, but just made a pretence as a matter of form.

"There remained the ferry. The murderer was about Grebe's

build. He quickly put on Grebe's cap and coat and went aboard, keeping his head down, and made straight for the bridge. *The ferry had to go*, otherwise there'd be a hue and cry and the whole business would come out. All the murderer wanted was time. He took the *Falbright Jenny* into the river, and there either his courage, or his skill, or his knowledge of the river failed him. Personally, I think he didn't know enough about the river and beached the ferry by mistake. Having done that, he'd to bolt across the sands as quickly as he could and get out of sight. He'd created a diversion. That would have to do. Still wearing Grebe's uniform, he crossed the bank and probably reached terra firma on the foreshore near the Peshall signpost. Thereabouts, at any rate. Jumping Joe was on his way home. He saw someone pass nearby dressed like John Grebe. Who else could it be at that hour, in his cap and greatcoat, fresh from the ferry? Then, when Joe heard the captain was dead about half-past ten the night before, he remembered in his fuddled way, he'd seen him later than that. He started to talk about ghosts. And when he grew sober, perhaps he thought of other things, as well. Perhaps he saw someone or heard someone talking to the ghost of Grebe."

Somehow, the atmosphere seemed to have lightened, as though relief was taking the place of anxiety. Horrocks leaned back, Bacon ordered drinks all round. Only Esther hadn't changed. She sat in her chair, looking straight ahead, her mind miles away. Littlejohn crossed to her.

"Can I get you another drink?"

"No, thanks."

"Then, if you'll allow me, I'll take this..."

And before she quite knew what he was doing, he drew the ring from her wedding finger and put it in his pocket.

She didn't even protest; just yielded as though used to having everything, peace, comfort, even the will to do as she wished, taken from her.

"What are you doing, Littlejohn? That's *her* ring. Play the game."

It was Horrocks, suddenly alive at what he seemed to imagine an insult to the woman.

"It isn't her wedding ring at all, sir. It's an intaglio ring which seems to have a spring locket which opens. If it contains what I think, sir, you shouldn't have given it to her, you know... It's wrong for a doctor to..."

"I don't know what you're talking about, Littlejohn."

"I'll explain in a minute. Mrs Liddell, have you anything to say?"

She sat there, a picture of defeat and despair. Littlejohn felt sorry for her. The members of this sordid drama seemed too intent on their own affairs to bother about Esther Liddell's isolation and distress.

"I killed John Grebe. It was as you say. I mistook him for Leo Fowler. I couldn't bear Fowler about me and I followed him to kill him. I'd had enough... Fothergill for years. I could handle him to a certain extent. But Leo Fowler was ruthless."

"Thank you."

Leo said it as though enjoying himself still.

"Shut up, Fowler."

It came from Cromwell, exasperated beyond endurance by the callousness of Leo and the relief of the rest of the party at hearing the case solved so easily.

Esther Liddell, for the first time, seemed changed. She even looked better for the confession. There was a flush on her cheeks and much of the lethargy had gone.

"You can arrest me, Inspector. I'll come along. I wouldn't have used the ring... I thought I might, when I asked for it, but I've been thinking it over."

The Chief Constable was busy now. An arrest, a warrant, that was all.

"You'll want the warrant before you charge her?"

"Yes, sir. Let Captain Bacon fill it in in the other room. My colleague, Cromwell, will go with him and explain."

Bacon, now! He almost looked proud as he rose and made his way out to the landlord's office to sign a warrant for Littlejohn.

"We'll be back in a minute."

Littlejohn spoke slowly and deliberately now.

"Did you find out whom you'd stabbed before you sent for the doctor?"

All eyes turned on Horrocks. The audience seemed to have thinned out considerably after the departure of Bacon and Cromwell, two big men who took up a lot of room.

"I knew it was the captain right away. It was horrible... He fell and...I...I had to get the knife... It was mine and they'd have known if I'd left it. I felt his beard... Then I knew. The doctor had a little flashlight, too..."

"So, you telephoned for the doctor from the callbox and he came?"

"Yes."

Horrocks intervened. He rose from his chair and without a move in Esther's direction, crossed to Littlejohn.

"I'll give you a full statement later. She sent for me. What could I do?"

"You pretended you'd come back for your stick. Instead you came to attend to Grebe."

"She thought he wasn't dead, but he was, when I got here. I know, as a JP, I ought to have acted otherwise."

"JP or not, you should have called the police."

"But she was an old friend of mine."

"Your mistress."

"If you like, until I grew old and passé."

"Yet, you educated her taste, you know. You made her want better things. Leo, whom she once fancied in the old days was, when he returned, quite loathsome to her after the education you'd given her among your Corots and your antiques and all the things you bought with the money you and Grebe made peddling the dope you shipped on the *Euryanthe*."

Horrocks's colour rose and he made a gesture as though to push away the revelations Littlejohn was making.

"Not here, Inspector. I'll give you a full account later."

"You'll do it now, sir. Mrs Liddell…"

Leo, full of solicitude for Esther Liddell now, had brought her another whisky. She turned as Littlejohn called.

"Was Grebe dead when you sent for the doctor?"

"I don't think so. He was gurgling in his throat. I think…I think the wound was in his lung."

"What kind of knife did you use? Keep your chin up… Don't think of the crime. What kind of knife?"

"A Bowie knife that was my husband's."

"I see. Did you leave the doctor alone with the body?"

Horrocks was interfering again.

"Why all this, Inspector? I've told you I'll give you a full written account."

"Don't interfere."

Littlejohn thrust Horrocks forcibly away.

"Mrs Liddell… You left the doctor alone?"

"He asked me to look out at the gates of the yard and be sure nobody was about whilst he moved the body."

"He was going to throw it in the sea?"

"He was the only friend I could trust. That's why I sent for him. He said he'd help me. If we didn't get rid of the body, I'd be had up for murder. Then there was the ferry. As you said, if the captain was missing it would bring a hue and cry and probably both of us would be involved."

"So I took the ferry over, Littlejohn. My motive was, I confess, to confuse matters and thus protect Esther. I put on Grebe's cap and coat. I'm about his height. In any case, it was dark enough to pull it off. Then, as I'd got in the river, I suddenly realised, it wouldn't be as easy on the Falbright side with all the light. Here, at Elmer's Creek, it's gloomy at the pier head; there it's as bright as day. I didn't know what to do. The *Jenny* made up my mind for me. I thought I knew the river and was used to handling craft. But not the *Jenny*. She's an old-stager and won't answer her helm promptly. I was silly to try. I beached her and had to bolt for it, just as you said."

"And met Jumping Joe."

"You're not insinuating... I saw nobody. I'd told Esther to get home as quickly as possible and I did the same when I got ashore."

"And you did it all for Mrs Liddell. Well, well..."

"No need to be offensive, Littlejohn."

"I'm not being. I *know*, Horrocks."

"You know what?"

Another diversion. The entrance of Cromwell and Captain Bacon. Bacon's face was a picture. It seemed to have changed its shape. Red, shifty, alarmed, like someone who'd been in mischief. Cromwell's face was set and firm, like one who'd fought a battle and won it. As they entered the room, Bacon turned and said to Cromwell what was now becoming like the refrain of a popular song: "I shall hold you responsible..."

The Chief Constable looked up suddenly, as though someone were using a phrase to which he'd sole rights. Cram was utterly confused. He didn't know what to do. First Mrs Liddell, now Horrocks. He wondered if it would be Fothergill's turn next.

Cromwell handed the warrant to Littlejohn, who took it and eyed it over.

"Alexander Horrocks, I arrest you for the murder of John Grebe."

There was dead silence as Littlejohn cautioned Horrocks and arrested him. Then pandemonium broke out. Above it all, Bacon apologising to his friend the doctor.

"Cromwell said if I didn't, they'd hold *me* responsible. I told him I'd hold *them* responsible for it all... You understand, don't you?"

Horrocks turned his back on him.

"Now, Littlejohn. Tell me what I've done other than answer a medical call and help a friend."

"Help a friend? Help a friend, did you say, Horrocks? You're an accessory on your own confession. You disposed of the body. You helped Mrs Liddell to evade justice."

"They can't hang me for that. I know it's serious and it's unfortunate it's all come out."

"It's unfortunate it didn't work out as you'd planned, you mean. All this business of the magistrates trying to push us into arresting Fowler for murder was done on your instigation, I'm sure."

"He persuaded us all. He was very convincing."

Bacon, finding his old friend on a murder charge, was now ready with his own stab in the back.

"But that's not all. You tried to persuade Mrs Liddell to take her own life if I arrested her. You were sure your share would come out if she stood her trial. So you gave her poison to take in emergency. You gave her your ring and she wore it with the receptacle on the inside of her finger to make it look like a wedding ring."

He took out the ring, pressed the minute catch, and the locket flew open. It contained white crystals.

"Looks like potassium cyanide. But Mrs Liddell was of better fibre. You've got to take your medicine, Dr Horrocks."

"You've accused me of murder when all I did was make sure Grebe was dead and help Mrs Liddell dispose of the body. I felt sorry for her at the time and acted impulsively."

"*You made sure Grebe was dead.* That's just what you did. Grebe wasn't dead when you arrived. Far from it. Let me read you the police surgeon's account of the wound."

Littlejohn opened his notebook.

"All right, Cromwell."

Horrocks's eye was on the door, but Cromwell stepped forward, slipped his arm through the doctor's, and handcuffed his own wrist to Horrocks's.

"This is an outrage. I'll make you pay for this."

Littlejohn was waiting with his open notebook.

"Perhaps this will explain why I'm holding you so firmly, doctor. *The wound was a strange one. A savage gash, and then a long tapering wound, right to the heart. It is difficult to even guess the type of weapon. Like a stiletto wound with part of the handle thrust in as well.*"

Horrocks turned pale now. He knew.

"If you don't mind, Leo, just ask the constable in the hall to come in and bring what he's holding for me."

The bobby, who'd had a drink in secret during his waiting, entered, trying to keep his distance lest the Inspector smell the beer on his breath. He handed over the walking stick and departed.

"What are you doing with that, and where've you got it from? It's mine."

Littlejohn gripped the stick in one hand and gave it a twist and pulled the handle with the other. It divided and revealed a short, strong blade.

"A swordstick, by gad! You never told me it was a swordstick, Horrocks."

Bacon sounded grieved at this lack of confidence.

"Shut up, Bacon."

"Really, Horrocks..."

It was pathetic.

"Grebe wasn't dead when you arrived, doctor. So you got rid of Mrs Liddell and finished him off with this sword. I don't know your real motive, but I think I can guess. You and Grebe were the sole beneficiaries from the drug racket before the war

DEATH DROPS THE PILOT

and you made a lot of money. Thieves must have fallen out. I can't see your quarrelling for love. It must have been the money, or else Grebe was in a position to blackmail you. Certainly Mrs Liddell's blow with the Bowie knife wasn't what killed Grebe. She played right in your hands by sending for you. You could have put him right or sent him to hospital to be put right. Instead, you had him in your power and you finished him off, just as you did Jumping Joe. You can cool off in gaol till we find out the real motive. We won't be long doing that. I must also arrest you, Esther Liddell..."

And he went through the usual formula again. Attempted murder, this time. The lawyers must fight out the rest of the complications in her case.

The Chief Inspector and Cromwell promised to follow the Chief Constable, Dixon, and the bobby from Falbright who crossed in a police launch with Horrocks and Esther Liddell. Everything seemed to fall flat after their departure. In spite of the noise of the patrons of the inn, excited by the night's events, and the flashes of the press photographers who got busy as the guilty pair went out into the night, the tension had gone, the case was solved, and Littlejohn and Cromwell would soon be on their way again.

Bacon, deprived of his boon companion, the one against whom he'd signed a warrant for arrest for murder, threw a stricken look in the direction of Horrocks's usual chair, drank up his whisky, walked into the darkness, and without another word went back to his moth-eaten hall and his shabby squiredom. Fothergill, the blackmailer, the public servant who held half the village in his power through reading their private letters, sat neglected where Dixon had left him on a seat by the wall. He had lost all importance and prestige, even at darts. He was on his way out to compulsory retirement and the digging of his own acres on the moss. Nobody spoke to him as he passed through the hall and left the *Barlow Arms* for the last time.

"Can I go?" he asked Littlejohn.

"Yes."

That was all. And Fothergill went.

For Leo, there was a bit of added excitement, a flash in the pan, before he went back to the *Saracen's Head*. "I'll look after things while you're away," he told Esther Liddell when they took her out. "When you come back, I'll be there with the place still ship-shape."

On his way for a drink in the public bar, where he also hoped to be feted by the gentlemen of the press, he met his offspring, Leo, back from hospital.

"Hullo, dad," said Leo. And as he said it, he palmed the two pound notes he'd cadged from his sister.

"What are those? Give them back to her. You're going to work now for any money you get."

"Sez you!"

Whereupon Leo Fowler, Senior, gave his son a clip on the jaw which rendered him unconscious.

"You don't know how to look after your money, my girl," her father told Lucy when she appeared again. "You're giving up this filthy job and coming to the *Saracen's Head* with me. You can look after things while I sit at the door and smoke my pipe and watch the stream roll past."

"I'm getting married. His name's Fred Heath."

"You can both come and live there, then..."

And they did! Lucy bought the pub with John Grebe's legacy.

At the Falbright police station, the Chief Constable allowed Dr Horrocks to smoke a final cigar before retiring to his cell. Colonel Cram was a bit apologetic towards the doctor, after all they were of the same class and had fished and shot together. The Chief looked as though at any time he might wake up and find it all a dreadful nightmare.

"After all," he said later, "he was an old friend and a JP. I never imagined he'd do me such a dirty trick. It wasn't playing the game."

For Horrocks dropped dead shortly after smoking the cigar he'd specially prepared for just such an occasion. He did manage to do his best for Esther before the poison started to act, however.

"She merely gave Grebe a scratch. She was off her head with worry. Blackmail, loneliness, and I'd not treated her very kindly myself. She thought a lot of me. But I'd got older and wanted peace without women mixed up in it. I finished Grebe off when I arrived. He'd collapsed from shock which made it easy. Esther thought he was dead, but he'd have soon come to. His age and the fact that he wasn't at all well had knocked him out temporarily."

A constable took it all straight down on the typewriter as Horrocks spoke.

"I'd arranged to meet Esther near the signpost. She never said a word against me when Littlejohn was questioning me. She thought a lot of me, that girl. Jumping Joe must have heard us talking near the signpost and recognised Esther's voice. He started putting it round about Esther meeting Grebe's ghost. He even approached her, and she gave him some money to keep him quiet. I couldn't have that. Once in the murder business, the rest was easy. I killed Joe, too. Neither Joe nor Grebe was any good physically. As a doctor, I knew they'd only a year or two to live. Funny... And I had to kill them instead of just waiting... You've got all that down, Constable? I'll sign it... Be quick... By the way, as regards my motive for killing Grebe, when my estate's dealt with, you'll understand... Good night."

He was right. They found that Horrocks and Grebe had thirty-thousand pounds in a joint account at the bank, both to sign, benefit to the survivor. The proceeds, or what was left of them, from the dope business of 1938. Horrocks was found to be hard-up apart from the little joint nest egg. Perhaps he was ready to ask Grebe for another share-out when he found it better to finish off a half-dead Grebe and get all instead of half.

Esther Liddell, on the strength of Horrocks's dying testimony, had her case put nice and tidy to a jury by a clever lawyer. She looked nice and tidy herself and to see her in court you'd have thought that the life she'd left at the *Saracen's Head* was bondage and what faced her was freedom.

She got seven years, and if she behaves herself, perhaps she'll get away with four or five.

ABOUT THE AUTHOR

George Bellairs is the pseudonym under which Harold Blundell (1902–1982) wrote police procedural thrillers in rural British settings. He was born in Lancashire, England, and worked as a bank manager in Manchester. After retiring, Bellairs moved to the Isle of Man, where several of his novels are set, to be with friends and family.

In 1941 Bellairs wrote his first mystery, *Littlejohn on Leave*, during spare moments at his air raid warden's post. The title introduced Thomas Littlejohn, the detective who appears in fifty-seven of his novels. Bellairs was also a regular contributor to the *Manchester Guardian* and worked as a freelance writer for newspapers both local and national.

THE INSPECTOR LITTLEJOHN MYSTERIES

FROM OPEN ROAD MEDIA

OPEN ROAD

INTEGRATED MEDIA